Matters of
Doubt

Books by Warren C. Easley

Cal Claxton Oregon Mysteries
Matters of Doubt

Matters of Doubt

A Cal Claxton Oregon Mystery

Warren C. Easley

Poisoned Pen Press

Copyright © 2013 by Warren C. Easley

First Edition 2013

10 9 8 7 6 5 4 3 2 1

Library of Congress Catalog Card Number: 2013933091

ISBN: 9781464201721   Hardcover
      9781464201745   Trade Paperback

Poisoned Pen Press
6962 E. First Ave., Ste. 103
Scottsdale, AZ 85251
www.poisonedpenpress.com
info@poisonedpenpress.com

Printed in the United States of America

To Marge, Greg, Sarah and Kate

Acknowledgments

Writing is reputed to be a lonely profession, but for me, at least, it took a village to get this book off the ground. I benefitted immeasurably from my 'in-house' editor, Marge Easley and her able assistant, Kate Easley. Their eye for detail, ear for authenticity and sense of plot kept me centered from the outset. Nor could I have written this book without my amazing critique group, Alison Jaekel, Debby Dodds, Janice Maxson, and LeeAnn McLennan. Here's to many more years of productive collaboration. Thanks to Richard Easley, Jerry Siebert, Rosann Jurestovsky, and Lanie Douthet, who slogged their way through early drafts and provided valuable feedback. Also, heartfelt thanks to the wonderful crew at Poisoned Pen Press, especially Annette Rodgers, who gave me early encouragement, Barbara Peters, whose insightful edits improved the manuscript greatly, and Jessica Tribble who cheerfully tied up more loose ends that I can count.

Finally, to the tough, courageous homeless kids in Portland, I say, keep the faith. There will be a better day.

Chapter One

Sometimes, when I'm working in my office, the sound of traffic out on Pacific Highway reminds me of a river. I close my eyes and there I am, hip deep in the current, casting my fly rod as ravenous trout and steelhead rise around me. But there was no time for fly fishing fantasies on that particular day. I was booked solid from nine until four. Not that being busy meant I was making much money in my one-man law practice. Money's tight in the small town of Dundee, Oregon, particularly since the downturn, and I found myself bartering for my fee more often than I'd like. Just the week before, I'd agreed to handle a man's divorce in exchange for his repairing the fence on the south side of my property. Thank God I have my early retirement from the city of Los Angeles to fall back on, meager as it is.

I was a chief prosecutor down there. You probably know the type—uptight, ambitious, nose to the grindstone. I called what I did for a living my *career*, like it was some precious thing one kept in a glass case to admire. That seems a lifetime ago, and now my needs are more modest up here in Oregon. Enough cash to cover the mortgage and underwrite my fishing habit does me fine.

It was noon, and I had just unwrapped a bagel with cream cheese, red onion, capers, and a thick slice of Chinook salmon I'd smoked the week before. I groaned when I heard a tentative knocking on my back door. The parking lot's behind my office, so most people come in at the rear, although I have a front door that opens directly onto the street.

"Crap. Can't a guy even eat lunch around here?" I asked my Australian shepherd, Archie, who, at the sound of the knocking, had let out a short, irritated bark from his favorite spot in the corner. Vowing to make short work of my visitor, I opened the door and said, "Can I help you?"

"Are you Calvin Claxton, the lawyer?" Maybe twenty, tall, pencil thin, he sported black, spiky hair and a silver ring thrust through his eyebrow that matched a smaller one through his lower lip. Tattoos decorated both forearms and one crawled out of his scruffy black t-shirt, disappeared around his neck, and reappeared on the other side. It was a strikingly realistic depiction of a coral snake.

"Yeah. That's me. What can I do for you?" My tone wasn't particularly friendly. I felt ambivalent about pierced, tattooed, dressed-in-black types. I'm all for rebellious youth—how else are we going to change anything on this damn planet? But there was an odd uniformity to their look that put me off, and I had a sense they were passive and uninformed when it came to the real issues battering this world. On the other hand, I felt just as ambivalent about most politicos dressed in blue suits and red power ties.

"I want to, uh, talk to you about something." Lightly pocked with acne scars, his pale cheeks joined his chin at a sharp angle. He had dark, liquid eyes that were clear and alert. I caught something in them—urgency, for sure, and something deeper with an edge to it I couldn't quite read.

"I'm taking a lunch break right now. You want to make an appointment?"

He shook his head and sighed. "I came all the way out here from Portland, man. I need to talk to you *now*."

I hesitated for a moment, then stepped back from the doorway. "What's your name?"

"Picasso. That's what everyone calls me. My real name's Danny Baxter."

"Okay, Danny. Come on in. I hope you don't mind if I eat while we talk."

He took a seat facing me across the desk. His high-top combat boots gleamed shiny black like the cheap plastic briefcase he was opening. He pulled out a file stuffed with papers, and while I munched a bite of my bagel, he said, "I want you to help me find the person who murdered my mother."

I set the bagel down and came forward in my chair. Not exactly what I expected to hear. My guess was he'd been busted for selling or possession or both. "I'm sorry for your loss, but I'm afraid that's a job for the police."

He sneered at the word. "They don't give a shit. I've given up on them, man."

"So, why me?"

"I met a kid in Portland from around here. He told me you helped his mom out. His old man was threatening to kill her. He said you're smart, that you don't give up. I want someone like you, someone who's *not* a cop."

I had to smile. I remembered the case. "I might've done that, but it sounds like what you need is a private investigator. I'm just an attorney. I don't do investigative work for a living."

His face remained impassive, but his eyes registered pain, like I'd just slapped him. "I can pay you. I've got money."

I'm not good at saying no. In fact, I'm lousy at it. Just ask my accountant. Sure, there was something about the kid I liked, his pluck, I guess. But my getting involved in some cold case in Portland made absolutely no sense. And his idea of money probably wouldn't cover my first day. *You've got bills to pay*, I reminded myself.

I stood up and said, "Sorry, but I'm not your man. I'd be glad to suggest someone who might be able to help you."

I expected him to push back, but instead, he tossed the file in his briefcase and muttered, half to himself, "Should've known better." The abruptness caught me off-guard. It was like he was used to being turned down, and considering his appearance, I supposed it was a regular occurrence. This tugged at me, but I resisted the temptation to ask him to stay.

I showed him out the back way. When I returned to my desk, I glanced out the side window just in time to see him pedaling north on a beat-up street bike with his briefcase bungeed to a rack over the back wheel. A dark band of clouds hung on the horizon in front of him. It was probably twenty-five miles back to Portland and I knew he'd get soaked, for sure. I shrugged and asked Archie, "Why the hell didn't he just phone me?" Then I turned back to my desk and opened the file of my next client.

I had work to do, but the thought of that kid slogging all the way back to Portland in the rain made it hard to concentrate.

Chapter Two

I didn't finish up at the office until late that day, and as I started climbing into the Dundee Hills toward my place, a hard rain let loose. It was early summer in Oregon, when sun and cloud vie for dominance with neither gaining the upper hand for very long.

A hand-carved sign outside the gate to my house says, Claxton's Aerie. Welcome. The sign was a gift from my daughter, Claire. The place is perched on a high ridge overlooking the north end of the Willamette Valley. I love it here, probably more than I should. Claire says it's not healthy to live alone in such an isolated place. But I have my dog, Archie. He's as fine a companion as any human could hope for. I have mornings when the fog burns off, and the colors in the valley come on like someone flipped a switch. I have nights when the stars glitter like big marbles, not the pinpricks you see—if you're lucky—in the city. I can hear owls and coyotes, too, and even the occasional cougar, whose calls during mating season sound like the wail of a grieving woman.

Okay, my leaky old farmhouse is a sitting duck for the storms that roar up the valley in winter. But I've gotten pretty good with a caulk gun, and every once in a while a storm leaves a perfect rainbow in its wake.

At my mailbox I jammed a ball cap on my head and hopped out to check the mail before climbing the long driveway, opening the gate, and popping open the back car door. Archie whimpered, but didn't move. Over-sized for an Aussie at seventy-five pounds and decidedly opinionated, he didn't care for rain, or water in general.

After dinner the rain subsided, but I could see more on the way. It hung like a gray veil below a line of fast moving clouds out in the valley. I called Archie in, and five minutes later more rain drummed in from the south. My thoughts turned again to the young man who'd visited me that afternoon. Surely he was home by now, I told myself. I'd made the right call. After all, my accountant keeps harping that I've got to think more like a businessman.

The rain had brought a chill to the air. I poured myself a splash of Rémy Martin, padded into my study, and logged on to my computer. I pulled up *The Oregonian* newspaper search engine and typed in the three words—"Baxter," "murder," and "Portland." This is what came up:

Deschutes River -------
Remains Traced to Woman Missing 8 Years

Skeletal remains found in a reservoir bed on the Deschutes River five weeks ago have been identified as belonging to Nicole Baxter of Portland, according to the Jefferson County Medical Examiner's Office. Chief Medical Examiner Dr. Ernest Givens stated the identification was based on the dental records of the deceased woman. He also stated that the preliminary findings suggest the cause of death was due to a single gunshot wound to the head. Ballistic tests on a single bullet found in the skull indicated a twenty-two caliber weapon was used. Baxter, an investigative reporter for *The Oregonian*, disappeared on May 18, 2005. An extensive investigation by Portland detectives at the time failed to identify any substantive leads. The missing person case became inactive in early 2006. Baxter is survived by her son, Daniel Baxter of Portland, and her sister, Amy Baxter Isles of Gainesville, Florida. A spokesman for the Jefferson County Sheriff's Department said the investigation of Baxter's death would be coordinated with the Portland Cold Case Unit.

The swivel chair creaked as I leaned back, my stomach tightening as I thought about what I'd just read. Eight years on the bottom of that reservoir. A young mother in the prime of her life, thrown away like so much trash. I thought about Danny Baxter's frustration with how the case was being handled. Out in sparsely populated central Oregon, Jefferson County didn't have a cold case unit to begin with, and they probably figured this was more Portland's case than theirs, anyway. And recent budget cuts had probably hit them as hard as the Portland PD.

As for Portland's Cold Case Unit, they—like all the others that had sprung up in the wake of the advances in forensic technology—were looking for cases with latent DNA evidence, a quick and easy way to score. There would be no DNA evidence in this case. So, although killing a reporter was close to killing a cop, I could see how this case might slip through the cracks like Danny claimed.

I remembered the thick file Baxter had brandished in my office and found myself wondering what information he had. I pictured him riding into that rainstorm, frowned, and shook my head. Maybe that glint in his eye—the one I couldn't read—was sheer determination. Tattoos and piercings aside, I liked that in a person.

I pulled up an earlier article describing the discovery of the remains of the then unidentified Nicole Baxter. I learned that a caretaker named Homer Burton had found human bones in the bed of a reservoir that had been emptied after a dam gave way. The reservoir was on the property of a private fishing cabin owned by Hugo Weiman, who, it was noted, was the head of Weiman and Associates, a lobbying firm in Salem. I wasn't that attuned to Oregon politics, but I knew Weiman was a big time power broker who'd amassed a small fortune by greasing the state's political skids.

As a regular on the Deschutes, I knew approximately where the cabin was located. I was also pretty sure the lodge was on the other side of a locked gate, meaning only owners and guests with keys could drive into the property. The article included the following quote from Hugo Weiman: "I was shocked to learn that human remains were found on my property. I have no knowledge of how or why this horrible crime was committed, and I am fully cooperating with the police to help find the person or persons responsible."

My eyes began to droop. I drained the Rémy, logged off, and took the back stairs up to my bedroom with Archie in close pursuit. I opened the window and stood there in the wash of a cool breeze as a throng of frogs down by the pond belted out their mating songs. Then, making a decision, I slipped quickly into a deep, restful sleep.

Three days later the phone rang at my office. It was my friend and sometime Portland business associate, Hernando Mendoza. My online search for the address of Daniel Baxter had proven futile, so I'd asked Nando for help. A Cuban exile with an intense appreciation of the US capitalist system, he dabbled in real estate, had an office cleaning business, and was the least known, but in my opinion, the best private investigator in Portland.

"Calvin. I have something for you," he said in his *basso profundo*. "This young man you're looking for, Daniel Baxter. He has no address because he lives on the street. Somewhere in Old Town, I am told."

"You mean he's homeless?"

"Yes. Like many other young people in Portland. I do not approve of children living under bridges. It is shameful. In Cuba, people are poor, yes. But if their families cannot take care of them, the state will."

"So why did you leave your island paradise?" I teased. Nando had rowed a boat of his own making to Florida eight years earlier—a five-day trip with very little food and water. He regarded his homeland with equal measures of love and disdain, and although he would never admit it, I knew he missed Cuba very much.

He laughed heartily. "It was a non-brainer, my friend. I wanted to come to America and get rich. You know—"

"I'm sure what you're going to tell me is fascinating," I interrupted, "but I'm a little jammed here, Nando." I really did love his stories about Cuba, but it was a topic he could expound on for hours. "How do I find the kid?"

"He is working at a community health center on Davis. Old Town Urgent Care. I am told he can be found there most days."

"Good work, Nando."

"I had no luck until I forgot about asking for Daniel Baxter and started asking for Picasso, the name he uses on the street. And the name seems to fit."

"How's that?"

"I am told this young man is an artist of exceptional skill."

After talking to Nando, I made a few more phone calls and cleared my calendar for the following day. This was something I did on a regular basis, although usually for different reasons, such as a good steelhead run. I'd make a quick trip to Portland to see if I could start over with the young man known on the street as Picasso. I wasn't sure he'd talk to me, and I sure as hell didn't know how I could help him, but it seemed like the right thing to do.

Chapter Three

I used to look the part when I worked down in L.A. I had a clean-shaven upper lip, razor cut hair, and wouldn't be caught at work without a suit of at least two pieces along with freshly shined shoes. I also exuded confidence just short of arrogance. That was part of the L.A. law enforcement culture back then. People on the street could read it a mile away, and I was mistaken for a cop more than once. But when I got out of my car in the old section of Portland the next morning, I didn't turn any heads. I had on a pair of jeans, scuffed deck shoes, and a faded polo shirt under a well-worn leather jacket. My hair was longer now, sprinkled with gray, and the moustache that sprouted after I moved north was full and ran to the shaggy side between trims. Somewhere along the way, I'd definitely lost that L.A. swagger.

As Nando promised, the medical center was on Davis, just down from the Chinese Garden, in a converted two-story office building. The sign above the front entrance read Old Town Urgent Care. Everyone Welcome. A young man with a cherub face and disks the size of quarters stretched into his ear lobes had his nose in a paperback at the desk. I wanted to ask how he'd done those discs, but thought better of it. "My name's Cal Claxton. I'm looking for Danny Baxter. He goes by the name Picasso. I was told he might be working here."

He gave me an annoyed looked. "Uh, he might be in the back. Let me check." He disappeared through a set of swinging doors.

It was only a little past nine, but the waiting room was nearly full. A medicinal smell mingled uneasily with body odor and a hint of bleach coming from a damp swath of the floor that had been recently mopped. I sat down between a young girl with dull, uncombed hair framing a pretty face and a twenty-something man with a backpack on his lap and his right foot wrapped in a filthy, blood-stained bandage. A sign across from me on the wall said, Tats Holding You Back? See if You Qualify for Free Tattoo Removal, and gave an address on Burnside. Another said, Do You Have Hepatitis C? Get Facts. Get Treatment. Here Every Thursday, 7 to 9 p.m.

Five minutes later a tall woman in a white coat came through the doors. She raised her eyes above a pair of reading glasses straddling the bridge of her nose and spotted me immediately. "Mr. Claxton?"

I stood up and smiled. I expected her to speak to me in the waiting room, but she spun on her heels so I followed her to a small, cluttered office on the other side of the swinging doors. In the harsh fluorescent light her eyes were the palest blue, her face devoid of color and slack with fatigue. Her hair was pulled back in a pony tail. It was the color of wheat, swirled through with veins of a lighter, almost golden color. "How can I help you?" she asked without introducing herself.

"I'm looking for a young man named Danny Baxter. His street name's Picasso. I understand he works here."

A strand of hair had broken free and hung down across one eye. She tucked it back in place and assumed a poker face. "What's your business with this person?"

I pulled a card from my shirt pocket and handed it to her. "I'm an attorney. Mr. Baxter came to me with a legal problem, but at the time, I didn't think I could help him. I've reconsidered."

She looked down at my card, pursed her lips slightly and then looked back at me and smiled ever so slightly. "You don't look like an attorney."

"I'll take that as a compliment."

She kept her gaze on me, as if trying to gauge my sincerity. "What sort of problem?"

I smiled. "I can't discuss that."

She smiled back and some color rose in her cheeks. "We seem to be at a standoff then. I'm sure you can appreciate that we have stringent confidentiality constraints here at the clinic." She motioned in the direction of the waiting room. "It's hard to gain the trust of these kids, and it's very easy to lose it."

"I can understand that." I glanced at the nametag pinned on her coat. "Look, Dr. Eriksen, I just want to talk to him. I think I can help him."

"This is about his mother, isn't it." It wasn't a question.

I nodded.

She shook her head and focused on something over my shoulder. "God, the things these kids have to endure," she said, more to herself than me. Then she caught herself and continued, "We've hired him to paint a mural on the side of our building. He's just getting started. He's a talented artist."

"I've heard that."

"He'll be in sometime this morning, I think. You'll have to wait for him to show."

I thanked her and as I turned to go, she offered her hand. "I'm Anna Eriksen."

"I'm Cal Claxton. Nice to meet you, Anna." And it was.

At a little coffee shop across from the clinic, I ordered a double cappuccino with skim milk and sat out front waiting for Picasso. From where I sat, I had a clear view of the side of the building where the mural was to be painted. It was a two story, windowless brick wall that extended nearly the length of the lot. The wall was blank, but a crude, one-tiered scaffolding was in place along maybe forty feet of its length. The lot next to the building was vacant.

While I waited I was asked for spare change by three different people, which explained, I think, why most customers were having their coffee inside. I was out of one dollar bills when the third—a twenty-something girl with both arms solid with tattoos—hit me up. Since I'd given to the other two, I felt obligated, so I handed her a five. As she walked away, I found myself wondering how much those tattoos cost. I decided that if I was going to spend any time around here, I needed to think through my approach to panhandlers or I'd go broke.

I'd finished the coffee, gone back for a blueberry scone, and read most of a *Willamette Week* before Picasso showed. He had on a paint-spattered sweatshirt and—despite the cool morning—a pair of cut-off jeans, which looked a little odd with his combat boots and spindly legs. He arrived on the same rickety bike, and when he got off it, I had to chuckle. He looked more like Ichabod Crane than a Goth or Punk, or whatever hip tribe he identified with. He locked his bike and disappeared around the side of the clinic. I decided to wait and watch for a while.

He returned carrying a backpack, a six foot ladder, a large bucket, and a scrub brush on a pole. He took a hammer and a sack of nails from the backpack and using the ladder to mount the scaffolding, shored up several of the rafters below the eaves. He handled the work with surprising ease, and I realized he wasn't as scrawny as I'd thought. His shoulders were bony, but they were broad and squared off. His calves bulged and knotted on his thin legs as did the muscles on his sinewy forearms. He was obviously no stranger to physical work, and I was willing to bet he'd put some miles on that bike of his.

He had begun scrubbing the wall with a soapy brush when I walked across the street to join him. "Wow," I said, "This is going to be a huge mural." And I meant it. Stepping up to the wall gave me a sense of the scale Picasso was tackling.

He turned around and squinted into the morning light at me, his forehead beaded in sweat. The skin above his eyebrow where his silver ring was inserted looked red and angry, like it was infected. His eyes finally registered recognition. "What do *you* want?"

"I was in the neighborhood. Thought maybe we could talk about your mother's case."

"I'm busy," he shot back.

"I can see that. Look Dan, uh, I mean Picasso. What the hell do I call you, anyway?"

"My friends call me Picasso, but that leaves you out."

"I don't blame you for being pissed. I should have listened to what you had to say the other day. I drove up here to make amends. Okay, maybe I should've ridden a bike, but here I am."

"I don't need your help. I've decided to handle things myself." He turned back to the wall and began scrubbing again.

I stood there for a while, but it was clear the conversation was over. Finally, I laid a card on the bottom rung of his ladder and said, "Okay. If you change your mind, give me a call." I took a couple of steps, then turned back and added, "You should have Doc Eriksen look at that ring in your eyebrow. It looks infected."

"Fuck off," I heard him mumble under his breath.

As I was leaving, the good doctor came out of the clinic with the young girl I'd seen in the waiting room. I caught her parting words as I approached—"See you on Monday, Caitlin. Remember your promise to me." The young girl—she couldn't have been a day older than sixteen—nodded her head solemnly and started down the sidewalk, her shoulders sagging under some unseen load. Anna turned to go back inside, but stopped when she saw me.

"Is she *homeless?*" I blurted out. I could scarcely contain my indignation at the thought of such a young girl on the streets.

Anna looked back at the girl and sighed deeply. "Almost all the kids we see here are runaways. Most for good reasons. The streets look better than what they're dealing with at home—physical abuse, sex abuse, parents that are drug-addicted or involved in criminal activity, the list goes on."

I shook my head in disbelief. "Surely there's a place for her."

She forced a smile, as if she'd dealt with my sort of uninformed, righteous indignation many times before. "It takes time. Resources are stretched to the breaking point and the kids are wary. The streets are dangerous, but there's a certain allure, too. They're free from a lot of the pressures we put on kids these days, and they fall in with others they feel they can trust. They form the families they didn't have." Then she glanced at her watch. "I'm running late. Did you see Picasso?"

"Uh, yeah. Doesn't look like I'll be helping him, though."

Her eyes were a deeper shade of blue in the sunlight, and her look said she guessed what had happened. She chased a strand of hair from her forehead before saying, "You're lucky to get one chance with these kids. They've pretty much had it with adults. Believe me, I know." Then she eyed me more intently. "Will he be okay, I mean with whatever's going on with the investigation of his mother's death?"

I shrugged. "I don't know. He feels like the police aren't doing enough to find her killer. He said he'd decided to handle the situation on his own."

She wrinkled her brow and absently nibbled on the cuticle of her thumb. "Oh, that doesn't sound good. He's carrying a lot of rage around. No, that doesn't sound good at all."

"Maybe you could talk to him. Persuade him to give me a call. I have some contacts in the Portland Police Department. I might be able to do something."

Anna agreed to speak to him on my behalf and then hurried back into the clinic. That didn't make me feel any better. I'd sent Picasso back to Portland empty-handed, and now I had a better sense of just what the young man was up against. I'd blown it, for sure.

Chapter Four

Nando Mendoza and I worked together on occasion, but the real basis of our friendship was a love of food. It was the following week and I was back in Portland having lunch with him at a Cuban restaurant aptly named Cuba Cuba. Nando was having the *churrasco cubana*, a thick skirt steak garnished with curled strips of bright yellow plantains. I ate a grilled fish that had been marinated in something remarkable. I closed my eyes and picked out lime, cilantro, cumin, and maybe some nutmeg. Damn, I asked myself, how do they do that?

I was on one of my infrequent business trips to Portland when he called and said he had a legal problem. I waited patiently for my friend to broach the subject, knowing from experience that this would not happen until most of the food on his plate was gone. Nando was a big man—six four, at least—with an ample girth, powerful arms, and a deep, resonant voice. His eyes were like black marbles, wide-set under thick, arching brows. More often than not, his eyes laughed at you or hinted they knew something you didn't. But all was forgiven when he smiled, an act that could light a dark room.

A funny thing about his English—it was Spanish inflected, of course, but it also had a British ring to it. He'd lived his first year in the states with a British philosophy professor at the University of Miami and his family. I suspected Nando liked the effect, because seven years in Portland had done little to soften it.

He tossed a plantain back on his plate. "These are not so good, but this steak"—he held up a piece speared on his fork—"ah, we could only dream of such meat in Cuba. Did you know I was an electrical engineer there, but went back to school for a degree in hotel management?"

"Why did you do that?" I asked. I hadn't heard this one.

"Simple, my friend. The best food went to the hotels for the tourists. I was a growing young man. I worked the desk at my first hotel job in Havana, but I became *very* good friends with the chef there. Her name was Catalina. She was ten years older than me." He whispered, "*Ay dios, es figura me tenia enloquecido,*" with closed eyes, then added, "We used to meet in the cooler where the meat was hung. From then on my family and I had enough to eat." Nando went on to describe the dishes his mother cooked from the food he smuggled from the hotel. Finally, as he was chewing the last bite of steak, he said, "Ramon got arrested last night."

Ramon Duarte was another member of the small, tight-knit Cuban community in Portland. He was a photographer who occasionally worked for Nando. "What for?"

"Assault."

"What happened?"

He waived his hand in disgust. "Ah. He was taking photos of a man with his mistress. I work for the man's wife. The man approached him and tried to take the camera away. That was a big mistake. Ramon beat the man up, and someone called the cops."

"Where is he now?"

"I bailed him out this morning. He should have just walked away. But, no. He had to break the man's nose. This is not good for business. The police are unhappy with me. I, uh, thought perhaps you could speak to your friend, maybe smooth things out. I don't want to lose my license."

My "friend" was Pete Stout, District Attorney for Multnomah County. I'd worked with Pete down in L.A. in my previous life, the life I'd come to Oregon to escape. We had re-established our friendship after he'd taken the job up here. I gave Nando a pained look.

He raised his hands in surrender. "I know, I know. This is a big favor to ask."

I let him squirm for a few moments. I only had so much capital with Stout, after all. Finally, I shrugged. "I'll talk to him, but I won't ask for any favors. I will tell him you're a good man and ask if there's anything *you* can do to improve your image with the department."

After lunch I interviewed a witness for an upcoming court case. I finished about three and as I came down 13th, realized I was only a couple of blocks from the Old Town clinic. What the hell, I said to myself. I hung a left on Davis and parked across the street from the building.

Picasso was up on the scaffolding sketching with white chalk. He was a leftie, I noticed. A large sketch book lay opened next to him. As I approached I could see he had divided the wall into a checkerboard grid of three-foot squares. It looked like the squares had been snapped in place using a carpenter's chalk line. I thought I recognized the pyramidal shape of Mt. Hood outlined on the wall. The volcano looked down on a foreground consisting of a set of undulating, horizontal lines that might represent the Willamette River. A gently curving path or road led from the mountain to the river, where it connected to a couple of diverging lines suggesting a wide bridge. Other groupings scattered east and west of the river looked like place holders for some of the landmarks in Portland, like the Big Pink, the twin spires of the Convention Center, and the graceful arc of the Fremont Bridge.

Unsure of the best way to announce my presence, I blurted out, "Da Vinci was left-handed, too."

Picasso swiveled around on the ladder and looked at me like someone awakened from a deep sleep. Without smiling, he answered, "So was M. C. Escher."

I chuckled. "You're in good company." I nodded toward the wall. "What's the theme going to be?"

"Doc Eriksen wants something on health care," was all he answered before turning and starting to sketch again. He was wearing a paint spattered pair of jeans I'd seen before, a t-shirt from a past Portland Blues Festival, and a ball cap that had *Dignity Village* written in script across the front. I knew the latter was some kind of tent city for the homeless. The red, yellow, and black bands of the coral snake tattoo stood in bold relief against the pale skin of his neck, and the piercing above his eye still looked infected.

"Buy you a coffee?" I asked.

He turned back around and considered my offer with narrowed eyes. I'd like to say it was my charm that won him over, but it was more likely that he figured this was the only way to get rid of me. "I only drink tea."

"Tea it is, then."

After we'd sat down with our drinks, a double cappuccino for me and a green tea for him, I said, "So, you're a muralist?"

"Yeah, that's my main interest. Murals that tell the truth." He'd brought his sketch book with him, but made no effort to show me the plan he was working from, and I didn't press it.

With little coaxing, he went on to tell me about the muralists and street artists he admired—Diego Rivera, Ras Malik, Keith Haring—people I'd never heard of doing a form of art I scarcely understood. I had, however, some familiarity with the political murals painted during the sectarian troubles in Northern Ireland. I'd leafed through a book about them once in a bookstore, and the stark images had impressed me so much that I bought the book. When I mentioned this, a faint crack formed in the ice between us. His dark eyes lit up for just a moment, and in that instant I could see the enthusiastic boy that was still in there somewhere.

"You've seen those? They're incredibly powerful. Kevin Hasson's a genius, man."

He went silent then, as if he feared he'd revealed too much of himself. We'd nearly finished our drinks when I brought up the topic of his mother's murder. I said, "The last time we spoke, I believe you said you were going to handle your mother's case yourself. What did you mean by that?"

He compressed his lips into a thin line. "Why do you give a shit, anyway?"

"I read about your mom's murder online. It made me furious. Someone needs to pay for that. And I'm not surprised the police dropped the ball. They're understaffed and overworked."

He kept his facial expression neutral and waited for me to continue. "Look, I don't always get it right the first time, Picasso. You know what I'm saying?"

He stroked his straggly goatee while seeming to ponder what I'd said. There was a long pause. "I know who killed my mom."

I set my cup down and leaned forward. "*You do?*"

"Yeah. His name's Mitchell Conyers. He was my mom's boyfriend when she disappeared."

"You have proof?"

"No. Not exactly. But I went to see the woman who gave him an alibi for the night mom disappeared. She was lying through her teeth."

"How could you tell?"

"She slammed the door in my face, that's how."

I resisted rolling my eyes. "Why are you so sure it's this guy Conyers?"

"The boyfriend always does it, man. Ask any cop. He and my mom fought like cats and dogs. Believe me, I was there. The night before she disappeared, they had a huge fight."

"Do you remember what they were fighting about that night?"

"Hell no, man. I'd learned to tune that shit out."

"Do the police know about the fighting?"

"Sure. I told them all about it. But who's going to believe a pimply twelve-year-old? Anyway, the thought of her at the bottom of that reservoir all that time made me crazy. I woke up a couple of days after they found her and decided to kill Conyers."

"Why all of a sudden?"

His face stiffened, and I realized he was forcing back tears. "When she was missing, I guess I always held out hope she'd come back. Pretty stupid, huh?"

"Not at all."

"When I heard they'd found her, it just crystallized. It was Conyers. I knew it. I looked up his address and started to think about how I'd do it. Shoot him, maybe, or bash his head in. But then I thought, wait a minute, that'd be way too quick. The dude needs to suffer. And mom would never forgive me for doing something like that, anyway. So I started to daydream about the cops arresting him, watching him do the perp walk, you know, hands and feet manacled, cameras flashing, a cop easing him into a squad car."

"Did you go to them with your suspicions?"

"I tried to." He laughed and shook his head. "They acted like I was radioactive, like I'd give them AIDS or something. Told me they'd be in touch. Nothing happened. Then Conyers has the balls to show up at my mom's memorial service." He frowned and shook his head. "I lost it, man."

"What did you do?"

"I told him to get the hell out. He just stood there, so I went after him screaming that he killed her. Got one good punch in and ripped the shit out of his Armani suit or whatever the hell he was wearing. My aunt Amy was so pissed at me, but I didn't care."

"What did Conyers do?"

"He took the hint and left. The press was there, so the whole sorry mess wound up in the paper." He laughed again. "'Son accuses mom's boyfriend of murder,' or something like that. Anyway, that's when I decided I needed help."

"When did this happen?"

"A couple of weeks or so before I looked you up."

I smiled and nodded. "Oh, yeah. Now I remember seeing that in the paper. That was you, huh?"

Picasso nodded and tried not to smile.

"You had a briefcase with you when you came to see me in Dundee. What's in it?"

"My evidence book, man. Everything I could lay my hands on that's related to my mom's disappearance—her appointment book, computer files, address book, newspaper articles, stuff like that. The cops gave a lot of it back to my aunt, and I had her send it to me after they found mom. I also made a list of her friends and the people she worked with at the paper, at least the ones I knew about. The cops probably talked to them when she went missing, but I figured after eight years they might remember something that didn't seem important at the time."

I drained my coffee, leaned back and met his eyes. "So, do you want me to take a look at this or not?"

He tugged absentmindedly on the silver ring through his lip and dropped his eyes, but the snake on his neck kept watch. Finally, he sighed and looked up, his eyes shining with a film of moisture. "Yeah, I could use some help. Either that, or I just kill the bastard." He paused for a moment while I chuckled. "What'll it cost me?"

"Tell you what, I won't charge you anything until I've looked your information over and done some preliminary follow-up, if it's needed. After that, if we decide to keep at it, we'll come up with a fair price. How does that sound?"

"Okay, I guess. Aren't I supposed to give you a retainer or something?"

I smiled and put a hand on his shoulder. "How much you got on you?"

He took out his wallet and opened it. "Uh, two bucks."

"Give me a dollar, then, and we'll call it a deal." We shook on it. I said, "One more thing. I know you're sure about who killed your mom, but I'm not going to start with any preconceived notions. You okay with that?"

Picasso face tightened as if preparing to argue. But he must have thought better of it. He nodded. "Fair enough."

Chapter Five

I had a lot more questions for Picasso, but he was anxious to get back to work, and I had another errand to run. We decided to get back together at the end of the day. I swung back to the clinic around five, and we threw his bike in my trunk since he lived several miles north, on the east side of the Willamette. Before we left he went into the clinic and brought out an old Dell laptop that must have been three inches thick. "Almost forgot this," he said as he slid into the seat next to me. "I charge it up here so I can use it at night. There's no electricity where I live."

As we pulled away, I said, "I thought you lived around here."

"Used to, but I kept getting my stuff ripped off so I decided to move. Old Town's still where I hang out, though, where my friends are."

"Where did you live after your mom was killed?" I asked, curious if he'd tell the truth about being homeless.

"Around," was all he gave me. Then he pointed up ahead. "Turn left at the light. I want to show you something." After we passed an acupuncture and medicinal herb shop called the Mystic Circle in the middle of the next block, he said, "Pull over and look back."

A huge mural covered most of the side wall of the building. I sat there taking it in for a few moments, then got out of the car for a better look. A man and woman stood next to an open grave. The man's head was turned toward the woman, a hand resting on her shoulder. Holding the photograph of a beautiful young girl, the woman looked straight ahead. As I approached, her eyes seemed to lock on mine, stopping me in mid-stride. Her eyes were clear and bright but filled with pathos, anger, and something else…accusation? Yes, that was it. Accusation. She was so deftly rendered that I half expected to see her chest heave and nostrils flare as she took a breath. To her left, Death stood in his hooded black robe, smiling with garish teeth, his familiar sickle replaced with an assault rifle sporting a large banana clip. In the background, tombstones dotted a grassy knoll with names etched on them—Columbine, Springfield, Aurora, Virginia Tech…and scattered between the tombstones were other groups of mourners. Like the woman, they stared out at me with the same haunting, accusatory look.

I stood there in stunned silence. Aside from the pictures of the murals in Northern Ireland, I'd never seen anything like it. Picasso had come up behind me. I dropped my voice to a whisper, "Beautiful work. Powerful." I shook my head. "Makes me ashamed to be an adult in this country."

Picasso nodded. "Thanks. I, uh, guess I'll have to add another tombstone now." Sandy Hook. He didn't have to say it. We fell silent for several moments before he continued. "Some of the best art in the world's going up on the sides of buildings, man. I started out with a spray can, but once I saw Malik's work, I knew what I wanted to do with my life."

"You used to do graffiti?"

"Yeah. I mean, a lot of guys started out that way. It's not all bad, you know. A lot of truth gets told with a spray can. Some good art, too."

"When did you go from spray cans to paint brushes?"

"When I was fifteen. I checked out this book in the main library about the murals in Philly. There was a picture of one of Ras Malik's murals in it, a bunch of children's hands overlapping, all different skin tones, the fingers kind of chubby so you knew they were kids. Covered the whole side of a two story building. I almost lost my breath when I saw it."

"So, you put the spray can down and picked up a brush?"

"Something like that." He chuckled and looked wistful. "I had to teach myself how to paint, first."

I looked at the mural again, then back at him. "I'd say you made the right call."

He allowed himself a smile. "Well, the folks at the Mystic Circle liked it. They bought the paint supplies and threw in a year's worth of free acupuncture treatments."

We continued to talk about the street art scene in Portland as we headed over to Picasso's new digs, which were in the Sunderland neighborhood, a sparsely populated outpost at the extreme northeast corner of the city. We pulled up in front of what looked like a campground of sorts, although a lot funkier. I said, "What's this?"

"Dignity Village. It's where I live now."

I thought of the ball cap I'd seen him wearing. "Oh, right. I've heard about this place." Actually, I wasn't very well informed. All I knew was that a small village had sprung up over night when a band of homeless people migrated en mass from the center of Portland. They'd been raising hell for several years and the offer of a vacant lot near the river represented some sort of compromise with the city fathers. It looked to me like the city got the better end of the deal. The village was squeezed between a correctional facility and a large warehouse complex. To the north across a vast, empty field, you could see planes taking off and landing at Portland International. Out of sight, out of mind.

Picasso had me sign in at a little blue shack at the entrance to the village. It was staffed by a thin, nervous woman with a cigarette cough and an enormous man with long silver hair and a black walrus mustache. As I followed him out, Picasso said over his shoulder, "This place is like a campground with shopping carts. I don't really dig it. I mean, I've been on the streets since I was fourteen. That's freedom, man. But I was sick of getting ripped off. There's hardly any crime here. If you screw up, they toss you out on your ass in a hurry."

The village spread itself over a sizeable chunk of city land, a crazy quilt of small structures, mostly wood, but I noted some stucco and straw-bale homes as well. Some were painted brightly, others stained by the weather. Bikes stood out front of some places and others had well-tended container gardens. Faint strains of music drifted on the air along with the smell of food cooking. The vibe was cordial, but I did get a couple of who-the-hell-are-you looks.

"I don't see any kids," I remarked as I followed Picasso down a narrow path through the camp.

"Not allowed. You can have a rap sheet and still live here. The powers that be decided kids would be a bad idea."

"Who are the powers that be?"

"Some kind of board. They're elected by the people living here. I don't pay much attention to the political stuff. They decide who gets in this place." He chuckled. "I think they let me in because they want me to paint them something."

"Are you going to?"

"Sure, but they haven't asked me yet."

Picasso led me to a small, wood-sided structure near the back of the lot. Built on a sturdy wooden platform, it reminded me of a tool shed from the outside. Across the path, a burly man sat in a director's chair in front of a hut with a tarpaulin roof. He had a full, black beard, muscular forearms covered with wiry hair, and intense, narrow set eyes. Picasso nodded to him. "How's it goin', Joey?"

"Every day's a holiday."

"Take your meds?" Picasso asked.

"Uh, yep. Sure did."

"Good."

"Who's that with you?"

"This is Cal, Joey. He's a friend of mine. I'm showing him around."

"Oh. Okay. Nice to meet you, Cal."

"Same here, Joey."

Picasso opened a combination lock, swung the door open, and invited me in. Light filtered in through two small windows screened with netting. The air smelled musty with notes of something pungent like a solvent. When my eyes adjusted, I saw a row of brushes soaking in jars at the back of the single room, next to a line of paint jars and a can of mineral spirits. In a lowered voice, Picasso said, "Joey's an Iraq vet. He saw a lot of action over there. The dude has PTSD now. Can't hold a job. His old lady left him, took the kids and the house."

I grimaced and shook my head. "Is he getting any help from the VA?"

Picasso laughed at my apparent naiveté. "He's tried, but the VA's fucked up, man. I've been trying to help him, but we can't even get his service records." He waved a hand dismissively and added, "But don't get me started on that."

The light was dim in the tent. Picasso lit a single propane lamp that hung in the middle of the room. A propane stove sat on a small, unfinished table beside a chipped porcelain pitcher standing inside a wash basin. Two folding chairs, a tiny cooler, and two wooden crates filled with books, clothes, and other items completed the furnishings. Propped on one of the crates was the framed picture of a woman I assumed to be Picasso's mother. The plastic briefcase I'd seen in my office sat next to the crates along with a backpack, sleeping bag, and small pillow.

Picasso watched as I took the scene in, then made a sweeping gesture with his hand. "See what happens? I get a roof over my head and right away I start accumulating shit." He seemed genuinely embarrassed by his new found acquisitiveness.

I shook my head. "Don't feel bad. You should see my attic."

"You want some tea?" he asked. I hesitated. "It's green tea—chock full of antioxidants—and a lot better for you than the stuff you drink." I nodded and he fired up the stove and put on a pan he'd filled with water from the pitcher. Then he picked up the briefcase. "So, you want me to take you through this stuff?"

I was tempted to dive in, but thought better of it. I didn't want his spin on anything. "I'd rather look at it myself first. I'll get back to you with questions. You have a cell phone?"

"Nope. Those suckers will give you brain cancer, man. Besides the security, the best thing about this place is the WiFi.

I bought my laptop from a tweeker—previously owned, you might say—and now I can go on line totally free." He gave me a gmail address.

As our tea steeped, I picked up the picture of his mother. She wore only the hint of a smile, as if to show a firm resolve. She had a thin, delicate nose, handsome cheek bones, and the same dark eyes, although they were more doe-like in her oval face and betrayed a degree of vulnerability absent in her son. "She was beautiful."

Picasso allowed himself a smile. "She'd bristle at that. She was first and foremost an investigative reporter."

"An endangered species these days," I responded. "Tell me about her."

He handed me a mug of tea and we sat down facing each other. "She was born and raised in upstate New York. Studied journalism at Columbia. She had a fling with some guy there, and I arrived nine months later." He chuckled and smiled. "She always said she got two great things from Columbia—a journalism degree and me. She was a single, working mom, never talked about my dad. Always made time for me, too. That's what's so hard, I guess. You know what self-absorbed shits twelve-year-olds can be. I never got a chance to tell her what a great mom she was, how much I loved her."

I winced inwardly. I knew firsthand the consequences of self-absorption. My wife had committed suicide, and I'd been too busy to see the signs of her depression. I kept those black thoughts to myself. "Moms have a way of knowing what their kids think."

He shot me a warning don't-bull-shit-me look. I was learning fast that Picasso had a low tolerance for anything remotely sappy.

"What happened after she disappeared?"

"My aunt Amy —my mom's sister—came and stayed at our place for a while. Finally, she had to go back to Florida. I think she made it clear she wasn't up for an instant family, and I was telling everyone who'd listen that I didn't want to leave Portland. So, DHS plunked me into a foster home with the Dougans. They lived over in the Hollywood district, which meant I had to change schools. I *hated* that, but old man Dougan had a coronary three months later, and I was put with another family. They had this posh place over by Reed College. I couldn't get along with their older son, so they gave me back to the system. By then, I was heavy into weed and art. School sucked, but I could get lost in painting, man."

"You still doing drugs?"

He gave me a sharp look. "Would that make a difference?"

I looked him in the eye. "I like to know what I'm dealing with."

He paused for a moment, as if he were considering his answer with some care. "I used to think drugs expanded my mind, but then I figured out art did that all by itself. But people like you shouldn't judge. Most people I know using drugs do it because they're in *pain*, not because they're bad people. Every kid on the street has a story, man, and none of the stories are good."

I nodded. "Just wanted to know. No judgment."

"I'm not saying I don't take a puff of weed now and then. You know, there's social pressure sometimes, like it's rude to turn down a toke." He took a sip of his tea and laughed. "Where was I? Oh, yeah, I wound up with a single foster parent next. Addie Jacobs was her name. What a trip. She was a big woman with a heart of gold and a gonzo cook. But she tried to force me to go to school. Finally I said, fuck it and ran away. I think I really hurt her, but I had to get out of there. I'd just turned fifteen."

"You've been on the street ever since?"

"More or less. I'd couch surf with friends sometimes, you know, mix it up. Never one place very long. When I turned eighteen, I got control of the money from my mom's estate. I don't want anyone to know about that. I'm saving up so I can go to art school." He looked around with a self-satisfied smile. "This place, the wood for the foundation—all donated, man."

"You'll need a high school diploma to get into art school."

"Not a problem. Got my GED. I studied online. The tests were a snap."

We talked some more about his life on the street, and then I changed directions. "You told me your mother and Mitchell Conyers fought a lot. Tell me about their relationship."

His face tightened. He got up and started to pace. "Conyers started showing up about a year before mom disappeared. She was a great mom, but she had lousy taste in men. He drank a lot and wasn't a happy drunk, man. He'd get wasted and then start accusing her of all kinds of things." He stopped pacing, smiled bitterly and shook his head. "He was a jealous little shit."

"Did he ever hit her?"

"Yeah. A couple of times, at least. Then he'd come crawling back."

"What about you?"

"He knew that if he touched a hair on my head, my mom would kill him."

"He's still in Portland?"

"Oh yeah. He owns a high-end steak joint downtown, on Second, I think."

"The Happy Angus?"

"That's it, I think. I'm not a regular there."

I smiled. "I've heard of the place. It's a Portland landmark." I drained my tea and waived off a second cup. Antioxidants aside, next to a cup of coffee, drinking tea's like kissing your sister. "Do you have any idea why your mom's remains wound up in a reservoir on the Deschutes River?"

He shrugged as a cloud of pain crossed his face. "No. I tried to find a connection between Conyers and the person who owns that property over there. His name was in the paper. But I didn't get anywhere."

"What about the woman you tried to confront. What's her name?"

"Jessica Armandy. I think she's a high-class hooker or something."

"A hooker?"

"Yeah, you know the look, right? Tits on display, too much makeup, and lots of sparkly jewelry."

"How does she fit in?"

"All I know is that Conyers trotted her out when he needed an alibi. Very convenient."

As our talk wound down, the lamp began to run out of propane. It started hissing, casting the room in a flickering white light. Standing at the door with the briefcase in my hand, I said, "I'll find my way out. I got what I need, at least for now. I'll look this stuff over and get back to you—by email, I guess. We don't have a lot to go on yet, so I need you to stay patient."

Picasso rolled his eyes. "We know who the fuck did it, man. All we need is a little proof."

"I hope you're right," I responded. As I started up the path, I saw the shadowy outline of Joey. I told him good night but he didn't answer.

It had been a long day, and I wasn't looking forward to the long drive back to Dundee. I worked my way over to the I-5, and when I'd cleared Portland heading south, I called Nando on my Bluetooth. "Calvin, my friend, what can I do for you?" he answered.

"I talked to Stout."

"So quickly? Thank you."

I laughed. "Don't thank me yet. It was brief. He's heard of you, Nando. He said you need to clean up your act, that the cops tell him your agency has a reputation for cutting corners."

Nando blew a loud breath into the phone. "I am not cutting the corners. I am running a *business*, and for a business to make money, it must get results."

"The police don't care about your results. They just care about how you go about getting them. There's a difference."

"So, is my license in jeopardy?"

"I don't think so. Stout said he'd look into the situation and get back to me." Nando grumbled something in Spanish I didn't catch, and I changed the subject. "Listen, I'm going to need your help on something." I filled him in on the murder of Nicole Baxter and answered his questions.

When I finished, Nando said, "Is this homeless artist able to pay you your usual fee?"

"Uh, yeah. His mother left him some money." I didn't tell him Picasso was saving that money for art school. "We'll work it out."

"Good. I know your weakness for charity cases, my friend. And you know my unwillingness to work for nothing. I do not wish to see you get hurt financially on this."

"Not a problem," I said, trying to convey more conviction than I felt.

"It sounds like you will be spending more time than usual in Portland on this case. Where are you going to stay?"

I shrugged. "I don't know. Haven't really thought about it."

"I have a small office building on Couch that is awaiting the funds to renovate it. It has a small apartment on the second floor. The former owner lived there. You could stay there, cut down on your overhead."

"That's a great idea. Thanks for the offer."

"We will call it even for your efforts with Mr. Stout."

Nando was right, of course. I couldn't afford to take a financial hit on this case. Not to worry, I told myself, chances are it won't go anywhere.

Chapter Six

When I drove up to the gate that night, my dog Archie greeted me with a fusillade of high-pitched yelps while jumping up and down and spinning madly in circles. You really can't beat the greeting an Aussie gives you, especially a hungry one. I fed him first, then took out a nice slab of Chinook salmon I had defrosting in the fridge and slapped it on the grill. That, together with some greens from the garden, roasted red potatoes, and a glass of Sancerre, made a fine meal.

After dinner I cleared the table in the kitchen and placed the contents of Picasso's briefcase in front of me—a three-inch-thick file folder and two thumb drives. It felt good to have something substantive to focus on, and I found myself wondering how much my decision to help Picasso was influenced by the sheer distractive power of a cold case. I read through the printed material first, taking a few notes and marking interesting items in her appointment book with sticky notes. When I came to the thumb drives containing his mother's back-up computer files, I groaned out loud. Each drive had dozens of pages of documents and emails. What did I expect from a reporter?

It would take hours to read through everything, so I decided to focus only on the most recent thumb drive. It wasn't full like the other one, covering from early February of 2005 up to the day she disappeared, May 18. I printed out everything that looked relevant to her disappearance.

The entire task took a little better than two hours, at which point I made myself a cappuccino and gave Archie a bone to gnaw on before sitting back down. I'd put the promising items into a stack and tossed the rest aside. The good news was that the stack was short, but that was the bad news, too. It contained Nicole Baxter's appointment book, printouts of four emails she had sent before disappearing, and in what I assumed was Picasso's handwriting, a note that gave the names and addresses of two of his mother's friends and three of her colleagues at work. That was it.

Furthermore, I didn't see anything pointing to a connection between the boyfriend, Conyers, and Weiman, the fishing cabin owner, nor was there any obvious connection between Nicole Baxter and Weiman. This didn't particularly surprise me—the fruit is seldom on the low branches.

From the news articles covering the disappearance, I learned Baxter had gone missing on a Friday night, after having a drink with a woman named Cynthia Duncan, one of the friends Picasso had listed. The article stated Baxter did not tell her friend where she was going that night and that she seemed in an unusually good mood. Her car was found abandoned in a SmartPark on SW Tenth in downtown Portland the following Monday, the day the investigation into her disappearance formally began. Mitchell Conyers was mentioned frequently in the articles, but he never rose to the level of a person of interest in the investigation. However, *The Oregonian* did report leaks from within the Portland Police Bureau to the effect that Conyers and Baxter had a "stormy" relationship, and that Conyers had refused a lie detector test.

Several entries in her appointment book caught my eye. Nicole Baxter was a busy woman who met with lots of people, and on several occasions she met or had a phone conversation with the same person—someone called, mysteriously enough, X-Man. Each meeting was at 8:00 p.m., and the last was just a week before she disappeared. I jotted the name down followed by a question mark. On three separate dates, one in April and two in May, she had written down phone numbers with no references to names or places, and on May 13 she had entered an address—5318 SW Macadam, along with the initials LV—in the 2:00 o'clock time slot. I would follow up on these, as well.

The three emails I printed out were all sent to Hank McCauley from Nicole Baxter, with no one copied. Judging from the context, McCauley must have been Baxter's boss at *The Oregonian*.

March 24, 2005

Hank,

I've got a potentially big story that's going to take a lot of time and energy to complete. I can't discuss any details now, and this email must be just between you and me. I have only talked to my source by phone and he has not revealed his name to me yet. I need you to cut me some slack on the Columbia dredging story. I think I'm the only reporter looking at it, so a little slippage won't hurt. What say?

Nicky

April 15, 2005

Hank,

My source is still talking but is nervous as a cat. He went to the police first, but apparently nothing came of it. He wants to remain anonymous and I'm still working to gain trust. I'm forbidden to discuss any of this with *anyone* (including you) until I'm given the "complete picture." I'll fill you in when the time is right. This story is a beaut. You're gonna love it.

Thanks for easing up my workload! You won't regret it.

Nicky

May 12, 2005

Hank,

Blockbuster alert! This story is huge. My source is
flowing like a river now. I've got to check several
things out, and then I'll be ready to sit down with you.
Thanks for the patience. You're a saint!

Nicky

It wasn't until I'd read the emails through again that I noticed
something else. The date of each one was the day *after* Baxter had
met with X-Man. The meetings were in the late evening, so it
would follow that Baxter would brief her boss the next day. "Of
course, X-Man must be Baxter's source!" I called to Archie, who
stood up and wagged his tail in apparent agreement. I turned
this over in my mind, wondering if Baxter or the source had
selected the name. I also wondered if the Portland police had
made the same connection. If they had, then they'd have focused
a lot of attention on identifying X-Man. Had they succeeded?

Then there was the question of the nature of the "blockbuster"
story Baxter was working on. What was it? And what had happened to her notes?

It was 1:20 a.m., and I was high on adrenaline and caffeine.
I pulled up a reverse phone directory on the net and tapped
in the first of the three phone numbers I'd copied from her
appointment book. It belonged to a psychologist in Lake Oswego
specializing in adolescent therapy. Thinking of the rings, snakes,
and tattoos now decorating Picasso's body, I had to chuckle. He'd
been a handful at twelve, I guessed. The second number was
for an auto repair shop specializing in Volvos, the make of car
Baxter owned. The third was for a bed and breakfast in Carlton,
a small town surrounded by vineyards that lay out my way, on
the north side of the Dundee Hills. I jotted down the date and
the name of the B&B.

I tapped the address on Macadam into a reverse address website next. It came up as the KPOC radio station, a Portland based AM station. I logged onto their website and scanned it for some hint of who the initials LV might stand for. There it was—their headliner was a man named Larry Vincent, who hosted a daily talk show called *Vincent's View*. Of course, I said to myself, I've heard of this guy. He's Portland's right-wing shock jock. But was he working there eight years ago? It only took a few more clicks on Google to verify that, in fact, he was.

I leaned back in my chair and stretched. Not a bad night's work, I decided. Of course, the first thing I should do is talk with the Portland Cold Case Unit, I told myself. The information I'd developed should be of interest to them and Jefferson County. At the same time, I felt more than a little protective of what I'd uncovered. Maybe I should hold off. Talk to Picasso and a couple of the key players first. Check a few things out. That's what I decided to do.

I took the back stairs to my bedroom and stood at the open bedroom window drinking in the cool night air. A few lights still flickered in the valley. They looked like a reflection of the stars in the night sky. An owl hooted way up in a Douglas fir next to the house, and a family of coyotes was chorusing merrily down in the quarry.

I was back in the hunt.

Chapter Seven

At seven the next morning I was roused from a deep sleep by Archie's barking and someone banging on the front door. As I staggered down the stairs cursing under my breath, I remembered it was the day the guy who'd agreed to repair my fence in exchange for a divorce was due to start work. He'd brought the materials we discussed and some beat-up tools, but it didn't take long for me to see he'd never fixed a fence before in his life. I wound up spending the day at the Aerie making sure the job got done. I was tired of skunks and coyotes wandering in at night through the holes in the fence, and Archie was, too.

This wasn't exactly the bargain the man and I had struck, but I decided not to make a big deal out of it. Plus, he was out of work and like so many people I represented, shattered by the failure of his marriage. Besides, he may not have known much about fence repair, but he put his back into the work.

When we broke for lunch, I sent Picasso the following email:

Hello Picasso,

I've read through your evidence book and have a couple of questions. I'm tied up today, but plan to come to Portland tomorrow. Let me know best time, place for us to talk. Meanwhile, think about the following.

1. Do you know or have you ever heard of someone using the nickname X-Man? Your mom met or talked with him several times and I'd like to know his name.

2. Do you know anything about a story your mom was working on when she disappeared? She might have described it as something big, a "block-buster," maybe.

3. Did your mom mention someone named Larry Vincent around the time she disappeared? He's a DJ at KPOC radio station. I think she had an appointment to meet with him a few days after she disappeared. Just wondering if you remember hearing the name...

Regards,

Cal

It was close to noon the next day when I cleared the Terwilliger curves on the I-5 and Portland's skyline burst into view, wounded as it was by the new high rise condos built on the river. To the east, Mt. Hood levitated above a sea of low clouds and to the north I could just make out Mt. St. Helens' decapitated profile. On the way up, the odometer of my three series BMW clicked past 200,000 miles, a milestone that gave me more than a little satisfaction. I'd bought it used at 50,000 miles and was getting my money's worth. I found a parking space on Couch and walked over to Nando's building. I was meeting him to check out the place he had offered me.

Nando showed up five minutes later, impeccably dressed as usual, in a silk tie, finely tailored blazer, sharply creased chinos, and hand-tooled Italian loafers. He opened the front door with a key and waved me in. "Welcome to your new home away from home. I hope you like it."

By the sign still hanging above the door—Caffeine Central—I knew it had been a neighborhood coffee shop that had almost certainly been put out of business by the Starbucks perched at the end of the block. "I hope they left the espresso machine hooked up," I said as I followed him into the building. The bottom half of the place was empty except for a huge, overstuffed couch that looked too heavy to move. A set of wide double doors through a dividing wall led to a rear area which housed a bathroom, kitchen, and storage areas, and a flight of stairs leading up to a small landing.

We took the stairs and Nando used a second key to open the door to the apartment. A narrow hall with a bath on one side and small bedroom on the other opened to a large room where light streamed in from three windows with slanted venetian blinds. A galley kitchen on the left and dining room/living room on the right completed the space.

Nando made a sweeping gesture with one hand. "I bought the place as is, furniture, TV, refrigerator, everything. The poor man who sold it was desperate, I think. What do you think?"

I walked over to the center window and spread the blinds to take in the view down on Couch. "This'll do nicely. Thanks."

He handed me a set of keys. "Use it in peace, my friend. I won't start working on it until later this year, God willing."

We had lunch at the Lemongrass, a little Thai joint on the other side of the river. Nando liked Thai almost as much as Cuban food, and the Lemongrass fare was as good as it was authentic. After railing about the state of the country, during which time he'd polished off a platter of roasted duck and vegetables in a smoldering hot curry sauce, he opened the business conversation. "Any word from Mr. Stout?"

I shook my head as I wrapped a last bite of larb in a lettuce leaf. "No news is probably good news."

"Would it help save my license if the man Ramon beat up dropped the charges?"

"Wouldn't hurt, but how're you going to arrange that?" I asked, fearing the answer.

Nando dabbed at his mouth with a napkin and smiled broadly. "Well, after all, I have photos of this man with another woman. I'm sure some—"

"Don't even think about it," I said. "You'll make matters worse with a stunt like that. I think Stout will come around in terms of your license, but Ramon will have to take his chances. Maybe we can get his charges reduced to a misdemeanor."

"Okay. Okay. It was just a thought. We will take the high street, then."

"Good. You won't regret it. Now let's talk about this case I'm working on." I went on to fill him in on what I'd learned from Picasso's information. When I'd finished I said, "So, there're a bunch of open questions. I'm on a tight budget here, so all I'd like you to do right now is see if you can look into the background of Larry Vincent. See if there's any way to tie him to Nicole Baxter."

Nando nodded. "What else?"

"Well, you might take a quick look at the woman Conyers was with the night Baxter disappeared."

"Jessica Armandy?"

"Right. I'm interested in her background as well."

That's how I left it with Nando. Picasso and I had agreed to meet at four that afternoon at the medical clinic. When I arrived, I didn't see him working on his mural. I walked over to the wall to see how it was coming. He hadn't started painting yet, but a few of the blocked-in figures I'd seen earlier were now drawn with more detail. It looked like some kind of parade or procession. A life-sized, yet small, lithe figure was sketched in at the front of the parade. I was pretty sure it was Mahatma Ghandi. He was walking ahead of a man in boots and a hard hat. Behind him was a tall figure in flowing robes and sandals. Jesus Christ? He was arm in arm with a woman in tennis shoes. Others were sketched in less detail, although there was a rough sketch of a tall woman with a stethoscope around her neck who looked suspiciously like Anna Eriksen.

Picasso had told me the mural will make a statement about health care. Just how, I wasn't sure.

I went into the clinic, slipped by the guy with the stretched earlobes, and peeked through the swinging doors. Anna Eriksen was reading at her desk. "Hi, Anna. I see you're being immortalized in Picasso's mural."

She put her glasses down, smiled, then wrinkled her brow. "*What?*"

"There's a tall woman sketched in out there that looks a lot like you."

She brushed a lock of hair from across her eye and smiled, crinkling the corners of her pale blue eyes. "*He didn't.*"

I returned the smile. "Might be your twin."

"We talked about that. He *promised*."

"Do you know where he is?"

"You just missed him. He said to tell you he went to meet with someone named Mitchell Conyers. He'll be back as soon as he can. I'm glad you two were able to work it out."

"*Conyers?*" I said, ignoring her last sentence. "How did that happen?"

"I have no idea. Is something wrong?"

"The last time those two got together, they wound up in a fist fight. Picasso's convinced Conyers killed his mother."

Anna put her hand to her mouth. "Oh, God. I thought that name sounded familiar. They had a fight at the memorial service, didn't they?"

"Right. Do you know where they're meeting?"

"No." She paused for a moment before adding, "But I think he used his computer to get directions."

"Where's his computer?"

Anna got up and I followed her to a storage room at the back of the clinic. Picasso's battered laptop was charging there. The screen was up, but dark. I hit the enter key and held my breath. An address on Westover Road and directions to get there popped up.

"Are you going to go over there?" She had more than a little concern in her eyes.

I nodded. "Yeah, I probably should."

"He's on his bike, so you're not that far behind him."

I took Burnside to 23rd and hung a right, then a quick left onto Westover, which started to climb into the West Hills, Portland's primo neighborhood. The street number on Picasso's computer corresponded to a three story Tudor, white with dark, half-timbering detail like something from Stratford on Avon. Artisan stone steps led up a steep, ivy covered bank to the house. I parked and took the steps two at a time. Picasso's bike was propped next to the front porch.

I started to ring the doorbell, when I heard the rattle of a gate to my left, then a muffled voice. I turned toward the gate and heard the next utterance with crystal clarity. "*Oh, Jesus Christ.*" The hair on the back of my neck straightened out. It was Picasso's voice.

The gate burst open and Picasso came into view. He was soaking wet and there was no question about it, his hands and arms were covered in blood.

Chapter Eight

I came off the steps and rushed over to him. "What the hell's going on?"

He looked at me as if I'd just materialized out of thin air, his eyes huge, strangely unfocused. He turned his head, looked back through the gate and pointed. "He's dead. Conyers is dead."

"*What?*" I said, pushing past him. The backyard looked like something out of the tropics—lush grass, big leafed plants in massive pots, and a profusion of flowers in beds and hanging baskets. A kidney-shaped swimming pool edged in jade green tile and surrounded with a stamped concrete deck sat toward the back of the yard, which was fenced and gated. The body of a man was lying at the shallow end of the pool, legs dangling in the water, arms outstretched, as if he were trying to pull himself out. His head was haloed in blood, the water in the pool a hazy, telltale pink.

I dropped to one knee next to him. His eyes were cocked open in a blank, dead-man's stare, his mouth agape, a look of utter surprise frozen on his face. From the newspaper photos I'd seen, it looked like Conyers. His head had a sizeable hole punched in it—a crater of splintered bone, oozing blood, and gray matter just above the right ear. I jerked my head away and heard myself say, "Shit."

I got up and returned to Picasso, who'd remained standing at the open gate. I gripped him by the shoulders and shook him. "What have you done, son? What the hell have you done?"

He twisted out of my grip and met my eyes. "I didn't do anything, man. He was floating in the pool when I got here. I jumped in to pull him out. He hit his head or something. Some kind of accident."

"*Accident?*" I went over to the diving board, a short fiberglass plank bolted to a low, round pedestal. It was as clean as a whistle. The tiles edging the pool were bullnosed, which seemed to eliminate the possibility that Conyers had somehow hit his head on them. At the deep end, around the corner from the diving board, I saw a distinct line of spattered blood. It was nearly dry on the warm cement. I backed away so as not to step on it.

Picasso remained standing at the gate, watching me intently.

I said, "He's been murdered. Someone either shot him or stabbed him with the mother of all ice picks." I pointed down. "I can see the blood spray. He was probably dead before he hit the water." I forced myself to take another look. "I'm guessing the ice pick. Doesn't look like a gun shot wound to me." I glanced around, looking for the murder weapon. "See anything lying around here?"

"No. I just found him floating there in the water."

I met his eyes and said, "Are you *sure?* Did you get angry and hit him with something?"

"*No.* I didn't. Please believe me."

"Why did you come here, anyway?"

"I got a message from Conyers. He said he had some important information about my mom and wanted to meet with me. Said there were no hard feelings." He dug into his pocket and pulled out a folded piece of paper. Here's the message. Milo said a bike messenger brought it for me."

"Who's Milo?"

"The guy who works the desk at the clinic," he answered, handing me the note. "Careful, it got wet."

I opened it gingerly, looked up and shook my head. "I can't read this. The ink's all over the page."

A car passed by on Westover. Picasso looked down at the street then back at me. "Shit, man, I'm getting the hell out of here."

"That would be the worst thing you could do. Tell me again, did you get angry and hit him?"

"*No*, I didn't do *anything*," he said. "He was face down in the pool." Picasso expelled a breath and shook his head. "I should've taken off, but I couldn't just leave him there. I thought he might still be alive."

He locked onto my eyes and didn't flinch. His appearance would scream guilty to the police—the coiled snake, the facial rings glinting in the sun, his hands stained with blood. But his eyes said something else to me. With that look and in that instant, something clicked into place, and I decided to believe him; at least most of me did. A small corner of my brain—call it the L.A. prosecutor piece—remained skeptical. Be careful, it warned.

He spun around and started out the gate. I caught up to him and grabbed his arm. "Don't do this, Picasso. Running's an admission of guilt. I believe you. I believe you didn't kill him."

My statement must've struck a chord. He stopped and gripped his head in his big hands and stood there with his back to me for what seemed an eternity. Then he turned around and folded his arms across his chest, "Okay, so I don't run. What the fuck happens now?"

"I've got to call 911. But before I do, tell me *exactly* what happened. Start when you arrived at the clinic this morning."

Picasso went back over the events. He hadn't seen the bike messenger arrive or leave. He was busy sketching. He didn't know much about Milo either, except that he was a recovering heroin addict. And no, he didn't think anyone had seen him leave for Conyers' place on his bike, and he sure as hell hadn't taken any murder weapons with him.

When he finished, he asked, "What's going to happen when they come, the cops?"

"They'll take preliminary statements here from both of us, then we'll go downtown to make it official. They'll take you in a squad car. They'll probably let me drive down."

"What about my bike?"

I started to tell him not to worry about it, but caught myself, realizing his bike was a major possession. "They'll probably impound it as evidence. If not, I'll put it in my trunk. In either case, you'll get it back. Now listen, Picasso, tell them *exactly* what happened, just like you told me. I'll join you as soon as I can. If they ask you something you're unsure of, do not speculate, and if they start asking you about *anything* other than what happened this morning, don't answer. Tell them you'd rather discuss it first with me. Got that?"

He nodded. "Are you still my lawyer?"

I almost said not for long, but opted to stay optimistic. "Good question. I am unless they charge you with something. If that happens, I'll have to bow out since I'm a witness. We'll cross that bridge when we get to it." I looked around the yard and added, "I'm going to take a quick look for the murder weapon. Stay here, you're still dripping."

I didn't see anything that could have been used to kill Conyers, and that bothered me. But, I went ahead and placed the 911 call. When I snapped my cell shut, Picasso looked down at his hands as if he were seeing the blood for the first time. He said, "Should I wash this shit off?"

"No. You can explain why the blood's there. You had to pull him out of the pool. You couldn't hide it anyway."

He shook his head and clenched his jaw. For a young homeless man like Picasso, the cops were to be feared even in the best of times. And this wasn't the best of times. He said, "I'm totally screwed. The cops are gonna be all over me." He held his hands in front of his face. "Shit, look at me!"

"If you didn't kill him, you have nothing to worry about," I shot back, but I didn't believe that for a moment. Picasso had a strong motive that was public knowledge, and with Conyers' blood literally on his hands, I knew his chances as well as he did, maybe even better. The criminal justice system was genetically programmed to rush to judgment in open and shut cases, and taking a menacing homeless man off the street rated bonus points.

But running was no answer, either. Hell, people back at the clinic knew he'd come here. That's when it hit me—this was all too convenient. I began to smell a frame-up. Not your garden variety frame, either. Someone had planned this with considerable care.

We heard the first *whoop whoop* of sirens in the distance. Picasso shook his head, looked at me and said, "I'm so screwed."

The sirens grew louder. I searched his eyes, a final gut check. They were a mix of fear and accusation. Flight to him probably seemed like his only chance, and I'd talked him out of it.

I said, "You're innocent, Picasso. When the cops get here, act like it." Then I heard myself add, "And don't worry, I'll get you out of this."

Who was I kidding?

Chapter Nine

A patrol car screeched to a halt down in the street, followed by an ambulance. The uniformed officers quickly sent the ambulance back and called in homicide and the ME. Lieutenant Harmon Scott was still puffing from the climb up the stone steps when he introduced himself. Scott had thinning brown hair, narrow eyes that squinted at me from behind thick glasses, and a belly that hung unapologetically over his belt. He looked more like a used car salesman than a cop, except for his eyes. They were the color of fog and had that glaze of practiced indifference that cops everywhere eventually adopt.

His partner, Detective Aldus Jones, was younger, trimmer, and still looked like he enjoyed his job. Smooth ebony skin accentuated a mouth full of perfect, white teeth, which he periodically flashed in a brilliant smile, even at a murder scene.

Scott and Jones looked the situation over, then separated us like I predicted. Jones took Picasso, Scott took me. We sat down at the table on the patio. Jones and Picasso had grabbed a couple of chairs and were face to face over by the gate. The uniforms were putting crime tape in place, and two medical techs and a young female photographer, who had just arrived, were setting up shop next to Conyers' body.

Scott pulled a spiral notebook from his shirt pocket and armed a ball point pen with thick, stubby fingers. "So, Mr. Claxton, I need your address and what you do for a living before we start."

I complied, adding, "Before I moved to Oregon, I was a deputy DA for the city of Los Angeles for twenty-two years. I worked closely with Pete Stout down there. Major Crimes." It was a shameless plug, but I wanted to get it in. It would add weight to my statement, and we needed all the help we could get.

Scott raised a single eyebrow and grunted but didn't write anything down. "Are you Mr. Baxter's attorney?"

"I am, but on a different matter."

"I see. What different matter?"

"I'm afraid that's privileged."

He nodded and jotted something down. "Start when you arrived here, and tell me exactly what happened." After I took him through the events and answered several questions, he said, "Why did you come to Mr. Conyers' house in the first place?"

"I was going to sit in on a meeting with him and Danny Baxter."

"What kind of meeting?"

"As far as I know, they were going to discuss some aspect of the disappearance of Danny's mother, Nicole Baxter." I told him about the message Danny had received but didn't explain what had happened to it. Picasso would cover that. The less said about our discussion before I called 911, the better. "She's been missing for eight years," I continued. "They found her remains over on the Deschutes River recently. I'm sure you heard about it."

Scott's eyes came up from his notebook and narrowed down to slits. "Right. Know the case. Were you invited to this, uh, meeting?"

"Not directly. Danny left word where he'd be and left it up to me as to whether I'd attend." That was close to the truth, and I saw no gain in implying I'd just barged in on the scene.

"What was Mr. Conyers' relationship to Mr. Baxter's mother?" I was pretty sure that was a question to which Scott already knew the answer.

"I believe he was Mrs. Baxter's boyfriend at the time she disappeared."

"I see." The eyes narrowed again. He was circling for the kill. "And how would you characterize the relationship between Mr. Baxter and Mr. Conyers?"

"I have no direct knowledge of that. I've only known Danny for a week or so."

"What about indirect knowledge?"

"I couldn't say."

A brief smile flickered across Scott's face, but he kept his eyes down as he jotted something in his notebook. Then he looked up. "Did you, uh, happen to see anything lying around here that could have been used to kill Mr. Conyers?"

"No, I didn't. But I really wasn't looking."

Scott closed his notebook and clipped his ballpoint in his shirt pocket. "Okay, Mr. Claxton, we're done for now. I'm going to need you to come downtown today for a formal statement." He handed me a card then glanced over at Picsasso and Detective Jones, who were heading out the gate. Picasso's shoulders were slumped, his face ashen. "You know we have to take Mr. Baxter in for further processing."

"Of course you do," I said. "If you have further questions for him, I plan to sit in."

Scott raised his eyebrows. "You're a witness to this crime."

"He and I *both* are, lieutenant."

At this point, we heard the thwop, thwop, thwop of an incoming news helicopter. Scott looked up, shaded his eyes and said under his breath, "Just don't crash in my friggin' crime scene."

I was going to make a quip about "if it bleeds it leads" but thought better of it.

As we were leaving I noticed the two ME technicians reenacting the murder at the edge of the pool, where I'd seen the blood spatter. One technician was standing where Conyers had stood, facing the pool. The other, who was behind him, raised his right hand and simulated a blow to the head. Then the man playing Conyers spun around, and the other man smiled and nodded.

I stopped dead when I saw that hand come up to strike the blow, that *right* hand. Why hadn't I thought of it sooner? Conyers' wound was above his right ear. If his assailant was directly behind him when he struck the blow, then he was most likely right handed.

Scott turned and gave me an impatient look as I stood there watching.

I felt a twinge of hope, maybe even vindication, and suppressed an urge to smile.

Chapter Ten

"Look, gentlemen," I said, allowing an edge of irritation in my voice, "Mr. Baxter's a witness to this crime, and he is more than happy to discuss what he observed at the Conyers' residence. He is *not* willing to join you in a fishing expedition. Now, if we can't move on, I'm going to advise my client to terminate this voluntary interview." We were downtown, in the middle of Picasso's second round of questioning. Scott and Jones kept coming back to the altercation between Picasso and Conyers at Nicole Baxter's memorial, and I'd heard enough of that. I guess they knew I wasn't bluffing, because after exchanging a glance, they moved on to another line of questioning.

They held us until about nine thirty that night, at which time we were informed they had a warrant to search Picasso's cabin at Dignity Village. The search was intrusive, owing to the flood lights that were brought in, and just about every person living in the village was milling around, trying to get a peek at the action. There was a lot of grumbling and more than a few choice epithets were shouted by the residents, who saw the cops, to a person, as the enemy. I turned around to say something to Picasso and noticed he was gone. I found him a few minutes later kneeling down next to his neighbor, Joey, the Iraq war veteran. Joey sat outside his shed with his head in his hands, sobbing.

"—It's okay, big fella," Picasso said in a low voice. "Nobody's hurt. Everything's cool. The cops are just looking around in my place. No big deal." He reached into Joey's shirt pocket and extracted a pack of Camels and a chrome plated lighter. "Here, man, have a smoke." Joey wiped his eyes with his forearm and took a cigarette. I turned around before Picasso could see me watching and blended back into the crowd.

Picasso had so few belongings that the search was over in less than an hour. I figured they were holding off on arresting him, hoping to find something more incriminating in the search. When this didn't happen, Jones, Scott, and the search team left unceremoniously at a little past eleven, after warning us both to stay in town.

As I was walking back to my car, my cell chirped. It was Nando. "What is going on, Calvin? I just heard you and some young fellow with a snake tattooed on his neck are being entertained by Portland homicide."

I had to chuckle. There wasn't a lot that happened in Portland that Nando didn't eventually hear about. I didn't bother to ask how he found out. "Yeah, it's true. The young artist you helped locate and I are witnesses in the murder of his mother's boyfriend. The guy got his head drilled this afternoon up in the West Hills. Picasso found the body, and I came on the scene right after that. "

"Witnesses, not suspects?"

"Well, there haven't been any arrests, put it that way. The police just finished up a search of Picasso's place over here at Dignity Village. They came up empty."

"Perhaps we need to talk?"

"That would be good."

Twenty minutes later, Nando and I sat in the apartment above Caffeine Central. He'd brought a cold six-pack of La Tropical, his favorite Cuban beer, mail ordered from Miami. Nando was slumped on a couch, and I was pacing the floor in front of him. I said, "Going disco dancing later tonight?"

A questioning look morphed into a smile as he reached down and fingered the heavy gold chain around his neck. "Disco was huge in Havana, but in those days, I couldn't afford a chain like

this. What can I say? The gold just feels good against my neck."
He dropped the smile and picked the thread of our conversation
back up. "So, how can you be so sure the young man's innocent?"

I took a pull on my beer. "It was gut feel at first, and the
more I pushed him, the more I believed his story. Look at it
this way—Picasso's a bright kid. If he wanted to kill Conyers,
do you think he'd announce to the world he was going to his
house, stab him in the head, then jump in the pool and pull
him out? I don't think so. And to top it off, I'm pretty sure the
medical examiner's going to conclude the killer was right handed.
Picasso's a south paw."

Nando smiled without showing his teeth and swung his left
arm away from his body as if stroking a tennis shot. "Perhaps
he has a wicked backhand."

"I don't think so. Someone dealing a death blow is going to
go for maximum power. Forehand, for sure."

Nando eyed me skeptically. "What if they struggled and
Conyers pulled him into the swimming pool before Picasso hit
him?"

I shook my head vigorously. "No way. There was a blood
spray pattern on the deck consistent with a single, sharp blow
to the head. That blow put Conyers in the pool, I'm sure of it.
And he didn't take anyone with him."

Nando smiled again, a fleeting gleam of white teeth. "I know
you are familiar with forensic evidence, but so much information from so little blood? As for the rest of your argument, you
know and I know, my friend, that passion and anger can cause
a man to do crazy things. It is not like you to make such a snap
judgment."

I pushed down a surge of irritation at Nando's skepticism,
although deep down I knew he had a point. The little voice in
my head reminded me of that. "It's the way I see it."

He nodded at my hand holding a beer bottle. "You're right
handed. I'm sure this fact is not lost on the investigating officers."

I forced a smile as a tiny flame of anxiety lit in my stomach.
"Who knows? If they give up on Picasso, they might turn on me."

Nando nodded. "You are a material witness to a brutal murder of a well known Portland business man. It would be easy for the police to drag you into this." When I didn't respond, he added, "Your defense of the young man is admirable, but do you think it is wise, Calvin? Perhaps you should distance yourself from this situation."

I stopped pacing and turned to face him. "Look, Nando, I gave the kid the benefit of the doubt, okay? He's being thrown to the wolves by someone, damn it. And you know as well as I do that the justice system will only be too happy to oblige. I can't just stand by and watch that happen."

Nando sighed heavily, nodded, and drained his beer. "So, someone is setting the young artist up?"

"No question in my mind. I mean, he'd already assaulted the guy once, and it was duly recorded in the newspaper. And to John Q Public he's nothing but a pierced and tattooed thug—the perfect fall guy."

"Who would do such a thing?"

I shrugged. "I don't have a clue, but I'm willing to bet it has something to do with the discovery of Nicole Baxter's remains. I think Conyers must have known something, something important enough to get him killed."

Nando popped another beer open. "It would seem so. Otherwise, one would have to assume the timing is coincidental, which, of course, it never is."

Nando left an hour later. I love the man, but he said absolutely nothing to make me feel better about my choice to stand by Picasso. I suppose that's what friends are for—to tell you when you're hell-bent for disaster whether you want to hear it or not. When I was wearing three-piece suits and worrying about my career down in L.A., I would have listened to my friend, but not now. It wasn't just misplaced idealism, either, damn it. The case just didn't sit right with me.

I logged on my computer, typed in a complete set of notes covering the day, then fell into bed. Sleep came quickly, but I had a repeating dream of Conyers' battered head floating past me as I fished a cold, swift river under a dark sky.

Early the next morning I called Gertrude Johnson, whose ten-acre spread sat uphill from mine. She was my accountant as well as my only close neighbor and had agreed to feed Archie in my absence. Before I could ask her about my dog, she said, "Listen, Cal, I hope the time you're spending in Portland is going to result in some receivables, because you were down almost twenty-five percent last month."

My stomach took a quarter turn. "Well, some months are like that, Gertie."

"*Some* months? This is getting to be a regular occurrence. You're down almost twenty percent, year over year," she shot back.

"Portland's not like the valley," I countered. "Business is still pretty good here." It was a true statement as far as it went. "How's Archie?" Changing the subject seemed like the best way out.

After that bracing conversation with Gertie, I headed to the medical clinic on foot with the objective of getting there ahead of Scott and Jones. I arrived at 7:50 to find the place locked and no police in sight. I grabbed an outside table at the little coffee shop and waited with a double cappuccino.

Ten minutes later I saw Anna Eriksen coming down Davis. You can tell a lot about someone by the way they walk. Anna moved with long strides, her gait fluid, athletic—the walk of someone with strong purpose. Dark slacks accentuated the length of her legs, and I decided she must have chosen medicine over dancing or marathon running. But her shoulders were slightly stooped, and as she juggled her briefcase and fumbled for her keys at the door, I sensed she was tired, maybe exhausted. I wondered when she'd last taken a day off.

I caught up to her as she was entering the clinic. She turned to speak and the sun lit the streaks of gold in her hair. "Oh, it's you, Cal. I used the number on your card to call you yesterday and last night, but only got your machine. I've been worried sick. Is everything alright?"

I shook my head. "Sorry. I didn't check my messages last night." After giving her my cell phone number, we went to her office where I took her through yesterday's events.

When I finished explaining my theory that Picasso was being set up, she raised a hand to her mouth and said, "My God, that *has* to be it. I know I told you Picasso was carrying around a lot of rage, but he would never hurt anyone." She said it with a matter-of-fact assurance I found comforting, although her conviction seemed to rest more on a judgment of Picasso's character than logic and evidence. I believed in him, too, but that small voice in my head would need proof, as well.

She continued, "Frankly, I'm amazed the police didn't arrest him. I mean, with all the hysteria about crimes committed by the homeless—"

"Oh, they wanted to arrest him, alright, but they had no murder weapon, and my story tended to corroborate his. But, there's more to come, I'm afraid."

Anna sighed and brushed back a lock of hair. Her eyes were the blue of glacial ice, but now they had warmth I could feel down to the soles of my feet. "Thanks for standing up for him, Cal. Most people either see these kids as a threat or a pitiful lost cause."

I mumbled something about her being welcome then added, "Uh, mind if I look around in the storeroom where Picasso keeps his computer?"

She raised her eyebrows in a question, pulled a ring of keys from her smock and, holding the key in question, handed the ring to me. "It's this one."

I wasn't looking for anything in particular, but it was the only other place I knew of besides his cabin that Picasso stored things. My gut said to check it out. I hated nasty surprises.

The storage room was at the end of the hall, next to the back door. Shelves covering one wall were crammed with general supplies for the clinic. A mop in a bucket, a push broom, and a wooden stepladder spattered with paint were propped in the corner. Picasso's computer sat on a narrow bench along with the backpack I'd seen in his place. At the back of the bench, eight or ten unopened cans of acrylic paint were lined up next to a jar of brushes.

I took a quick look in his backpack. The main pouch contained his sketchbook, a half dozen pencils, a Philip K. Dick paperback, an apple, and the hammer I'd seen him use outside. In a smaller compartment, I found a pair of pliers, a pocket knife, a measuring tape, and a Phillips head screwdriver. His computer would be of great interest to Scott and Jones, so I disconnected it from the charger and put them both under my arm. God knows what he had on that machine.

I handed the computer to Anna and told her to only give it up if it was specifically asked for. I stepped outside just as Picasso rode up on his bike. I glanced at my watch. "I'd like you to take a quick look in the store room before the law arrives. I already removed your computer. Doc has it in her office."

"Why?"

"The cops don't need to see it."

He shrugged. "I've got nothing to hide."

"Good," I answered, "but they still don't need to see it." As he followed me around to the back of the building, I said, "I want to know if anything's there that shouldn't be or if anything's missing."

He entered the room ahead of me, looked around for a few moments and shrugged. "Looks cool to me. What's the big deal?"

"See anything out of the ordinary?"

He glanced around again, half-heartedly. "Nothing."

I nodded in the direction of his backpack. "Those tools in your backpack, are they all there?"

He took a cursory look. "Yeah."

"You don't have something to open your paint cans with?"

His eyes might have flared ever so slightly, but I wasn't sure. "Yeah. It's probably back at the village. I've got more sketching to do before I start painting."

"Okay."

Picasso took his backpack and went out the back door to begin working on his mural. I went down the hall to find Anna. She was just entering an examination room with a file folder in her hand and a stethoscope draped around her neck. "When does Milo get in?" I asked.

She looked at her watch. "He's late. I asked him to come in at eight this morning to help with some filing." She sighed, and her eyes seemed to lose what little color they had. "He's really not working out. I think he's using again."

I went over to the coffee shop, bought Picasso a cup of green tea and brought it to him. He was busy sketching in another figure in his parade, Martin Luther King, maybe. I handed him the tea and said, "You doing okay?"

He blew on the tea and took a sip. "I guess so. Had a hard time sleeping last night. Every time I closed my eyes I saw Conyers' face." He shuddered. "That look, you know? Like he was so surprised he was dead."

I nodded. "Know what you mean."

"I hated the son of a bitch, but I can't say I'm glad about what happened. Maybe I was wrong about him. Maybe he didn't kill mom."

I shrugged. "We just don't know at this point. What can you tell me about the kid with the stretched earlobes—Milo?"

Picasso smiled and tugged playfully on his own earlobe. "They're called *gauges*, man. If you don't make them too big, the holes will grow back when you take them out. Milo's probably won't. You think he's in on this thing?"

"He brought you the note, right? I talked to Doc this morning. She didn't see any bike messenger yesterday, either. She's checking with the rest of her staff, but I doubt if there was any messenger."

Picasso nodded. "Well, I never trusted the dude."

"Why do you say that?"

He considered this for a few moments, and seemed hesitant to talk. A code of the streets, I figured. "We used to call him Captain Smack before he got into that program over on Twelfth.

They got him the job here. He had to agree to start using his real name, and get some of his nastier tats removed, and stay clean, of course. Dude used to move some heroin, man. Said he was straight, but I never bought it. I mean who's ever straight after being on smack?"

"Know where I can find him?"

"I think he has an apartment now. Doc would have his address." He looked around. "Where are the cops? You said they'd be around first thing."

"They'll be here soon enough. And the media might show, too. *Don't* talk to them. Not one syllable. Got that?"

Anna was with a patient, but one of her nurses looked Milo's address up for me, and I was off before Scott and Jones arrived. Milo lived over in Northeast, off Mississippi, in a tired old Craftsman that had been converted to a duplex. M. Hartung was written in child-like block letters on a card thumb-tacked next to the second floor buzzer. I rang twice but got no reply, although I could hear the thrum of music coming from the second floor. I tried the first floor buzzer. No reply there either.

One swipe of a credit card against the lock and I was in the foyer, which greeted me with the aroma of bacon grease and mildew. The music—an incessant techno beat—was much louder now and definitely coming from Milo's apartment. I took the stairs and rapped on his door, which was slightly ajar. Nothing.

I pushed the door open enough to insert my voice. "Hello in there. Anybody home? Milo?" Nothing. I would have left it there if the narrow opening in the door hadn't afforded me a clear view through the living room and down a short hallway to the bathroom. The door was ajar, too, and something lay on the floor across the opening.

It was a thin, pale human leg.

Chapter Eleven

The apartment felt unheated when I stepped in, and Milo's body was as cool to the touch as the room. Clad only in a pair of navy blue boxers, he was slumped to the right side of the commode, face up. His skin was the color of wet plaster, and with closed eyes, he looked like he'd just fallen into a peaceful sleep. A greasy syringe dangled from his arm where the vein, now collapsed, had apparently carried a lethal fix to his heart and brain. A Bic lighter, a soup spoon, and a small red party balloon with its stem cut off sat on the rim of the sink. The bottom of the spoon was blackened with carbon and the inside stained with a dark brown residue. There didn't appear to be any dope left in the balloon.

The residue in the spoon smelled faintly of vinegar, a dead giveaway for black tar heroin. I knew the drug when I smelled it. I knelt down next to him and gently nudged his arm. It was rigid. I saw no needle marks on either arm. His right leg was twisted awkwardly under his body, affording a view of the back of his leg. A trail of red dots, some fainter than others, ran up his calf, tracing his saphenous vein. Anna was right—he *was* using, and he was going to great pains to hide it from her.

I stood up and shook my head, struck by the senseless waste of it all. His young face was a mask of serenity now, almost innocence, but the silver discs piercing his earlobes reflected in the harsh light like garish mirrors. There'd be no growing back of the holes now, that's for sure.

As the radio blasted away in the living room, I took a quick look around. On a small plastic end table next to a thread-bare sofa bed, I found a baggie with a half dozen white pills spilling out of it. I had no idea what they were. I put one in my shirt pocket. I saw nothing else out of the ordinary except a half-dozen long necks in an otherwise clean trash can. Either Milo was a beer drinker as well, or he could've had a visitor the night before.

I wiped my prints clean and as far as I knew, got out of the building without being seen. After clearing the neighborhood, I called Nando. "What are you doing?" I asked when he picked up.

"Slaving in my office."

"Which one?"

"My detective agency."

"I'll be right over."

The office was in Lents, a diverse, blue collar stronghold in Southeast Portland. It was in a storefront just off the Max Green Line next to a used book store. A sign in the window said, *Se Habla Espanol.* Nando's long-time secretary, Espinoza, waved me through to his office, which reflected his belief in low overhead. It was small and sparsely furnished and the walls unadorned except for a framed copy of his license, and a large photo of Barack Obama hanging next to one of Fidel Castro. Nando saw absolutely nothing incongruous about that. The only exception to his frugality in the room was the top of the line MacBook he was frowning at when I entered.

"Como fastidian estas computadoras!" he muttered as he snapped the lid down, turned to me and forced a smile. "So, what is up, my friend?"

I slumped down on a straight back chair and sighed. "I went to talk to the kid who gave Picasso the message to see Conyers. He works the desk at the clinic. I found him dead in his apartment with a heroin needle in his arm."

"Hmm. Another coincidence?"

"*Right.* Looked like an overdose. Trouble is, he'd been shooting up in his leg to conceal his habit. So, why the needle in his arm?"

"I see. Any idea when he died?"

"The body was cold, so he'd lost maybe twenty, twenty-five degrees. That'd make the time of death around, let's see, fourteen hours ago, give or take. And that fits with the fact that he was in full rigor mortis."

"Excellent. You and the young artist were guests of the police last night, so you have an alibi."

"We were due a break."

"Do you have any idea how this Milo could be connected to the murder of the boyfriend?"

"Like I said, he was the one who gave Picasso the message from Conyers, which was probably a forgery. Other than that, I've got nothing. I saw some pills in the apartment and grabbed one." I pulled it out of my pocket and slid it across the metal desk between us. "Looks like a prescription med. Any idea what it is?"

Nando looked the pill over, which had the number 512 imprinted on it. "Definitely a pain pill of some kind. They are very popular these days. It seems our young people are in a lot of pain. I will check it out. Have you reported the death?"

"No. That's why I'm here. Can you do that for me? I really don't need Portland homicide to know I was snooping around there."

"Of course. I always keep a prepaid cell phone handy."

I gave him Milo's address. "Just tell them you're a concerned neighbor and his radio's been blasting for hours."

"What about his story about the bike messenger? It would be easy for me to check it out with the messenger services."

I hesitated as Gertrude Johnson's warning about my finances rang in my head. But Nando could get the answer much quicker than me. "Yeah, I guess you should go ahead with that."

As I was leaving, I said, "Anything on Larry Vincent yet?"

"I have feelers out but have heard nothing back yet. Have you ever listened to his rantings on the radio? The man is a case of nuts."

I chuckled and shook my head. "I only know him by reputation. Talk radio's not my thing. I'd rather listen to mating cats."

"This Larry Vincent lives in constant fear—people of color, the homeless, illegals, Muslims. He thinks they are all plotting against him and America. My father had a saying for men like him, '*Al espantado, la sombra le espanta*'—he finds his own shadow frightening."

I got back to the clinic around nine thirty. Scott and Jones' unmarked sedan was parked in the loading zone directly in front of the building. On the mural side of the building, Picasso was up on his scaffolding surrounded by a tight knot of people. I saw a jumble of cameras and microphones. He looked like he'd been treed by a pack of dogs.

As I approached the group, someone at the front said, "Hey, Baxter, do you still think Mitchell Conyers killed your mother?" I was surprised by the aggressive tone. The Portland press, like the city itself, was known for its civility. Picasso looked at the man from his perch on the scaffolding, but to his credit and my relief, didn't say anything.

I worked my way to the front of the crowd and put up my arms. "Okay, folks, we're through here. The circus is over." Then I turned to Picasso and said, "Come on, let's go inside."

As we rounded the corner of the building, the reporter who'd called out the question fell in step with us, as the others followed. There was some jostling, and I got separated from Picasso. The reporter, who was doubling as his own photographer, took some video clips of Picasso with a small, expensive looking digital camera. Then he got up in Picasso's face and said, "That's a poisonous snake on your neck. Does it signify anything?"

Picasso stopped and looked at the man, as if seeing him for the first time. His face tightened and lost what little color it had. The reporter moved in even closer. "Did you attack Conyers again yesterday?" He snapped. "He deserved it, right?"

I shoved my way past someone to step between them, but it was too late. Picasso's long leg shot out and his foot caught the man's hand holding the camera with pin-point accuracy and bone jarring impact. *Whack.* The camera flew in two different directions, and the man clutched his hand, screaming, "You broke my camera. You broke my goddamn camera." I was pretty sure his hand was broken, too.

I grabbed Picasso's arms and hustled him into the building, only to run smack into Lieutenant Scott and Detective Jones, who had just finished up inside. Anna was in the process of showing them out. She sucked a breath. Scott and Jones assumed a ready stance. "What happened?" she asked.

"Oh, just a little dustup out there," I said. "Some jerk reporter got a little too aggressive."

Scott and Jones ducked out the door to see for themselves. I grasped Picasso by the shoulders like I had at Conyers' place. "Why the hell did you do that? All you had to do was ignore the idiot."

He turned his head to avoid my eyes. "That prick had it coming."

"That's not good enough. You're under a microscope right now, and you've just demonstrated to the whole world that you can't control your temper." As I said that, all my confidence in Picasso's innocence threatened to bleed away. Had I made a mistake?

"I, um—"

"I don't want to hear it. Now stay here with Doc while I see how much damage you've done." To Anna, I said, "Take him into your office and shut the door. Please."

The media crowd was now knotted around the injured reporter, who held his kicked hand against his chest while clutching the pieces of his shattered camera in his other hand. He was talking to Jones and Scott, who both had their notebooks out. I worked my way through the crowd and introduced myself to the reporter.

"Mr. Baxter would like to apologize for his actions. He's understandably upset by recent events and sensitive to the memory of his mother." The reporter looked down at the remains of his camera, and I found myself adding, "He'll be glad to replace your camera." I fished a card from my wallet and handed it to him. "Call me, and I'll arrange it." I spun on my heels and went back into the clinic, wondering what I'd just committed to.

It was quiet when I entered Anna's office, but the look on Picasso's face told me she'd been at him, too. I said, "Well, you just bought yourself a broken digital camera." He started to protest, but I shushed him with a raised hand. "I don't know whether he's going to press charges or not. You'd better hope his hand's not broken." Anna glanced at her watch and excused herself.

Picasso said, "If I'd wanted to hurt him, I would have kicked him in the face. I went for his camera. I could tell he had a hard on for it."

The fluid, graceful move he'd made replayed in my head, and I realized he was telling the truth. "Well, that may be so, but nobody out there knows that. They probably think you tried to kill him and missed. Where'd you learn to kick like that, anyway?"

"I did a series of paintings for a kickbox studio over in Southeast, on the inside walls. They gave me free lessons in exchange. I was a fast learner. They asked me to stay on and teach."

"Did you?"

"And become a working stiff? No way. I wanted the skill for self-protection. Comes in handy on the streets, you know. Two skin heads jumped me under the I-5 bridge one night." He smiled and shook his head. "Boy, were they surprised."

"Well, you need to keep your kickboxing prowess to yourself. Like I said, you're under a microscope, and the last thing you need is for information like that to get out. Understood?"

The smile dissolved, and he nodded.

Scott and Jones didn't return, which was good news. Anna told me they'd interviewed her and the staff, then taken a brief look around the clinic. The question of Picasso's computer didn't come up. It probably didn't occur to them that a homeless youth would actually own a computer.

The media finally cleared out, and Picasso went back outside to work on his mural. I was sitting in Anna's office checking my phone messages when she came in to jot some notes about a patient she'd just seen. I flipped my cell shut and said, "I'll get out of your way. Thanks for the use of your office."

"You're welcome to stay. You can work the front desk," she said with an impish smile before adding, "Just kidding. Milo still hasn't shown up, but we'll manage."

Milo's gray visage flashed across my mind as I groped for something to say. He was probably in a body bag by now. "Well, I'm flattered by the job offer, but I've got this other job in Dundee that I've been neglecting."

She laughed, then her look turned serious. "How's he going to pay for that camera, Cal? He doesn't have any money."

Apparently, Anna didn't know about his savings. I shrugged. "We'll worry about that if and when I get a bill. I just hope that's as far as it goes."

"You've been through the wringer. I hope you're not sorry you're standing up for him."

I chewed my lip for a few moments. "Nah, I'm not sorry. But I'm concerned about that stunt he pulled. It's not going to help his cause a bit. Does he always go off like that?"

She shrugged. "I don't honestly know, but people on the street have hair triggers. It's a survival mechanism. And honestly, I'd say he did what a lot of us would want to do in that situation. We just lack the courage."

I nodded and smiled. "Yeah, I guess you're right. We've all got a little paparazzi rage."

She reached out with both hands and took mine. Her skin was soft and warm, her eyes burning like a flame that's gone from blue to white. "I hope you'll continue to have faith in him, Cal. He did *not* kill that man. You've got to believe that."

The little voice in my head had gone quiet again, and I left the clinic feeling pretty good. I would need an ally in this fight—someone to remind me why the hell I'd gone all in—and I knew I could count on Anna for that. There was that soft, pale skin and those haunting blue eyes, too. I found myself wondering if there was room in her world for anyone besides the homeless and needy. The jury was out on that question.

Chapter Twelve

By the time I got to the Aerie that Friday, the sun was low, and dirty white clouds were churning up the valley, threatening rain. I'd stopped first at my office to meet with a prospective client and pick up my mail, which had accumulated in a pile below the slot in the front door—an overdue check from a client, three fliers, two catalogs, and four bills. The ratio of bills to checks was not encouraging.

However, when I saw Archie at the gate, my spirits rose. You'd think I'd been gone a month the way he carried on. Then he calmed down, bolted off, and returned with a slobbery tennis ball in his mouth and a manic gleam in his eye. I threw the ball long and high and he caught it on the first bounce. We kept this up until rain thrummed over the ridge from the valley and chased us into the house.

I fed Arch, and after pouring a glass of wine, began looking for something to eat. My search was cut short when I found a covered bowl of meaty beef stew in the refrigerator. I raised my glass and said, "Bless you, Gertie." Gertrude Johnson had not only fed my dog, but left a meal for me. A phone call of thanks was in order, but I ate the stew first.

I was exhausted by the events of the last two days and turned in early. It had cleared off and a waning moon hung between the Doug firs like a bruised lemon. I stood at the open window in my bedroom and watched it for a while in the company of my friend the owl, whom I could hear but not see. I envied that damn moon, moving around up there in a predictable path, no matter what. I'd come to Oregon to find some kind of order, some peace in my life. And now, for reasons I couldn't quite explain, I felt that what little stability I'd cobbled together was threatened.

I pushed the dark thoughts down and took several lungs full of cool air and exhaled them slowly. I thought of Picasso and all the other kids out there trying to make it on the cold streets. How the hell did it come to this? They all have a story, Picasso told me—don't judge. But I would judge—not the kids, but the adults who'd let them down. I closed the window and climbed into bed. Archie settled onto his mat with his muzzle between his paws, and I fell asleep thinking about Anna. Anna,—a female Holden Caulfield—trying to catch all those kids before they slipped into the abyss.

I awoke the next morning determined to get some exercise. As I laced up my jogging shoes, Archie went out in the hall and stood by the staircase, whimpering and wagging his tail. A run with me would prove things were completely back to normal. But our run was delayed when I stopped at the mailbox for a quick look at the morning paper. I'd already seen the initial coverage of Conyers' murder in yesterday's paper—a factual account containing no surprises or new information. Picasso and I were described as witnesses and not persons of interest in the article.

Today's paper was a different story. The headline read "Murder witness and journalist clash." It was accompanied by a photograph of me grappling with Picasso right after he'd drop-kicked the camera. I took one look at it and shook my head. I had his arms clamped in my hands, and his head was thrown back, affording a view of the coral snake decorating his throat and showcasing his eyebrow and lip jewelry. The reporter was bent over next to us holding his hand. The caption below the picture mentioned that the reporter worked for a small, online newspaper.

The article described the altercation and what provoked it and went on to give the backstory surrounding Nicole Baxter's disappearance and the discovery of her remains on the Deschutes River. In other words, it put Picasso and to a lesser extent, me, squarely in the crosshairs of *public* as well as police scrutiny for Conyers' murder. I suppose I knew it was bound to happen, but I was taken aback at the speed of it. It didn't help that the article gave Picasso's address as Dignity Village. I figured there were more than a few readers who would associate the address with drug use and violence, although both were expressly forbidden at the village.

I quickly scanned the rest of the paper. Milo Hartung's death hadn't made that news cycle.

I put the paper back in the box and to Archie's delight, started jogging up the hill toward the cemetery. We hadn't gotten more than a mile when my cell rang. I'd reluctantly brought the damn thing with me. I pulled up and managed a hello while still panting.

"Cal? It's Anna. Are you alright?"

"Yeah. You caught me jogging. I'm a little winded."

"I'm at the clinic, Cal. The detectives are here again. They just told me Milo Hartung was found dead in his apartment."

I cringed inwardly at the prospect of having to lie to her. "I'm sorry to hear that, Anna. What happened?"

"They said it looked like a drug overdose. Oh, Cal, he was so close to turning his life around."

"You mentioned that you suspected he might be using again."

She sighed, and I felt a stab of guilt for having left the young man crumpled on the floor in his bathroom. "I know I did," she said, "but I was hoping I was *wrong*." I heard a single sob.

"You did all you could for him, Anna."

She laughed with a bitterness that surprised me. "No, Cal. We *never* do enough for these kids." We lapsed into silence. Finally, she continued. "Right now, the detectives are talking to the janitor, Howard. They asked him to come in this morning. They're back in the storage room, I think."

My gut tightened. "Is Picasso there?"

"No. I didn't see him."

"Good. If he comes in, remind him not to talk to *anyone* unless I'm present, okay?"

"I'll tell him, but the detectives have no reason to suspect he's involved in Milo's death, do they?"

"No, I don't think so. He can account for his whereabouts after the Conyers' murder. Look, Anna, if anything unexpected comes up, call me."

After our conversation, I turned my phone off and resumed my jog. Usually a sure-fire remedy for what ails me, the run had hardly made a dent in my stress level. Afterwards, I went into the kitchen and fixed a three egg omelet fortified with smoked salmon, tomato, red onion, jalapenos, and a sharp Tillamook cheddar. Good food was another way to deal with anxiety.

For the rest of the morning, I lost myself in an all out assault on the weeds in my vegetable garden. At noon I checked my voice mail at the office. There were half a dozen calls from reporters wanting a statement from me. I ignored them. Later that afternoon I was fertilizing my blueberry patch when my cell rang again. It was Nando. After we kicked around the newspaper article, he changed the subject. "The pill you removed from Milo's apartment is Oxycontin."

I considered this for a moment. "So, someone could have brought those over to Milo's apartment and after they got him blitzed, overdosed him with the heroin. That would be simple enough to pull off."

"Yes, and extremely hard to prove. Mixing the two drugs is common."

"You're right. So, even if Scott and Jones dislike coincidences as much as we do, they probably won't get anywhere with this."

"I have something else. The young artist was correct. Jessica Armandy *is* a woman of the night, a madam, actually. She owns an escort service called Eros' Dreams. I am told Mitchell Conyers and she had an arrangement—"

"An arrangement?"

"Yes. Some of her, ah, most attractive employees work out of his restaurant, the bar, actually. You know, clients meet them there, for drinks, perhaps dinner. It is good for both businesses. But here is the interesting point—one of her best clients is Weiman and Associates, the political lobbying firm. I believe you mentioned that Hugo Weiman is the owner of the property where Picasso's mother was found."

"Nice work, Nando. That was fast."

He chuckled. "Thank you. I have some contacts in the industry. It is very competitive, but there are few secrets. Eros' Dreams is at the top of the chain of food."

"Any direct links between Conyers and Weiman?"

"My sources know of none, but they're still making inquiries." I thanked Nando again and before we signed off he said, "You know, Calvin, this could get ugly, and it won't be cheap, either. Are you sure you want to continue?"

"Yeah, I'm sure." What else could I say?

I was stretched out on the couch later that afternoon trying to catch up on my sleep, but a couple of pesky flies kept buzzing around and landing on my face. Just as I finally dozed off, my cell phone buzzed like another irritating insect. I thought seriously about throwing it through the window before I answered it. It was my old buddy Pete Stout, the District Attorney for Multnomah County. We exchanged greetings and he asked me how it was going.

"Never a dull moment," I answered. "It's starting to feel like the old days in L.A."

"So I hear. I, uh, can't make our racketball date tomorrow. Something's come up."

My mind raced for a second. I'd completely forgotten that we'd made the date during my last conversation with him. I forced a laugh. "Something's come up for me, too." There was no way we were going to socialize now, and we both knew it. Not with the probability that his office would be prosecuting my client in the near future. In fact, I was surprised he'd even called.

"Listen, Cal, regarding this matter you got involved in. I don't know what happened or what your plans are going forward, but my guys tell me the crime scene looks a little hinky, like somebody's screwed with it." He paused, but I chose not to speak. "Just a word to the wise." He hung up without waiting for my reply.

I sat there staring at the blank phone screen, feeling like I'd just been slapped in the face. It was a warning pure and simple. I guess Stout figured he owed me one. This was about the murder weapon, or the lack of one. I was sure of it. Why would someone try to set up Picasso and not leave the weapon behind? It was a question I should have faced up to before being blindsided like this. I didn't have any answers, but what I did know was that Scott and Jones now suspected me of helping Picasso dispose of the weapon. That made me an accessory to murder.

I sat there as the room slowly darkened. Archie finally came in from the kitchen and laid his muzzle in my lap and whimpered a couple of times. He was hungry. I fed him and tried to figure out what I was going to do for my dinner. But the fact was, I'd completely lost my appetite.

Chapter Thirteen

The call I was expecting came on Sunday around noon, although I didn't necessarily expect it to come from Anna Eriksen. For a moment, I entertained the possibility that it was a social call, but I had no reason to expect that. Her tone set me straight in a hurry. "Cal? It's me again, Anna. I'm at the clinic. The police just took Picasso away. He was here working on his mural."

"Did they cuff him?" I asked.

"No. I saw them put him in their car. He wasn't handcuffed."

"Good. That means they didn't arrest him. They're going to question him again. Maybe they're hoping they can get him to talk without me being present."

"I told him not to talk to anyone, like you asked me. But I'm not sure I got through. I'm never sure with him."

I told Anna I was on my way. Then I called Central Precinct in Portland and got Scott's voice mail. I left a message. Then I repeated the process and asked for Jones. I got him live. I told him I'd be there in an hour and that there were to be no interviews until I arrived. He shot back that I'd saved him a call, since they were going to bring me in for more questioning anyway.

I threw some clothes, toiletries, and a couple of books in an overnight bag and went down the backstairs and through the kitchen to the study for my laptop and briefcase. I was almost out the door when I thought of the information Picasso had given me. I still had some papers and another thumb drive I hadn't looked at. I went back and added his briefcase to my load.

Archie confronted me in the front hallway. His ears were down, an anxious look in his eyes. I hesitated for a moment, and he whimpered a couple of times. "Okay, big boy, you're coming this time." I grabbed his leash and doubled back into the kitchen for his food and water bowls and a bag of kibbles.

I worked my way through the vineyards to Dundee, and as I headed north on 99W, began to turn the situation over in my mind. The biggest question mark was the murder weapon. If Picasso was telling the truth about the absence of a weapon at the scene, then either the murderer took it with him for some reason or hid it somewhere on the property. No way the killer would *take* the weapon. That made no sense at all. That meant the killer stashed the weapon somewhere after piercing Conyers' skull. I didn't buy that either, but there was a lot I didn't understand about this case, so I held it out as possible but not probable.

The other possibility was that Picasso had hidden the weapon and lied to me about it. I thought about his reaction when I asked him about the paint can opener. *What if I'm wrong about him?* I pushed the ugly thought down. After all, I told myself, I crossed that bridge, right? I had, but the little voice in my head was still there.

The traffic slowed to a crawl on 99W, seeming to mimic my thought process. Out of frustration, I turned off at Sherwood and cut over to the I-5. It was smooth sailing from there into Portland.

I parked on Second Avenue, fed the meter, and rolled the windows half way down for Archie. Central Precinct was an imposing hexagonal midrise occupying the entire block on Second between Madison and Main. After I'd cleared the metal detector and signed in, Lieutenant Scott came down to meet me. Following brief pleasantries he said, "Thanks for coming in counselor. We just need to go over a few things with you and Mr. Baxter." The overhead fluorescents glared off his glasses, which kept me from reading the look in his eyes.

"We're glad to help, Lieutenant."

I saw his eyes now, dark slits, all business. He looked tired. "Your boy came in without any trouble. You must be relieved, considering his temper."

"He's not my boy," I snapped back. "About today—we're happy to respond to questions regarding our earlier statements, but that's it. We're not breaking any new ground here."

"Sounds like you've decided not to cooperate. It's your call, counselor, but don't whine to me if the press picks that up and runs with it." With that, Scott left me at the door to the room where Picasso was waiting.

He was dressed for work in ragged jeans, combat boots, and a t-shirt with something written beneath the paint spatter that took me a few moments to decipher—Live Simply So Others Can Simply Live. He looked tired, too, and tense. His three day growth made the snake on his neck look like it was hiding in the grass.

When we bumped fists, I noticed his eyebrow ring was missing, and the punctured eyebrow itself looked less red and swollen. I pointed. "Where's the ring?"

He touched the spot with his finger. "Doc took it out. Infected, like you said. She gave me something to put on it." Then he smiled. "Don't worry, it's going back in."

I opened a hand and said, "It just wouldn't be you."

He tried to stifle a smile, but failed. "You heard about Milo Hartung, right?"

I nodded. "What do you think happened?"

His dark eyes studied me for a moment. He shrugged. "It's easy to OD, man, especially with smack. But the timing's weird."

I nodded again. "If Milo set you up with a fake note, then he knew too much."

His eyes enlarged and he tugged absently at his lip ring. "You think he was snuffed like Conyers?"

"I can't prove it, but my gut says that's what happened."

"Wow, two murders related to me? Should I be feeling important here?"

I laughed in spite of myself. "You *are* important. Someone wants you to take the fall in the worst way."

Picasso sighed like the world was resting on his shoulders. "What about the guy I kicked? Is he cool?"

"I haven't heard a thing, but I seriously doubt he's cool."

He hung his head in his hands. "Oh, man, that was *stupid*. I did some checking on that freaking camera on the net. I'm pretty sure it was a Canon XL2. Those suckers cost over four thousand bucks."

I whistled involuntarily. "Look, we'll deal with that when the time comes. Right now, we need to focus on this interview. I told Scott and Jones that we'd answer questions about our statements, but nothing else. Don't be surprised if they spring something on us."

"Like what?"

"I don't know. Maybe they found the murder weapon." I was watching him carefully.

His face clouded over, and he said in a lowered voice, "Is it cool to talk about this shit in here?"

I tensed up. "Yeah, it's okay. Why? Do you have something to tell me?

He lowered his eyes. "No, man. You know everything I do."

"Good," I said, sounding more positive than I felt. I didn't particularly like his reaction, but his tells were inconclusive once again. And this was no time to bring up doubts.

Scott and Jones interviewed me first, taking me back over every detail and bringing up absolutely nothing new. The only exchange of note occurred before the cameras were rolling. Jones flashed me a mock-friendly smile and said, "Mr. Claxton, Pete Stout says you're a standup guy. And I gotta say on a personal note, I admire what you're doing."

I met his gaze and waited to see where he was going with that. I saw Scott shift in his seat out of the corner of my eye.

Jones continued, "It takes guts to help out a kid like Baxter. I mean, it can't be good for your practice in Dundee. Folks down your way don't understand these Portland street kids. They think they're all pierced and tattooed killers. They're probably wondering why you'd want to get mixed up with one."

"Haven't heard any complaints."

"Glad to hear that," Jones replied, glancing at Scott and flashing a toothy grin.

Scott chuckled and added, "It's early days, counselor."

Jones said, "You know, you're seeing the street scene here in Portland for the first time, but we've worked with a lot of these kids. There's one thing you can say about nearly all of them—they're great cons, right, partner?"

Scott nodded. "A few years on the street, they have their PhDs in it."

Jones went on, "Like I said, counselor, I admire you for believing in a kid like Baxter when so many factors suggest otherwise."

I said, "I'm a lawyer. I don't have to *believe* in my clients. But since you brought it up, I do happen to believe Danny Baxter didn't kill Mitchell Conyers. He's an intelligent young man. He wouldn't have killed Conyers shortly after telling several people he was going to meet with him. Furthermore, if he had just killed Conyers, he wouldn't have dived into that pool and pulled him out, thinking he might still be alive. And if he did it, where's the murder weapon?"

Scott and James exchanged glances but remained silent.

"So, who did kill Conyers?" I went on. "It was public knowledge that he and Mr. Baxter had an altercation at Nicole Baxter's memorial service. Shortly after the incident, Conyers is murdered and Mr. Baxter lured to the crime scene with a phony message given to him by Milo Hartung. Hartung turns up dead the next day. How convenient. So, gentlemen, I hope you're looking hard at any enemies Mr. Conyers might have had. Oh, and one more thing. Danny Baxter's a lefty and the person you're looking for is right handed."

They exchanged glances again but maintained their half-bored cop expressions. Finally, Scott said, "Can we get started now?"

Nothing new came up in Picasso's interview either, and it was a lot shorter. It was going reasonably well until we got to the question of the murder weapon. Scott said to Picasso, "Okay, you told us that you came in the side gate, saw Mr. Conyers in the water, jumped in without hesitating and pulled him out. What happened after that?"

Picasso rolled his eyes and looked at me. I nodded for him to go ahead. "I, uh, kind of panicked and decided to go for help. I came out of the gate, and that's when I saw Claxton standing on the front porch."

Jones said, "So, you pulled the body out of the pool and went directly out the gate?"

"Yeah, that's what I just told you."

Scott said, "You also told us that you did not see anything lying around that could have been used to strike Mr. Conyers. Is that right?"

"That's right."

"Tell me," Scott continued, "How could you be so sure there was nothing lying around if you were so panicked?"

I tensed again and held my breath.

Picasso glanced at me then back at Scott. The color in his face seemed to deepen a shade. "I didn't see anything, man. What can I say?"

Jones said, "Maybe you heard Claxton out there and hid the weapon?"

Scott glanced at me and chimed in, "Or maybe Claxton here helped you hide it?"

Picasso started to reply but I waived him off as I stood up. "That's it, gentlemen, we're out of here."

Picasso and I walked out of Central Precinct without saying another word. When we reached my car, I said, "Come on, let's take a walk."

I leashed up Archie and the three of us went down to the river, crossed under the Hawthorne Bridge, and stopped at a bench near the Salmon Springs Fountain. A gaggle of screaming kids were playing in the fountain, and an army of tough looking workers were setting up carnival rides on the grass strip running up to the Morrison Bridge. It was nearly Rose Festival time.

We sat down and Picasso's gaze drifted to the kids running under the arcing jets of the fountain, kids who had parents watching them and homes to go to. He sighed. "I'm so screwed. Those two cops don't believe anything I've said."

I scratched the top of Archie's head while I thought about how to reply. The sun went behind a cloud, and suddenly the fountain looked dark and cold, but the kids were oblivious. "That's what cops do—try to fluster you and then see how you react."

"Yeah, and we stomped out of there. That can't be good."

"Not if we left because we were unjustly accused, right?"

He chewed his lip and nodded. "I'm sorry I got you mixed up in this."

I chuckled. "Don't worry, my skin's plenty thick. But, look, why do I get the feeling you're waiting for another shoe to drop? Are you sure you've told me everything?"

"*Jesus*, Cal, how many damn times are you going to ask me that? I told you, man, you know everything I do."

Archie raised his head to look at Picasso, and I raised my hands. "Okay. Just so we're clear on that."

We sat in silence as the sun broke free again, dappling the river in silver light. Finally, Picasso said, "So, what happens now?"

"They don't have enough to hold you, so we've got some time. We need to figure out who wanted Conyers dead and who was smart enough to come up with this elaborate frame."

"How in the hell are we going to do that?"

"I'm not sure yet, but my hunch is the whole thing's related to the discovery of your mom's remains."

"You mean whoever killed Conyers killed my mother?"

"It wouldn't surprise me."

Chapter Fourteen

The light was good that afternoon, so Picasso went back to the clinic to work on his mural. He was unsettled by the interview, but I knew by now he didn't allow much to stand in the way of his art. It provided a tight focus for his life, and I admired him for that. He used a key Anna had given him—a demonstration of her trust—to open the back door of the clinic. I went down the hall to Anna's office with Arch on his leash. She was typing away on her computer with her back to the door. I knocked softly so I wouldn't startle her.

"We're back."

She swiveled around, swept a lock of hair off her forehead and smiled. Our eyes met, and just for an instant I got caught up in the pale blueness of hers. I broke eye contact. "How did it go, Cal? I've been worried."

"About as well as it could have. Picasso's back at work now." Her eyes dropped down and took in Archie.

"Is he okay in here?"

"Sure. Just not in the treatment rooms. He's an Aussie, right?"

I nodded. "A tricolor. Name's Archie. Why don't you join us for a walk, and I'll fill you in. It's Sunday. You deserve a break."

Anna wanted to go down to the river, and Archie and I didn't mind a second trip. We walked over to Burnside and at the bridge took the stairs back down to Tom McCall Park. The clouds had blown to the north, and the park was filling with sun-starved Portlanders anxious to cure their vitamin D deficiencies. The sun made us squint, and the brisk, shifting breeze had polished the day to a diamond brilliance. As we walked, I filled her in on the day's events and where the case stood. I left out the part about Scott and Jones accusing me of tampering with the crime scene. I had a feeling that would only worry her needlessly. By this time, Anna had Archie's leash, which seemed to please them both.

When I got to my theory about the killer being right handed, Anna whirled to face me, her eyes enlarged, excited. "Picasso's *left* handed, Cal."

I smiled. "I know. Just like da Vinci and Escher." Then I went on to tell her about the position of the wound, the blood spatter I'd seen and how I'd watched the crime scene techs re-enacting the death blow.

Relief flooded her face. "Then you've proved he's innocent!"

I shook my head. "It's not that simple. It's an argument that can be made, but it's not ironclad by any means. It could have been a backhanded blow, but I don't believe that's the case."

She nodded slowly and turned to face the river. The afternoon light had dulled somewhat, like silver to pewter, and the air off the water smelled fresh and clean. Across the river, cars spilled silently down the I-5 ramp from the Marquam Bridge like lemmings. "I see," she said. "Well, it's a start." She put a hand over mine and looked at me. "Cal, you have no idea what your support means to Picasso. He's never had any kind of male role model in his life."

I nodded, feeling a tinge of discomfort. I wondered just how much she expected from me. But I shrugged the thought off. After all, the sun on my skin felt good, and her hand felt even better. We stood there looking out at the river while I finished talking about the interviews. A cruise ship passed by, heading upriver. Tourists in sunglasses and shirt sleeves were lined up on both decks. It seemed they were all gawking at us—a handsome dog, a beautiful woman, and a lucky man.

I said, "Tell me about yourself, Anna. What brought you to the clinic and a seven day work week?"

She hugged herself, as if suddenly chilled. "I grew up in lower Manhattan, Tribeca. I would've probably stayed back east, but after my brother died, I wanted to get away, far away. I came out here to do my residency at OHSU. A local nonprofit was looking for someone to run a clinic for the homeless just about the time I finished up. It was my dream job, and it didn't hurt that I'd fallen in love with Portland and the Northwest by then. So I applied, and here I am."

"Sorry about your brother."

"Thanks. It happened over seven years ago." She hugged herself again and smiled wistfully. "I still miss him like crazy."

"I'm sure you do." I waited, sensing she had more to say.

"Peter was my little brother. There were just two of us. He was the screwup, the poor student, and I was little miss straight-A perfect. At least that's how my parents saw it. Actually, Peter was brilliant. Too brilliant. School bored him to tears."

"There's nothing worse for a bright kid."

"That's right. Anyway, he started acting out, using drugs, and wound up on the streets. He died in some kind of fight over a sleeping bag. Stabbed to death."

"Oh, that's terrible."

She gazed out on the river and nodded her head slowly. The wind twirled a lock of her hair. "It *was* terrible. My parents essentially disowned him when he started using drugs." She turned to face me, her eyes suddenly shiny with moisture. "Of course, *I* was too busy at medical school. *I* didn't have time for his problems." She dropped her eyes and raised a hand to her mouth. "Oh, God, there I go. I'm getting morose."

"No, no, it's okay. I understand."

She glanced at her watch. "I need to go."

With Archie between us, we headed back. At the Burnside Bridge stairs a young man sitting on the sidewalk asked us for change. Despite the warm day, he wore the hood of his sweatshirt up. He had a cherub face roughened by a sparse, uneven beard and a large, raw scab on his lip. I started to reach for my wallet, but Anna waived me off with her eyes. She said, "Are you new in town?"

"Yes, ma'am."

"Hungry?"

He cast his eyes down and nodded, as if ashamed to admit it.

"The best and cheapest food is at the Sisters of the Road Café. It's at Sixth and Davis. If you can't pay they'll let you work it off." Then she added, "You need to have that sore on your lip examined."

He raised a finger to his lip and touched the sore gingerly. I had the impression he hadn't seen his reflection in a mirror in a long time.

Anna handed him a card. "The clinic at this address is free. Drop by and I'll treat it for you."

He thanked her and as we walked away, I said, "I liked the way you handled that. I never know what to say or what to give these kids."

Anna laughed. "Yeah, I know. I used to be like an ATM, but I'm older and wiser now. You can buy meal tickets at the Café and give them away when you're stopped. That way you know your money's not going for drugs."

Picasso was still hard at work when we got back to the clinic. There were six or eight kids in their teens or early twenties lounging on sleeping bags and propped against backpacks there on the field behind him. The mood was festive, enhanced, no doubt, by the joint that was being passed around. Anna said, "They've heard about Picasso's problem. This must be a show of support."

Up near the front, right below the scaffolding, I noticed Caitlin, the young girl I'd seen that first day. She was leaning back on her arms, watching Picasso sketch. She wore a pink sweatshirt with the sleeves cut off, jeans, and hiking boots. Her oval face and bright amber eyes were framed in dark, stringy hair that cried out for shampoo. She had a delicate nose and a wide, full mouth that seemed to smile, even at rest. The angry red blotches of acne on her cheeks did little to detract from her soft beauty. A tall young man sat next to her wearing grubby black jeans and a studded leather jacket. He stood up, stretched, and ran his fingers through shoulder-length blond hair. Anna said, "Uh oh."

I looked at her. "What?"

She nodded at the young man and said under her breath, "I think that guy's a member of the family Caitlin used to belong to."

"Family?"

"You know, they hung out together, five or six of them, for safety. They were into petty theft and survival sex. She promised to stay away from them."

"What's survival sex?"

"Sex for food and money. Some of these kids are forced into it." She averted her eyes. "Caitlin's seen her share of that."

I cringed inwardly, thinking of my own daughter, a graduate student at UC Berkeley. I felt a surge of anger bordering on nausea for all the so-called adult males who would stoop to such behavior.

We stood in silence for a while. The rough sketch of the mural was coming together, one square in the grid at a time; each square a proportional representation of a corresponding image in Picasso's sketch book. A stream of humanity spilled from the flanks of Mt. Hood west to the river and across into the center of the city. Ordinary people arm in arm with folk heroes, spiritual leaders, and cultural icons as Picasso saw them. I chuckled and said to Anna, "Look, you're still in there. Who's that next to you?"

Anna laughed. "That's Bono, I think. That's the price I extracted for being in the mural. See the guy on the other side, the one with the beard? I think he's Alan Ginsberg."

I looked again. "Or Karl Marx."

We both laughed. "No, it's Ginsberg, for sure," she said.

When I left the clinic that afternoon, Picasso had finished up for the day. He was standing with his bike on the sidewalk talking to Caitlin. A full head taller than she, he was bent over, listening intently. Her hair jounced as she gestured and talked. Just two young kids hanging out.

Anna went back to work, I dropped my gear off at Caffeine Central, and after feeding Archie, walked over to Jake's Famous Crawfish for dinner. Since I was living rent free, I decided to treat myself to what might be the best seafood restaurant anywhere. I ordered dinner and a glass of Argyle reserve chardonnay, and while I waited for my food, called Nando. I planned to spend at least two days here in Portland, and I needed to get my ducks in a row.

Of course he was appalled I was dining alone. No self-respecting Cuban would ever do such a thing. "At least you are eating well," he commented, "although some of Jake's dishes are a bit on the bland side for my taste."

"I'm having the razor clams."

"A case in point," he said. "A dish of fried clams should leave your brow dripping with sweat. Unfortunately, Jake's will not have this effect."

I chuckled. "I'll suffer through." Then I filled him in quickly on the police interviews.

"I'm not surprised the police think you might have helped the young artist," he said when I'd finished. "I warned you about getting involved, my friend."

"I knew that was coming," I said, barely masking the irritation in my voice. "They were just trying to get a rise out of us, and you know it. To his credit, the kid held up pretty well."

"What makes you think he didn't kill this man and hide the weapon before you arrived on the scene?"

I struggled for an even voice. "We've been through this already."

"They will surely find the weapon. What if they accuse you of helping him hide it?"

They already have, I said to myself. I'd left that part out. "Not likely," I shot back. Leave it to my friend to show me the downside to my behavior. Anxious to change the subject, I asked, "You got anything for me?"

"We have confirmed that none of the messenger services were used to bring Picasso a message," Nando answered. "So, it looks like Hartung was lying."

"The cops will check this, too. Trouble is, they'll think Picasso was lying, not Milo. You got anything else?"

"No. What are you planning to do next?"

I took a sip of wine. "I've been thinking about that half the afternoon. I might as well jump in and start talking to people. See if I can shake something loose."

"Who did you have in mind?"

"Larry Vincent, Hugo Weiman, and Jessica Armandy, not necessarily in that order. Any way you could set me up?"

"I can probably help you with Armandy and perhaps Weiman. But I have no contacts in the world of radio."

"Do what you can," I responded.

My dinner arrived just as Nando and I finished up. The razor clams were exquisite.

Later that night in the apartment above Caffeine Central I worked at my computer while streaming jazz from the local twenty-four-hour station. I was trying to ignore the floral print wallpaper that swirled biliously on the walls of the alcove where I was sitting. During a really good Clifford Brown track, Archie's ears popped up, and he began growling. I turned the volume down and heard someone knocking on the front door of the building. I slipped on my shoes, followed Archie downstairs, and switched on the lights. I started to open the door but thought better of it. "What is it?" I called out.

"I'm looking for Calvin Claxton. I was told he stays here." The voice was deep, accented.

"What do you want him for?"

"I'm Jessica Armandy's driver. I've been sent to pick him up."

As usual, Nando hadn't wasted any time. I opened the door. A tall, athletically built man faced me with his arms crossed. He was backlit by a streetlight and all I could make out was a protruding brow, a hawk nose, and a chin like a cinder block. Archie made a low, guttural sound from behind me, signaling his distinct disapproval of the situation.

"Hang on," I said. "I'll get my coat."

Chapter Fifteen

I rode in style to the meeting place in a black Lexus with tinted windows next to a sullen, taciturn Russian. I did manage to get his first name—Semyon— and the fact that he'd emigrated from the city of Kursk. His blond hair was cut high and tight, military style and he had a discontinuous, vertical scar on his right cheek that resembled an exclamation point. He was tall and lean and even though he wore a black blazer, I sensed he had a rock-hard upper body. I was surprised when he stopped in front of Mitch Conyers' steak house and said, "She's in the bar, corner table." I was to learn later that Jessica Armandy held court at this table every night.

I wasn't a high-end steak fancier, so I hadn't eaten at the Happy Angus. The dining room was a traditional affair with tables clad in white cloth and set with silver and crystal in a surround of dark hardwoods, brass fixtures, and somewhat garish art. A wide spiral staircase in the back led to a bar on the second floor that was jammed with a crowd that, from the sound of it, didn't seem too concerned about the passing of Conyers or the approaching work week.

I spotted a corner table with three women seated at it, and as I approached, the older woman in the middle dismissed the other two with a nod of her head in the direction of the bar. Young and attractive, the two women slunk away, drinks in hand, but not before eyeing me with brazen interest. The remaining woman appraised me coolly. "Mr. Claxton. I recognize you from the picture in the paper. I'm Jessica Armandy." She pointed to a chair across from her with an open hand. "Please join me." A waitress appeared and I ordered a Mirror Pond. Armandy ordered another Courvoisier with ice.

I could see she was probably in her midforties, but flawlessly applied makeup took a decade off, at least from a distance. She was a striking woman with finely sculpted cheek bones, quick, intelligent eyes, and a wide, sensual mouth. Even seated it was clear her body was sculpted as finely as her face. She wore a richly brocaded silver blouse, black pants, and a lot of jewelry that didn't just *look* expensive.

"Nando Mendoza tells me you want to talk about Mitch Conyers," she said after the drinks were ordered.

"I understand he was a friend of yours, so first let me offer my condolences." She acknowledged my statement with a nod. "I'm looking into the murder of Nicole Baxter and wanted to ask you some questions."

She arched her eyebrows theatrically. "I thought you were the lawyer for that tattooed bastard that killed Mitch."

"You mean Danny Baxter, Nicole Baxter's son. Actually, he's a witness in the Conyers' case. Despite what you've read, he hasn't been charged with anything. I'm trying to help Mr. Baxter find out who killed his mother."

Her eyes flared in anger for a moment, and I thought she might lash out at me. But instead she said calmly, "Well, if you think Mitch killed that woman, you're wasting your time."

"I don't know who killed Nicole Baxter, and Mitch Conyers had a solid alibi thanks to you."

"That's right. It's all in the police record. They must've questioned me a half dozen times."

"Was being with him a regular occurrence?"

She rattled the ice cubes in her drink and stared down at them as if deciding whether or not she was going to answer any questions at all. A few moments passed. "He was my mentor. I was just starting out in business, and he gave me lots of good advice."

"While you were with him, did he ever mention a newspaper story Nicole Baxter was working on when she disappeared, an important story?"

She shook her head. "We never talked about that woman. The only thing I knew about her was that she was some kind of reporter for *The Oregonian*."

"Did Conyers love her?"

She smiled and looked down at her drink again. "She was a cute little thing, no doubt about it. But the only thing Mitch ever really loved was money."

"How about somebody nicknamed X-Man? Does that mean anything to you?"

She wrinkled her brow and smiled. "You're pulling my leg, right?"

I didn't answer.

She took a pull on her drink and shook her head again. "Isn't that some damn superhero movie? Last time I checked, Portland's fresh out of superheroes."

When I asked about Larry Vincent, the conservative talk show host, she told me she knew of no connection between him and Conyers, and that she didn't know him personally. However, she did admit to being a loyal listener of his show. At that point, she said, "I admire the man. He stands for the second amendment, and he's tough on crime."

Fortunately, I was between mouthfuls of beer, or I might have sprayed the table. The madam of a high end prostitution ring a law and order type? You've got to be kidding me.

I saved my best shot for last. "I understand Hugo Weiman's a good customer of yours. Did you know he's the owner of the property where Nicole Baxter's remains were found?"

Her eyes widened, then flared anger again as she forced her collagen-laden lips into a tight line. "My customers are *none* of your business, Mr. Claxton," she said before glancing over at the bar, where Semyon had taken a seat without my noticing.

"Did Conyers and Weiman know each other?"

She wagged a finger at Semyon, and a moment later he was standing next to my chair. She said, "Mitch Conyers was a damn good man. He's not even cold in the grave, and you come around trying to cook up some excuse for the kid who killed him. Well, I can tell you, people in this town won't appreciate that. If you know what's good for you, you'll go back to that hick town in the valley. You're in over your head, Claxton." With that, she turned to Semyon. "Take him back to Couch Street."

I stood up. "Thanks for the chat, Ms. Armandy, and thanks for the offer of a ride, but I'll manage on my own." Then I fished a ten out of my wallet and tossed it on the table. "That's for the beer."

Cabs don't roam around Portland looking for fares; you have to call them. I didn't feel like doing that, so I decided to walk the six or eight blocks back to Caffeine Central, despite the light mist I encountered out on the street. By the time I crossed Burnside a stiff breeze had kicked up, and rain was dripping from the chins of the twin lions guarding the ornate gate leading to Chinatown. But I didn't feel so cold and damp after passing people bedded down for the night in doorways and alcoves.

I'd decided my chat with Jessica Armandy hadn't been a total bust. After all, I was pretty sure she knew more than she was telling me, particularly about how Hugo Weiman played into this, and her reference to Nicole Baxter as a "cute little thing" was interesting. Did I detect a note of jealousy? Finally, her threats didn't strike me as idle. I made a mental note to watch my back.

I got up early the next morning and walked with Archie over to Whole Foods in the Pearl and stocked up on food. Around nine I clicked on KPOC.com and began streaming their radio broadcast while I worked on a legal brief and made some phone calls. I drifted in and out of listening, catching the beginning of the Larry Vincent show. A resonant voice clicked through an introduction that included phrases like "a voice of sanity and reason in the maelstrom of our political discourse," and "a gun toting, God fearing, pro-life warrior."

Ten minutes into the program, which featured frenetic commercials for gold coins and mortgage refinancing made easy, Vincent said, "We're shocked and sickened at the murder of Mitchell Conyers, a leading business figure in Portland." I snapped to attention. "You probably saw this in the paper, folks. Mitchell Conyers was stabbed to death in his own backyard. A young homeless punk was found at the scene with blood all over him. He has a snake tattooed on his neck. Real wholesome type. He claims he got there *after* Conyers was killed. *Sure he did.* We've talked many times on this program about the dangers these homeless people present to the community. They usually kill each other over drugs or booze, but this time it was an upstanding Portland citizen who got killed. Here's the thing, folks—it's been *four days*, and that homeless dirt bag is still on the streets. My question for the Portland police is, 'What's taking so long to lock up *snake boy*?' Believe me, folks, we're gonna follow this story until justice is done."

That unleashed a fusillade of angry phone calls lasting the next forty minutes—"hobo teens" were a criminal threat, panhandling was chasing tourists and shoppers out of downtown, tougher laws or outright eviction from the city were needed. At one point a caller said, "Yeah, Larry, show me a homeless criminal who's free on the street, and I'll show you some bleeding heart liberal with a law degree who's working pro bono to keep him out of jail. Those are the people that ought to be run out of town."

Shaking my head, I clicked off the web site. Archie looked up at me expectantly. "Well, at least I'm not working pro bono," I said to him. And that reminded me—I needed to talk to Picasso about my fee.

I called KPOC to see if I could get Larry Vincent to meet with me. The receptionist told me he handled his own appointments, and since he was still on the air, gave me his voice mail. I left a message. I figured the chance of him calling back was low, so I looked up the address and drove over to the studio, a small building on Macadam, south of St. John's Landing. I figured he'd be looking for lunch when he finished, so I parked in the lot and waited. At one end of the Staff Only section I noticed a new, cherry red BMW M3 with a cloth top and a vanity plate that read IMRIGHT. I figured that was Vincent's car.

At twelve eighteen, a man came out of the station and headed for the BMW. He was of medium height with a high forehead and thinning, brownish hair. Nearly pear-shaped, his torso widened below narrow shoulders and a thin chest. I recognized him from the picture on the KPOC website. "Mr. Vincent," I said as I approached, "can I have a word with you about Nicole Baxter?"

He turned and gave me a pained look. "Who?"

"Nicole Baxter. She's the woman whose body was found recently on the Deschutes River. She'd been missing eight years. "

"What about her?"

"My name's Cal Claxton." I handed him a card. "I'm an attorney looking into the case for her son, Daniel Baxter."

His eyes narrowed as he looked me over more carefully. "You mean you represent that kid who killed Mitchell Conyers?"

"Last time I checked Danny Baxter hasn't been accused of anything."

He pulled a ring of keys from his pocket and spun around. "Get lost, asshole."

"I'd like to know why you had an appointment scheduled with Nicole Baxter for the week after she disappeared," I shot back.

"I don't remember that," he answered with his back to me.

"Yes you do. You handle your own appointments. There's no way you wouldn't have made the connection, considering what happened to her. We can either discuss this now or later at your deposition." Using the d-word is often a good bluff. I had no grounds for deposing *anyone* about Baxter's disappearance, but I was hoping Vincent didn't know that.

The driver's side door lock released with a solid click, but instead of getting in, Vincent turned to face me. His narrow-set eyes were sepia colored, evasive. He had a thick, crooked nose and a chin that fell away too abruptly below thin, bloodless lips.

"She called one day and made an appointment. Said she wanted to interview me for a story she was doing. She didn't show, and then I realized she was the missing woman I'd heard about. That's it. That's all I know."

I took him through the rest of my questions and got nowhere. So much for shaking anything loose, I said to myself as he drove off in his shiny new M3. However, there was one thing that caught my attention. By the time we stopped talking, a couple of beads of sweat had formed on his brow, and it was a cool Oregon morning.

I went back to Caffeine Central and spent the afternoon on the phone with clients who thought they were going to meet with me in Dundee. Needless to say, they weren't particularly pleased to be talking to me on the phone rather than in person. By the time I'd finished up and fixed something to eat it was getting dark, but both Archie and I needed some exercise. I leashed him up and we headed for the river. From the Burnside, we jogged past the Hawthorne Bridge, then turned around and came back. The night was clear with a soft wind, and the city lights shimmered on the dark mirror of the river.

I let us back into the building through the front door. The moment I closed it behind me I knew something was wrong without knowing why. Archie halted beside me and we stood silently in the dark, listening. There wasn't a sound. Then it hit me—I was feeling a cool breeze wafting in from the rear of the building, which could only mean the back door, the one I'd left bolted, was open.

Chapter Sixteen

Arch and I moved cautiously through the swinging doors and stopped dead when we saw what had happened. The back door was open alright, and the battered door knob hung from a single screw. The dead bolt was on the ground among splinters and scraps of wood that lay in a spray pattern in front of the door. Arch whined nervously and pulled at his leash in the direction of the stairs leading up to the apartment on our left. I couldn't tell whether he thought someone was up there or whether he just locked onto the scent they'd left. In any case, I hustled us out of the building and called 911 and Nando Mendoza, in that order.

No one was in the apartment, and the cops left after dusting for prints and completing an incident report. They told me break-ins like mine were a common occurrence, perpetrated by druggies looking for cash and electronics to sell. Nando got there shortly thereafter bearing a tool box and an assortment of lumber. As we worked to temporarily secure the door, he said, "So, they cleaned you out, huh?"

I shook my head in disgust. The enormity of what had happened was settling in. "Shit, not just my computer, which wasn't backed up by the way. They got Picasso's briefcase. It was filled with important stuff about his mom's disappearance. And my briefcase, too, with a bunch of client files. I should have been more careful, but with that deadbolt on the back door, I just wasn't worried about a break-in. How do you think the bastard did it?"

Nando scratched his head and scrunched his bushy eyebrows together. "Someone used a very heavy lead pipe or steel bar. One sharp thrust and *bang*, the deadbolt is ripped from the wall. Very violent, but very effective. This was not the work of a common burglar or someone seeking money for drugs. They look for easier prey. I think whoever broke in had decided how to take that deadbolt out ahead of time. Besides, most people would think this is a vacant building, hardly a target for burglary."

I nodded in agreement. "I think someone wanted my computer and anything else that would tell them why I'm here in Portland and what I'm up to."

"Will they learn much from what they took?"

I shrugged. "There was a summary of a discussion I had with Picasso, an email I sent him, as well as a bunch of emails and files from Nicole Baxter's computer, her appointment book and some notes I made. Hell, I hadn't even finished reading it all. But, who knows? At the very least, whoever stole the stuff knows my initial take on the information."

When we'd finished the temporary fix of the door, Nando said, "I'll send someone over tomorrow to replace it and put on a heavier lock. You're welcome to stay at my place tonight, if you wish."

"No. I'll stay here."

My friend looked at me and smiled. "I thought you would say that." He reached behind his back and pulled a revolver from his belt. "This is a Glock 19, nine millimeter. It will stop a man, even one with a large pipe." I didn't reach for it, so he extended the gun to me, handle first. "Don't be foolish. Take it. These people you are playing with are dangerous."

After Nando left, I set about cleaning up the mess upstairs. I had to chuckle about my reluctance to accept the Glock, a testament to the power of Picasso's anti-gun mural. It's a handgun, I told myself, not a damn assault rifle. I straightened my clothes up, placed the books I'd brought back on the nightstand, and put the mattress back on the bed and the cushions back on the couch. Tomorrow I would have to go buy a new laptop, a depressing thought. Even more depressing, I would have to call at least four of my clients and inform them confidential information contained in their files had been stolen and would have to be replaced. I wondered how many of them would fire me after hearing the news. And worst of all, I'd have to tell Picasso I'd lost the information he'd entrusted to me.

When I finished, I put the Glock on the nightstand and fell back on the bed without undressing. It was clear that the break-in was both fishing expedition and warning. I thought about the hostile reactions from Jessica Armandy and Larry Vincent to my questions, the veiled warnings from Pete Stout and detectives Scott and Jones. Hell, even my friend Nando had questioned my involvement in this case. The message seemed to be—walk away, this homeless kid doesn't really count. But I wasn't about to walk away. I don't know which act I loathed more, the murder of a young mother or the attempt to frame a young man for a murder.

This was war. The only question was—who the hell was the enemy?

I woke up the next morning with my clothes still on. After a shower, a shave, and a bowl of granola, I made phone calls to the clients whose files had been stolen. I was handling a divorce for the first client I reached. She was irate and downright rude when she heard the news. The second client was facing a DUI and took the news gracefully. I left messages for the other two. I slipped across the street and bought a copy of *The Oregonian*. There was a follow-up article with photos on the Conyers' murder on page two, which gave more of the victim's background and stated that his restaurant, the Happy Angus, would continue to operate under the management of Conyers' stepbrother, a man named Seth Foster.

I was surprised to read that Conyers owned similar establishments in Seattle and San Francisco. That got me wondering what Conyers' will looked like, if he had one. The article also mentioned that a memorial service would be held that day at eleven at the Old Church, a landmark in the center of the city.

I turned to the editorial page and read the letters to the editor, which bristled with dire warnings about the homeless menace. Portland had a reputation as a progressive haven, but Larry Vincent's message seemed to hit a nerve. I wondered if part of the anger was simply because these kids were there, on the street, reminding the rest of us of an unpleasant truth—that we all owned a piece of the blame. I know I felt that way most of the time.

I leashed up Arch and headed over to the clinic to touch bases with Picasso. It was half past eight, and the clinic was closed, but his bike was leaning against the corner of the building. I walked around to the side of the building and stopped dead. Picasso was standing with his hands on his hips looking at his mural. The words *Murderer* and *Go Back To Dignity Village Snake Boy*, accompanied by a liberal sprinkling of swastikas and obscenities, had been spray painted across his work.

"No!" I exploded. "Who the hell did this?" Archie started barking.

Picasso turned to face us, his demeanor catching me completely off guard. He looked calm—a lot calmer than me and my dog—and almost amused by what had happened. He ran a hand through his spiky hair and shrugged. "I don't know who did it. There're plenty of assholes out there with spray cans, and this guy's no Jerry Moses, that's for sure, although I kind of like the name Snake Boy.

"Jerry Moses? Who the hell's Jerry Moses?"

Picasso smiled, fueling my exasperation. "He's a Haitian graffiti artist, works with a spray can in each hand. The guy's awesome."

I rolled my eyes and turned my hands palms up. "Aren't you *upset* about this?"

"Sure I'm upset. Shit, I was about ready to start painting. This is going to slow me down."

I exhaled and Archie stopped barking. "You mean you can fix it?"

"Yeah, I can fix it. I'll have to paint over this shit, then re-sketch what's lost. That'll go pretty fast, I think."

"Aren't you worried this will happen again?"

"A little bit. I'll have to think about how to protect it until I have a finished product. After that, the work is on its own. See, the thing is, if your work's good, really good, it will last, people will respect it. If not, well…"

"That's a high standard to hold yourself to. Like you say, there are a lot of assholes out there."

"Yeah, I guess so. But it's reality. It's not like art hanging in a gallery somewhere. A street artist has to accept the fact that his work won't last forever. That's part of the beauty of it."

I nodded. "You're right, I guess. There really aren't any guarantees."

"Nope. No guarantees."

"But what about all the work you put into it?"

He smiled and scratched the spot where his eyebrow ring had been. "It's the *journey*, man, that's what's important. Not the ego trip. When I finish a mural, I'm done with it. I try to say something true and then I let it go. It becomes part of the city."

"How are you going to protect it when you're not working on it?"

"I don't know yet, but I have a couple of ideas." With that, he turned on his heels and sauntered off toward the back of the building to get his supplies. When he returned, I handed him a green tea I'd gotten across the street. While sipping my double cap, I began filling him in on what had happened the night before.

"So, screwed again, huh?" Picasso said when I'd finished.

"No, not at all. I remember most of the significant points out of the stuff you gave me," I answered. "One thing, though. I read in one of the newspaper articles you gave me that your mother had a drink with a friend the night she disappeared. Do you remember her name? I'd like to talk to her."

"Her name's Cynthia Duncan, my mom's best friend. She came to the memorial. She works for one of the small newspapers in town. The *Zenith*, I think."

I called the *Zenith* and used their automated system to confirm she worked there and then ring her extension. She picked up on the third ring, and an hour later I was in her office sitting across from her. She wore her blond hair in a pixie cut, and her big, expressive brown eyes were in constant motion, like a hummingbird. Her body, too, was charged with a kind of kinetic energy even at rest, and although her handshake was firm, she looked disturbingly thin in a beaded chevron dress, black tights, and lace-up boots.

She told me she had gone to the memorial service and witnessed the outburst between Picasso—Daniel, as she called him—and Conyers. She had lots of questions about Picasso, and I filled her in as best I could, trying to put a positive spin on a pretty desperate situation.

When she asked about the kicking incident, I told her I'd witnessed it, and that he was provoked by the freelance reporter. She said, "I'm not surprised. I know that creep Ronnie Lutz. The reporters in this town are a tight-knit group."

"Maybe you could say something to him. I'm afraid he's going to want a lot of money for that camera. That could be a big problem for Picasso."

She nodded. "I'll see what I can do."

I began asking her what she remembered about Nicole Baxter's disappearance but didn't learn much until I said, "Do you remember anything about her state of mind around the time she disappeared?"

Her answer surprised me. "Yes, I do. She was very excited, exhilarated, I would say."

"Why?"

"Well, for one thing, work was going really well for her. She was working on some big story. But that wasn't all. She'd been seeing someone else for a while, and it was heating up."

"Who?"

"Wouldn't tell me." She smiled for a moment. "Nicky was good at protecting her sources. The guy was married and, of course, she was still going with Mitch Conyers. But she'd finally realized what a loser he was," she said, rolling her eyes. "This new guy told her he was going to leave his wife for her."

"Did Conyers know or suspect anything?"

"I don't really know." She shook her head. "Conyers was such a contemptible bastard."

"Did you tell the police about the affair?"

"Yes, I did. But I don't think anything ever came of it. I mean, I don't think they ever found out who her lover was."

"What about the story she was working on? Did she tell you anything about it?"

"Like I said, Nicky was scrupulous about confidentiality. The only thing she told me was that someone big was going down, or something like that, meaning the story was going to hurt someone important."

"Any idea who that was?"

"Not at the time, but after Nicky disappeared, I made this crazy connection." She dropped her eyes and focused on something on the cluttered desk between us. "I'm not sure I should tell you. I'm probably way off base."

I slid to the edge of my chair. "I'm careful with my sources, too."

She held her eyes on the desk and drummed her fingers for several beats before saying, "Well, right after Nicky disappeared, this rumor popped up around here about a local celebrity who was involved in some kind of scandal. A really juicy one."

"Who was it?"

"His name's Vincent, Larry Vincent. He's a radio personality, the darling of Portland's far right wingnuts."

"Why did you connect the two events?"

She laughed and looked back down at her desk again. "The timing, I guess, and the way Nicky talked about it. You know, she was relishing the thought of taking this person down, and she hated bigots with a passion. Then this rumor pops up about this blowhard right after she's gone. It just seemed a little too coincidental, that's all."

"Did you tell the police about this?"

"Are you kidding? I didn't have the nerve. It was pure conjecture on my part."

"What became of the rumor?"

"The accusations never surfaced, although Vincent's wife left him right after that. I never heard anything more about it."

I thought about Vincent's appointment with Nicole Baxter, but she didn't need to know about that. "Thanks. That's something I can look into."

"Well, it's just a theory, you know. I'd say it's much more likely that Mitch Conyers found out she was going to leave him and killed her. I don't care how good his alibi was."

I took her through several more questions, including who the hell X-Man might be, but nothing else important surfaced. I thanked her and wrote my cell number on a card for her in case something else came to mind. I sat in my car outside the Portland *Zenith* building thinking about what Cynthia Duncan had just told me. Nicole Baxter had a lover who was apparently never identified, and she may have been writing an exposé about Larry Vincent.

The pot wasn't boiling yet, but I could see some steam.

Chapter Seventeen

The only discount electronics shop I knew of in Portland was over in Southeast, on Eighty-Second, a tough area of Portland known as Felony Flats. The electronics shop was located between the headquarters of the Oregon Cannabis Foundation and Duke's Gun Shop, which claimed to be "Portland's Last Real Gun Store." I hated to rush into a big decision like buying a new computer, but didn't feel I had much choice. An hour later I had a new laptop with a four gigabyte RAM and a backup hard drive that I vowed to use religiously. I also bought a prepaid cell phone for Picasso in the hopes of stimulating better communications. As I wrote the check, I remembered that I still hadn't talked to him about getting paid. That discussion, it seemed, kept being overtaken by events.

I locked my new computer in the trunk of my car and crossed the street to a pharmacy, where I bought a green ball cap with *Oregon* written in yellow script across the front. I wouldn't call it a disguise, but I hoped that with the cap, my dark glasses, and my fleece zipped and collared-up, I might go unrecognized if I kept to the fringe of Conyers' funeral. I glanced at my watch. If I hurried, I could get there before the service ended.

I managed to score a parking space a block and a half down from the Old Church, a nineteenth century Gothic gem that a group of citizens had rescued from the wrecking ball in the sixties. The buttressed belfry tower still jutted skyward emphatically, but it was missing a cross—a testament to the building's secular use, I assumed. It was 11:25, about time for the building to disgorge Conyers' mourners.

I suddenly felt apprehensive. What if someone recognized me, like that reporter Picasso kicked, or worse, what if Scott and Jones showed up? And what the hell did I expect to learn anyway? I had no answer except that I knew funerals were a powerful draw, and I was curious to see who would show up.

I put on the cap and glasses and joined a small group of onlookers who'd gathered next to a group of TV reporters and their technicians. People I didn't recognize trickled out first, and it wasn't until several minutes later that Conyers' stepbrother, Seth Foster, emerged. He was younger than I judged from the news photo, broad through the chest with the florid complexion of someone with a taste for alcohol. His face was drawn up in a tight, controlled expression, and I thought his eyes betrayed genuine sadness. Jessica Armandy was next to him, dry eyed and grim-faced, her hand resting on his arm.

The cameras were rolling, but out of respect none of the reporters approached Foster. Then Larry Vincent emerged, and I heard a murmur from the onlookers. He went straight to a reporter he seemed to know, said something I couldn't hear, and then up popped her microphone. She said, "Mr. Vincent, would you like to comment on Mitchell Conyers' memorial service?"

"Yes, I would, Casey. It was a beautiful service to commemorate the tragic loss of an outstanding citizen of Portland. Mitch Conyers will be sorely missed. This is a wakeup call, a stark reminder of what the city's permissive policies toward the homeless can result in. I hope and pray the police bureau will bring Mitch Conyers' killer to justice and do it soon. And I call on the mayor and the city council to crack down on these unwanted and potentially dangerous people. Thank you."

Vincent stepped away, a self-satisfied look staining his face. The woman behind him looked familiar, but I couldn't place her. She wore a tight black dress that accentuated an eye-popping body and thick mane of honey blond hair. Most of her eye makeup was on her cheeks, which were red like her nose. She was the only one I'd seen crying in the whole crowd. Then it came to me—she was one of the women sitting next to Jessica Armandy the night I met her. I fell in step with her and offered my handkerchief. "I'm sorry for your loss. Mitch must have been a good friend."

She waved off my handkerchief and shot me a sideways look. "Who the hell are you?"

"I'm Cal Claxton. I'm trying to figure out who killed your friend."

She looked at me again. "You don't look like a cop."

I laughed. "Thanks, I'm not. I'm an attorney. I was, uh, wondering if I could talk to you about Mitch Conyers."

She stopped and faced me. She was tall with the skin and hair of vibrant youth. Her big, doe eyes were as green as the sea, and her mouth wide with lips that were naturally round and full. She reached up and took my cap off, the stones in her tennis bracelet glittering with authenticity. "You're the guy at the bar the other night who was talking to Jessica. You represent that snake kid, right?"

I smiled hesitantly, half expecting to get shut down. "Uh, yeah. I represent Danny Baxter."

She nodded, then sniffed, and I offered my handkerchief again. She took it this time, dabbed her eyes and looking down on it, said, "Shit. There goes the makeup." Then she looked up, studying me for a few moments. "I'm not going to the cemetery. What I could use is a stiff drink. My name's Bambi."

"I could use a drink, too." I pointed up the street. "My car's on the next block." As we started walking, I glanced back toward the church and saw the imposing figure of Jessica's driver, Semyon, getting into her Lexus. I was pretty sure he hadn't seen us, but I couldn't say the same for the passengers behind the heavily tinted windows of the sleek, black car.

We drove over to a tiny watering hole Bambi knew that was located in a turn of the century flatiron building across from Powell's Books. A clutch of homeless kids were lounging in the sun near where we parked and one—a pudgy girl with bad teeth—asked if we could spare some change. I hadn't bought any of the meal vouchers Anna had suggested yet, so I reached into my pocket so as not to look cheap in front of Bambi. Before I got my hand out, Bambi fished a five dollar bill out of a small purse she was carrying and placed it in the girl's outstretched hand. "Damn spangers," she muttered as we walked away.

"*Spangers?*" I asked. I hadn't heard the term.

She looked at me in disbelief. "Spare change artists. You'd be surprised how much money they can make."

"Why do you give her money then?"

She shrugged. "I usually don't. It was the girl. I felt sorry for her."

When we were seated at the back of the bar, I asked her about her name. She laughed. "My real name's Stephanie, but Jessica wanted me to be called Bambi. She said older clients would really dig it. I used to hate the name, but I got used to it."

Jessica was probably right about the name, although given Bambi's physical attributes "Ralph" would have worked just as well. As we waited for our drinks, I said, "How did you meet Jessica?"

She had repaired her makeup in the restroom, and her eyes seemed less innocent now. "Actually, she discovered me."

"How so?"

A smile brightened her face. "I was hanging out one day in Pioneer Square, seven years ago, I guess. I was seventeen, living on the street. Got kicked out of my house in Boise. Anyway, Jessica walks up to me, introduces herself and asks if I want a job."

"What kind of job?"

She shot me a look, like I was some sort of idiot. "Escorting, what-a-ya think? She told me I had real potential."

Potential must mean being beautiful and looking five years younger than your age, I thought to myself. "Was Mitch Conyers one of your clients?"

Our drinks had arrived. She took a pull on her whiskey sour as her face clouded over and her eyes began to tear again. "Yeah, but it was more than that. I was his special girl. He always told me that." She raised her wrist to show me the bracelet. "He gave me this."

"It's lovely."

She dabbed her eyes carefully with a napkin and laughed with a bitterness that saddened me. "He told me he was going to get me out of the life, you know. Now he's dead."

I nodded in a show of understanding. "It must still be possible to get out, Bambi."

"Yeah, well, it would be nice, but it's not as easy as you think. I make a good living, you know. I have bills to pay, too."

I had a feeling there were more formidable barriers to her leaving but set them aside for the time being. "Do you have any idea who killed Mitch?"

She lowered her napkin and met my eyes. There was a steely resolve in her face I hadn't seen before. "It wasn't your snake boy, that's for sure."

I set my beer down. "Why do you say that?"

"Right after they found that woman's bones, Mitch started acting kind of nervous. Even had trouble getting it up one night." She allowed another smile, wistful this time. "That wasn't like him at all. I asked him what the problem was, you know? He didn't want to talk at first, but after a couple of drinks, he tells me he's worried."

"About what?" I coaxed.

"I'm not sure, exactly. But it wasn't your boy. He wasn't scared of some homeless kid. He said he'd been squeezing someone and maybe they'd had enough."

"*Squeezing* someone?"

"You know, he was being paid to keep quiet about something. Blackmail."

"Did he say who he was blackmailing?"

"No. Anyway, then he says, 'Bambi, I'm going to give you an envelope. If anything happens to me, give it to the cops.' You know, like right out of the movies."

"Do you have the envelope?"

She shook her head. "No, he never gave me anything. He got killed two days later."

I dropped my head and sighed. "Have you told the cops about this?" I asked the question, but I already knew the answer.

"I don't talk to cops. Jessica would kill me."

"Would you talk to them if I came with you?"

She shook her head emphatically. "*No way*. And if you tell the cops, I'll lie," she said defiantly.

"Then why are you telling me this?"

She rattled the cubes in her drink. "Looks to me like you're the only one trying to find Mitch's real killer. Maybe this'll help. Besides, I feel sorry for that homeless kid. I've been there. I know what it's like."

I nursed my beer and bought her a second whiskey sour, which made her a little tipsy. She told me Seth Foster's mother was Mitch Conyers' dad's second wife, and that Foster had been active in Conyers' restaurant business, but she didn't know any details. She did add, however, that Foster had a real thing about Jessica Armandy, although she apparently didn't feel the same way about him. When I asked whether she knew Hugo Weiman, the owner of the Deschutes property, she told me his name sounded vaguely familiar, but didn't know anything about him.

After I ran out of questions, I drove her back to her car. As she was getting out, I handed her a card and said, "If you think of anything else, give me a call. And, if you decide to change jobs, let me know. Maybe I can help."

When I got back to the clinic, I noticed a plastic tarp was hanging from the eaves of the building, partially covering Picasso's mural. I walked over to the side of the building for a closer look. The offending words were already painted over, and I could see where Picasso had started resketching.

As I started into the clinic a tall man in a blazer crossed the street and headed me off. An obese man with a full beard waddled like a duck behind him. The beard had a camera.

The blazer said, "Mr. Claxton, I'm Arnie Simms from *The Oregonian*. I understand you're representing Daniel Baxter. Is that right?"

"Not for the murder of Mitchell Conyers, I'm not. Mr. Baxter hasn't been charged with anything." It had clouded over. The camera flashed twice.

"That's true. But I just came from a press briefing at the Portland Police Bureau. They announced that Mr. Baxter is now considered a person of interest in the murder of Conyers. Would you care to comment on that?"

The camera flashed again. I felt the blood rise in my neck. The term "person of interest" pissed me off. "Well, I'm not sure what that term really means. Is this an attempt to placate certain interests in this city who seem bent on rushing to judgment? The fact is, Daniel Baxter hasn't been charged with anything, so he should be considered a person of innocence. I'd advise the police to broaden their search. There's a vicious killer out there, and it's not Danny Baxter." At that point, I caught myself. "That's all I have to say."

I ducked into the clinic, which was jammed with people. Anna was with a patient, and I found Archie in her office snoozing with his nose between his paws. He raised his hind quarters and stretched luxuriously before standing and wagging his stump of a tail.

We found Picasso in the spare office across from the storage room. He was sitting at a table next to Caitlin, an open book between them. He was saying, "…in algebra, whatever you do on one side of the equation, you have to do on the other side." Caitlin was chewing on her pencil, a pad of lined paper in front of her covered with equations. They looked up and Picasso said, "Hey Cal, this is Caitlin. I'm helping her study. She's going to the alternative high school over on Twelfth Street."

Caitlin averted her eyes and smiled shyly, an act that bracketed her mouth with a pair of perfect parentheses. Her chestnut brown hair looked freshly washed and gleamed in the overhead lights. We chatted for a few minutes about the joys of algebra, and then I looked at Picasso. "Arch and I are heading back to Dundee tonight. After you finish up here, can you swing by Caffeine Central? We need to talk." I turned to leave and added, "Great job on the mural. What's the tarp for?"

"Privacy. Me and some of my friends have decided to take turns sleeping out there to keep an eye on things. Plenty of room for a sleeping bag next to the building."

My thoughts went straight to what would happen if the vandals came back, but I let it slide.

I was packed up when Picasso arrived two hours later. He was wearing a faded, long-sleeve cotton turtle neck and a pair of jeans that had more holes than cloth. I stepped back and eyed him. "You're not so scary looking with your tats covered."

He smiled. "But deep down I'm still Snake Boy."

I showed him the new back door and told him the details of the break-in. When we got upstairs he reached into his pocket and handed me a folded check. "Here. I figured you needed this." It was a check made out to me for two hundred and fifty dollars. I looked up at him and he said, "We never talked about your fee, but I figured I owed you at least that much."

I looked back at the check and shook my head. "Things have happened so fast, I'm not sure how much you owe me. Can you afford this?"

He shrugged. "It's only money, man."

He still wasn't forthcoming about his finances, and I didn't press it. I said I wouldn't charge him for last week and would charge fifty bucks an hour going forward. My going rate was one hundred and twenty-five, but I figured art school wouldn't be easy for him to afford. Call it a scholarship.

With that behind us, I said, "Look, I was cornered by a reporter outside the clinic this afternoon. He told me that the cops have declared you a person of interest in the Conyers murder."

"I thought I already was."

I laughed. "This makes it official. They had to tell the press something. It'll be in the paper tomorrow. Don't worry about it. Every day that goes by without them arresting you means the chances are less and less likely." I went on to fill him in on what I had learned the last couple of days. After describing my conversation with Cynthia Duncan, I said, "Do you remember anything about your mom seeing another man before she disappeared?"

His brow wrinkled above an incredulous smile. "*What?* Mom was running around on Conyers? She never let on to me." He shrugged. "She wouldn't have told me, anyway. I would have ratted her out to Conyers just to see the expression on his face." Then he paused for a moment. "You know, there were a few times around then when mom didn't come home. It was no big deal. I was twelve and she always told me she'd be home in the morning. But she swore me to secrecy. Maybe she was with that guy."

"Any idea where she went?"

He shook his head. "I have no idea. You think this guy could've killed her?"

"Maybe your mom got cold feet, and he became angry." Then I changed directions. "Like I asked in the email I sent you, did your mom ever mention the name Larry Vincent."

"Who's he?"

I chuckled. "You don't know him, but he knows you. He's a talk show host on KPOC. He's the one who named you Snake Boy. Cynthia Duncan thought your mom might have been doing some kind of exposé on him. Apparently, he has some dirty laundry."

"Man, I got teased all afternoon about that name, but two people approached me today about doing art for them. Word spread fast about what's happened, and people want to support me."

"Good. But you don't remember hearing his name?"

"Nope."

"I didn't find a trace of any big story or exposé on the thumb drives you gave me, but I know she was working on one. Could your mom have stashed another thumb drive or printout someplace else? You know, some favorite hiding place she used?"

He tugged on the ring in his lip while he thought about it. "If she did stash something away, it's long gone. My aunt sold the place over on Knapp Street about eighteen months after mom disappeared. I don't know what happened to her stuff."

"What about Conyers? Could he have gotten hold of it? Remember, your mom's computer was never found."

He looked at me and shook his head. "I just don't know."

"I went to Conyers' memorial service today. One of Jessica Armandy's hookers told me he'd been shaking someone down and got nervous after they found your mom's body. Maybe he was using the story against someone and tried to up the ante after she went from a missing person to a murder victim."

"So this guy Vincent killed him, and my mom, too?"

"It's another possibility. If not Vincent, then whomever your mom's story was about to expose."

"Well, Conyers could have easily found something. It was chaos after mom disappeared, and he was probably in and out of our place."

Finally I asked him about X-Man. He laughed and said, "This is getting weird. I was a big fan of the movie *X-Men* back then. Mom must've gotten that name from me."

"There's more than one X-Man?"

He laughed again. "Sure. They're a collection of superheroes who work for a man named Professor Xavier. I suppose he's *the* X-Man." Picasso went on to tell me more about the movie than I really wanted to know, but I made a mental note of the name Xavier.

When Arch and I walked Picasso down to the street, I handed him the cell phone I'd bought that morning. "Here. Take this. And don't worry about brain cancer. The phone's only temporary. I'm going to be in Dundee for several days. If anything comes up, call me *immediately*. And look, if those idiots with the spray cans come back, use the phone to call the cops, okay? Don't get into it with them, understood?"

Picasso nodded, but the look in his eye was not reassuring.

I turned to leave, and Picasso stopped me. "Uh, there's something I wanted to ask you. It's about Joey. He's getting worse, man. Some mornings I come out and he's sitting right where I left him the night before. He doesn't sleep. Just sits there and smokes all night. He needs help bad, but the army and the VA are fucking him over. I've been trying to help him, but he needs an attorney." He stopped there and rested his eyes on me.

I should have said no, damn it, but how could I do that when this young man—who was being framed for a murder and slandered in the media—seemed more worried about his neighbor than himself? I smiled and shook my head in resignation. "I'll take a look at it when I get back in town, okay?"

The drive back to Dundee was punctuated with gusts of wind that spun and twirled the fine mist of a light rain. When I turned onto the long driveway leading up to our gate, Archie began to whimper with excitement. Portland was full of new sights and smells, but the Aerie was his five acre slice of paradise, his domain.

As the headlights illuminated the gate, two facts that had been floating around in my head came together—Picasso had mentioned there were times when his mother didn't come home, and her appointment book had a telephone number that I'd traced to a bed and breakfast somewhere out in the wine country. It made sense—what better romantic getaway for Nicole Baxter and her lover than a B&B in the wine country?

There was only one problem. I was drawing a blank on the name and location of the bed and breakfast. It just didn't seem very important at the time. I'd jotted it down in my notes, but they were long gone along with everything else I'd lost in the break-in. And besides, even if I found the place, what were the chances they'd have records or remember anything? Very slim, I figured.

Chapter Eighteen

Archie and I were hungry. I fed him some kibbles, then took a nice bone from the refrigerator and tossed it out on the porch. "Behave out there," I warned. "Don't chase any skunks." I searched the fridge again and came up with a frozen steak the size of my fist and two big globe artichokes I'd forgotten I had. With water heating on the stove for the 'chokes, I nuked the steak to defrost it, pricked a nice yam with a fork and slathered it with olive oil and popped it into a hot oven. When the 'chokes and yam were nearly done, I ground pepper onto the steak and seared it in a hot skillet, leaving it red in the center, then served it all up with a bottle of five year old Rioja. It was good to be home.

I was shaving the next morning when a bank of dormant synapses suddenly began firing in my brain. I said, "*Carlton*, that's where that B&B was, Carlton." I dropped the razor, toweled off the shaving cream, and took the back stairs down to the study with a patch of stubble still bristling on my chin.

Like Dundee, Carlton was a small farming town given a new lease on life by the pinot noir grape. It was straight west of the Aerie, maybe ten miles. Google said there were three bed and breakfasts there, but none of the names sounded familiar. The first place had only been in business five years, I learned with a quick phone call. The next two, the R J Simpson House and the Logan House B&B and Vineyard, had been around nine and twelve years, respectively. However, the woman running the

R J Simpson House explained they only kept their records for three years per the tax code. She laughed when I asked if there was any chance she'd remember a couple from eight years earlier. That left the Logan House. The gruff-voiced proprietor, a man named Harry Winthrop, said his wife was a compulsive record keeper. Why, she even had Polaroid snapshots of most of their guests in addition to their comments about the stay. But he was leery of sharing information about their customers. I gambled on a direct approach, telling him I was helping a son investigate the unsolved murder of his mother, and that I would hold the information in the strictest confidence. There was a long pause before he said I could stop by, and they'd see what they could do for me.

I wolfed down a cup of coffee and a piece of toast and dashed back upstairs to finish shaving and get dressed. Twenty minutes later I turned off the highway onto a long drive that wove through a well-tended vineyard and ended in front of a Queen Anne Victorian mansion. The place was up there on the charm scale, with an arched, second story balcony and a generous supply of brightly painted gingerbread. Better yet, it was isolated and boasted only a single room, which made it more likely a furtive couple like Nicole Baxter and her lover would choose it for a get-away.

I parked in the circular drive and told Arch to stay put. Harry Winthrop met me on the porch. He was a big man with a crushing handshake and quick, friendly smile. The oak floor creaked musically as he showed me into the formal dining room. His wife was busy, he explained, but he'd managed to find the guestbook corresponding to the year 2005. A leather-bound tome, it sat on the dining room table below an ornate crystal chandelier. Before he opened the book, he asked more questions about the case. I was relieved that he hadn't heard about it. The notoriety might have caused him to think twice about becoming involved. He said, "What month was it, again?"

"Nicole Baxter disappeared on May 18, so I'd say April to mid-May, in that time frame."

We opened the book, started thumbing through it and found the couple almost immediately. They had come in on May 8, a Tuesday, and stayed one night. A faded but well-focused photo showed a woman in a turtleneck sweater and teardrop earrings beaming a smile from the same dining room table. She looked older and decidedly happier than in the photo Picasso had shown me, and there was no question she was Nicole Baxter. She and her son shared the same dark, liquid eyes, and she had a delicate lift at the corners of her mouth I now realized Picasso had as well. She would be dead a week later. The thought of it brought a stab of anger and a sense of the loss Picasso must have felt as a twelve-year-old boy.

Her companion was less visible. He was turned toward her, his left hand partially obscuring his face. I couldn't tell whether this was deliberate, or he was simply caught in the act of saying something, an aside, to Nicole. I could see the contour of his left cheek, part of a heavily browed eye, and dark, wavy hair that was swept back. He wore an expensive looking watch on his left wrist, a blazer with three brass buttons on the cuff, and a button-down oxford shirt, no tie. The watch looked like a Rolex. The photo gave me a sense of the man, but there was no way I could use it to make a positive identification.

The couple had registered as John and Nicole Baxter and had paid their bill in cash. An entry, in what I took to be Nicole's handwriting read, "To Harry and Florence, Thanks for sharing your lovely home with us. The breakfast was magnificent! Best regards, Nicole and John."

"You remember anything about this guy?"

Harry put on a pair of reading glasses and leaned in to the picture. "Nah, they only stayed one night. I don't remember either one of them. She was pretty, though. Did he kill her?"

I shrugged. "I don't know. How about your wife? Would she remember anything?"

He looked at me and shook his head. "Florence doesn't remember *me* half the time. Alzheimer's."

I expressed my sympathy, and we went on to talk about other things, including the pinot noir grapes he was cultivating. I took a picture of the snapshot with my cell phone, but it didn't come out worth a damn. Harry surprised me by saying, "Take the picture, I don't need it, and Flo won't miss it."

Arch and I headed straight from the B&B to my office in Dundee, because my first meeting that day was scheduled for ten. The sun was out, so instead of skirting the Dundee Hills I meandered through them on Worden Hill Road. I had a back window down for Arch. The air smelled of fir with a tinge of something sweet, plum blossoms maybe, and down in the valley the last flecks of a morning fog traced the path of the Willamette River. To the west, banks of cumulus clouds lined up along the Coastal Range like white-washed fortifications.

Risking a buzz kill, I switched on the radio to hear what Larry Vincent was up to. I caught him in the middle of a tirade about the current mayor of Portland. Vincent was bragging about showing up at a recent city council meeting to hector the mayor for joining a national mayors' group calling for gun control. A caller described Vincent's performance as a courageous act, a characterization Vincent brushed off as nothing more than his patriotic duty.

After a commercial for some new, enriched form of fish oil, Vincent said, "I vowed to keep the heat on the mayor and on the police bureau to bring Mitchell Conyers' murderer to justice. In today's *Oregonian*, I was pleased to see that the police finally named Daniel Baxter a person of interest in the case. You remember Baxter, folks. He's the homeless thug with a snake tattooed on his neck and piercings that make his face look like a pin cushion. We call him Snake Boy around here. Anyway, this cretin was caught with blood on his hands, *literally*, next to Conyers' bludgeoned body in the man's own backyard, but Portland's finest haven't seen fit to arrest him."

Vincent went on about the particulars of the case, before getting around to me. He said, "Snake Boy's lawyer is some bleeding heart from out in the valley named Calvin Claxton. Honestly, folks, I don't know how a man like that can look at his self in the mirror. Judging from his comments in the paper, he's upset that Snake Boy's under suspicion. *Upset? Are you kidding me?* Conyers was an outstanding citizen, a pillar of this community, and now he's dead. *That's* what Claxton should be upset about."

I switched the radio off after listening to a couple of angry callers who chimed in after Vincent's comments. My cheeks felt hot and my mouth dry. Just for a fleeting instant, I fanaticized about going back to the radio station and waiting for him in the parking lot. I also found myself wondering how many fans Vincent had out where I lived in the northern valley. I suspected there were quite a few.

Chapter Nineteen

I heard a soft *tok tok tok* on my bedroom door, and fear gripped me like a hand to the throat. I swung my feet from the bed onto the floor while trying to decide who or what was out there. That's when I woke up and realized the sound I'd heard was rain that had begun dripping from a leak in my window, a leak I'd been trying to fix since the day I moved in. I got up and put a towel on the sill to absorb the water and dampen the sound. Arch got off his mat and came over to supervise. Getting back in bed, I reached out unconsciously to the empty space beside me and felt the cold sheets. Thoughts of my wife, the touch of her warm body in bed, flooded back to me. I could feel the contours of her body nestled against me and hear her soft breathing. She's gone, a familiar voice within me said. You don't get a second chance at something that good.

I lay there until the ache subsided. By that time sleep was no longer an option. I sat back up again but lingered there like an inert lump until Archie came over and coaxed me to my feet. He had a knack for doing that.

I took the back stairs down to the kitchen and put my nose into the bag of coffee beans and breathed deeply before pouring a charge into the grinder. I was on my second cappuccino and nearly through the online *New York Times* when Nando called.

"What are you doing up so early?"

He chuckled. "It is not of my doing, believe me, Calvin. It is necessary to meet with a plumber this morning. The man is an insanely early riser."

"I've got some new leads on the Conyers' murder," I answered, "but you go first. I'm sure you didn't call just to wish me good morning."

"You asked me about Hugo Weiman, the lobbyist. He divides his time between Portland and Salem. This is his Portland week. However, my contact tells me he's harder to get in to see than God."

"So, any suggestions?"

"Well, I'm told he has lunch every day between one and two at the bar in the Heathman. A liquid lunch. I suppose a man with big *cajones* might go there and wait for an opportunity to present itself."

I had to chuckle. "I'm flattered. What else do you have?"

"I managed to dig something up on the radio man, Larry Vincent."

"He's got some dirty laundry," I shot back.

"Impressive, my friend. How did you know this?"

"Nicole Baxter's best friend's a reporter at the *Zenith*. She told me. Did you get any specifics?"

"It's very strange. I could find out very little, and I shook the tree hard. All I know is that it involved sexual misconduct of some sort."

"Do you have a name?"

"Nobody is talking."

"Keep digging. There could be something to this." The last bit of news Nando had was that the street was not suspicious about Milo Hartung's death. It was generally conceded he died of a simple overdose. I filled him in on what I'd just learned. He wanted to see the photo of Nicole Baxter and her lover, and we agreed to cover that when I got back to Portland. He agreed to take a look at Conyers' stepbrother, Seth Foster. I was particularly interested to know what he stood to gain from Conyers' death, a question I hoped Scott and Jones were looking at as well.

I spent the day at my office in Dundee. It was *not* a good day. One of the clients whose files had been stolen fired me, and a prospective client with an insurance issue called and abruptly cancelled her meeting without any explanation. To top things off, there were three threatening phone calls waiting for me on my answering machine. As far as I could tell, they were from separate callers. Couched in colorful language, they invited me to perform an impossible biological act and assured me they knew where I lived.

After dinner, I googled Hugo Weiman. I needed to acquaint myself with his appearance since I was planning to join him for lunch. His dossier was extensive and impressive. His consulting firm, Weiman and Associates, was active in issues that spanned the Oregon political spectrum—from salmon restoration and logging to the silicon forest, Portland's nickname for its high-tech industry. The genius of Hugo Weiman, as one columnist put it, "…is that he has managed to stay above the backbiting political partisanship in Salem, thereby opening up his shop to do business with both sides of the aisle."

But nearly overshadowing his lobbying exploits was his charitable work. An item covering a high-end cancer fundraiser in *The Oregonian* included the line, "Since the tragic death of Eleanor Weiman from breast cancer four years ago, her husband, Hugo Weiman, has probably done more than anyone in this state to advocate for a cure." Another article announced he had received the governor's top award for volunteer work. An accompanying photo showed Weiman standing between the mayor of Portland and the governor at the award ceremony. He was taller than both men, with silver hair swept back from a high forehead, horn rim glasses and a full mustache. He'd be easy enough to spot at the Heathman.

Out of curiosity, I went back to the year 2005, getting better than a dozen hits. Two items caught my eye. The first appeared in *The Oregonian* on May 18, reporting that Weiman accidentally shot himself in the hand while cleaning his gun at his home in Lake Oswego. He was expected to make a complete recovery from the self-inflicted wound. The second was a brief article in the *Statesman Journal,* accompanied by a photo, with the headline "Hugo Weiman to speak on gun safety." The article, dated August 21, stated that Weiman, a gun enthusiast, was planning to talk at a Salem gun club about the lessons learned from his recent gun accident. The article went on to mention he was injured while cleaning his twenty-two caliber target pistol.

I looked at the date of the first article again, pushed myself away from the computer and sat there frozen, as it sunk in. May 18. That was the day Nicole Baxter disappeared. I pulled up the later article and looked hard at the photograph of Weiman. His hair was darker, and there was more of it. His upper lip was clean shaven. I fetched the photo Harry Winthrop had given me and compared the two. I couldn't say it was a match, but then again, I couldn't say it wasn't, either. Then another fact clicked in—he was shot with the same caliber weapon as Baxter, a twenty-two.

I grabbed my phone and speed-dialed Nando. "Listen, Weiman got shot in the hand on the exact day Nicole Baxter disappeared. I want you to drop everything else you're doing for me and concentrate on this. I want to know the time it happened, where he went for medical attention, everything. It was supposedly an accident, self-inflicted. Is there any way to verify that? Did anyone witness it? I don't know, a friend or neighbor or something? Not his wife. She's dead. I need a name."

We kicked around the theory that Weiman was Baxter's lover and the shooter for a while. There were lots of nagging questions, like if he was the shooter, how did *he* wind up getting shot? And, where was Weiman when Mitch Conyers was killed? We agreed to touch base when I got back to Portland, which I decided was going to be the next day. Before he hung up, Nando said, "I hate to bring up money, Calvin, but you are into me for better than fifteen hundred already."

"But all I've asked for so far is information, Nando. No stakeouts or anything that takes a lot of manpower."

"True. But information also costs money, my friend."

"Okay, okay. I'm good for it. Pull out all the stops on this. This could be the break I've been looking for."

Chapter Twenty

While driving into Portland the next morning I called to arrange a meeting with Cynthia Duncan. She agreed to meet at a little espresso shop near her building, and while she waited in an overstuffed chair I got our drinks—a double cap for me and a bottle of raspberry-flavored water for her. I threw in an almond croissant, and when I offered her half she told me she was dieting. *Dieting?* I could encircle her bicep with my thumb and index finger.

I sat down and she said, "I talked to Ronnie Lutz about the broken camera. I told him Daniel was homeless and couldn't afford to replace it. Oh, and that he was very sorry. Lutz was noncommittal, though. I think I could have changed his mind, but I wasn't going there." She rolled her brown eyes, which sparkled with flecks of gold in the overhead lights. I must have looked puzzled, because she added, "You know, he wanted me to sleep with him."

I chuckled and might've even blushed. "Oh. That would've been beyond the call of duty."

"For sure. Anyway, one of my coworkers told me the camera's insured, so the whole thing is bullshit anyway."

"Good to know." I then pulled the photo of Nicole Baxter and the man out of my shirt pocket and handed it to her. "Do you know who this man is?"

She raised a hand to her mouth and her eyes filled. "When was this taken?"

"Shortly before Nicole disappeared. At a bed and breakfast out in the wine country."

She looked at the picture for several moments before saying, "Oh, Nicky, I miss you."

"The man, Cynthia, do you recognize him?"

She sniffed and dabbed her eyes with a napkin. "No. I have no idea who that could be." She continued to study the picture, though, noting the Rolex and pointing out that the blazer he was wearing looked hand tailored. "Looks like he has money," she remarked. "That would be like Nicky."

"Did Nicole ever mention the name Hugo Weiman?"

"The lobbyist? No, I don't remember her ever mentioning him." She looked back at the photo. "Are you saying that's *him?*"

I shrugged. "I don't know. It's a possibility." Then I added, "Look, Cynthia, this is sensitive stuff. I'm trusting you to keep this confidential."

Her eyes flashed at me. "I get it, okay? You can trust me." Then the corners of her mouth turned up ever so slightly. "I would like to ask you for a favor."

"Shoot."

"When you get this figured out, I want to be the one to break the story."

"You got it," I said, then added, "You know, I've got my hands full right now, but I'm still intrigued by your theory that Larry Vincent could be the focus of Nicole's story. I haven't come up with anything more than what you told me about the scandal. Any chance you could come up with a name, or something else that might shed more light on what happened?"

She didn't hesitate. "Okay, I'll see what I can do."

I went from there to Caffeine Central to stash my gear and give Archie a quick walk before dropping him at the clinic. Picasso had agreed to keep an eye on him. At 12:45, I was sitting at a small table near the entrance to the bar at the Heathman Hotel. My leather coat didn't help me blend in with the affluent clientele, who were sipping nine dollar "signature cocktails" and speaking in low tones. I ordered a Mirror Pond and waited.

At 1:05, three men entered the bar wearing dark suits and power ties and were immediately shown to a corner table. Weiman was one of the three, and I could have touched him as he strode past my table.

Three vodka martinis later, he got up and headed toward the gents. I followed and standing next to him at the urinals, stole a quick glance at his face. I caught it at just the right angle. The heavy brow, the line of his cheek bone, the swept-back hair—grayer now, but no matter—they all fit. He reached his left hand up to the flush lever and there it was, the Rolex and, of course, the jagged scar left by a bullet wound he sustained a week after the photo was taken. It was him. I was sure of it.

Or was I? By the time I got back to my table, I was second guessing myself. Maybe I just wanted it too much. A lot of affluent men wear Rolexes, I told myself.

The three men left the bar at a little past two, and I fell in behind them with absolutely no idea what I was going to do next. One of Weiman's companions headed toward the Schnitzer Concert Hall, and the other walked north with him for a block before crossing Broadway at Salmon Street. Suddenly it was just Weiman and me. I followed him into the lobby of the Fox Tower, and when he used his security pass to enter the elevator I stepped into the otherwise empty car with him. He gave me a sharp look, and I raised my hands and said, "Sorry, forgot my pass."

He turned back to the control panel and punched the top button for the 35th floor. When I didn't follow suit with a lower floor, he turned to face me. The doors closed, and the car started moving. "Do you have business on thirty five?"

I smiled affably. "I hope so. I'm Cal Claxton, Mr. Weiman. I'm an attorney looking into the murder of Nicole Baxter on behalf of her son, Daniel. I'm wondering if you could spare me a few moments out of your busy schedule." I extended a business card.

He left my hand hanging there between us, and with eyes narrowed took the measure of me. "I don't appreciate being ambushed."

"I understand that and apologize. I just have a few questions. It won't take long at all." I smiled again. "And it'll probably save you a deposition." What the hell, I figured. Threatening a deposition might work on him, too.

He took the card, looked down at it, then back at me. I was glad I wasn't wearing a suit and tie. Better the chance he might underestimate me. His eyes were a little shiny, but otherwise the vodka martinis seemed to have had no effect on him. The elevator lurched to a stop, a bell dinged and the doors opened. "Okay, Claxton, let's get this over with."

I followed him down a corridor and through a set of imposing glass doors. A bronzed plaque on the right announced we had entered the domain of Weiman and Associates. We filed past an elegantly furnished seating area facing an attractive receptionist behind a mahogany desk, then through another set of glass doors into a suite of offices. Weiman stopped at an alcove in front of the corner office and told a male assistant named Charles that he was going to meet with me for thirty minutes and to hold his calls.

Weiman's office wasn't what I expected. Instead of the obligatory pictures attesting to his lofty station in the halls of Oregon power and influence, the walls were covered with photographs, prints, and paintings taken in and around the Deschutes River. I knew this because of the countless hours I'd spent fishing there. I was drawn to one particularly exquisite print of a large trout breaking for a salmon fly. The artist had drawn it from the point of view of the fish, which was looking up at the insect floating on the surface of the water. The curve of the trout's thick body captured the coiled-spring power of the animal, and filtered sunlight illuminated its iridescent red side.

I stood admiring the print. "*Mykiss Iridus*, my favorite fish."

Weiman raised an eyebrow and smiled. "I agree. There's nothing like taking a redside with a dry fly," he replied, using the nickname for the species of trout found only in the Deschutes River.

I nodded toward a photograph of a low building with a flat roof and a porch facing the river. "I took a twenty-two incher right in front of your cabin last year."

He laughed heartily this time. "No wonder I can't catch any fish in front of my place." He walked behind his desk and motioned for me to take a seat. "There's a grassy bank two hundred yards downriver from the cabin. Maybe the best stretch on the river."

My turn to laugh. "I thought that was *my* secret place." I let the conversation drift in this vein for a while, which was easy because I loved to talk fly fishing as much as he did. Finally, I explained I'd forgotten my briefcase and asked to borrow a pad of paper to make notes. By this time, I was pretty sure I represented no threat to him. Eat your heart out, Columbo.

I started off by chucking him a couple of softball questions about the disappearance of Nicole Baxter and the discovery of her bones in the reservoir on Weiman's property and got no surprises back. I asked him if anyone else had access to the cabin—friends or business associates, for example. The answer was no. He had never allowed unescorted guests at the cabin, although there was often evidence—trash and other detritus—of trespassing fishermen, rafters, and the like. After several more questions along those lines he glanced at his watch and reminded me he'd gone all through this with the police. I said, "Okay, let's move to the present tense. I'm sure you're aware that Nicole Baxter's boyfriend at the time she disappeared, a man named Mitchell Conyers, was recently murdered."

He met my eyes and looked faintly amused. "Did your client do it?"

The question shouldn't have surprised me. A man like Weiman reads the newspapers. "No. He did not."

He shook his head slowly but not, as I thought initially, to refute my statement. "A homeless kid makes a tempting target. It makes me sick to see someone tried in the media like this. You've got your hands full, I'm sure."

Surprised again, I had to chuckle. "It's been interesting." Then I shifted in my seat. "Did you know Conyers?"

"Never met the man."

I nodded and smiled. "I see. I just thought you might've met him through Eros' Dreams. He was a regular customer, and I understand you are as well."

Weiman looked at me for a moment, then laughed with what seemed genuine amusement. "Nice try, Claxton. Like I said, I didn't know him. Hell, I'm not involved with that escort service *personally*. I use them for business purposes now and then. You know politicians—they crave companionship." He laughed again, winked at me and added, "Eros' Dreams is on the up and up, you know. Says so right on their website."

I didn't get the rise I was looking for from that question. Weiman seemed completely at ease, and despite his cavalier attitude toward the exploitation of young women, it was hard to completely dislike the guy. We talked a few minutes longer, and then I got up to leave. At the door, I turned and fired my last round. "Oh, one more thing. I was sorry to read about your gun accident. Did you realize you shot yourself in the hand on the same day Nicole Baxter disappeared?"

He launched a cover smile, but the mirth in his eyes cooled and the skin of his face tightened ever so slightly. "How extraordinary. I didn't realize that." He shook his head and slid his eyes off of me, focusing instead on something over my shoulder. "If it hadn't been for my wife, Eleanor, you know, I might've lost my hand. She found me and drove me to Meridian Park Hospital." Then he chuckled and added, "I'm still embarrassed about that accident."

"Well, we all make mistakes. Thanks again for the chat." With that, I closed his door and left. As I walked back to my car, I mulled over what had just transpired. I wanted to learn as much as I could without tipping my hold card—that I suspected he was Baxter's lover. I felt like I'd succeeded. His "accident" was somehow related to Baxter's disappearance. I was pretty sure of that now. Did he know or have contact with Mitchell Conyers? I was less certain of the answer to that question. If he *didn't* know him, then my assumption that Baxter's and Conyers' murders were related might be wrong. That seemed improbable.

Finally, he made sure I understood his wife had taken him to a local hospital after his accident. That gave him a strong alibi. After all, Baxter was apparently shot better than a hundred miles from Weiman's house in Lake Oswego, the *alleged* site of the accident.

At the same time, I had to admit my suspicions didn't mesh completely with my sense of the man. There was something disarming about him, his modesty, I suppose, his sympathetic take on Picasso's situation, and of course, his love of fly fishing. These factors militated against him being Baxter's killer in my mind, although as an ex-prosecutor, I knew that jealousy and passion could darken the heart of any man.

Chapter Twenty-one

"Wow. You're making great progress," I said to Picasso, who was up on the scaffolding with a paint bucket in one hand and a brush in the other. It was nearly four, and I'd just gotten back to the clinic.

He nodded, grunted something unintelligible and dabbed some black paint on Bob Dylan's 1970s afro. In the background, a fully rendered Mt. Hood stood in stark relief against a bluebird sky. Several other marchers had emerged, infused with life by the miracle of acrylic paint. A striking depiction of Anna Eriksen was nearly complete. She was caught in mid-stride, a lock of gold hair looped across her forehead. She had that resolute half-smile I'd come to know, and her eyes beckoned as if to say "step in, join us." The image made me realize I'd missed her, a thought that caught me by surprise.

"Where's my dog?"

"Try Doc's office. He's either there or out walking with Caitlin."

I found Archie in Anna's office, but Anna was busy in one of the examination rooms. I waited around for a while, then decided to head back to Caffeine Central. As I was leaving, I called out to Picasso, "Call me when you finish up." He nodded and continued to paint.

I drove to Whole Foods and laid in some provisions for my stay. You can't beat that grocery store for selection, but the people who call it "Whole Paycheck" have a point. I didn't have enough cash, so I used a credit card. An hour and a half later, I was up in the apartment sipping a glass of pinot with my feet up when I heard someone knocking. Weiman may have been a likeable guy, but who knows? I went into the bedroom, took Nando's Glock from my suitcase, and after releasing the safety, tucked it in my waistband at the small of my back.

I followed Arch down the narrow stairway to the first floor. "Who's there?" I called out, standing at the front door.

"It's Anna, Cal. Anna Eriksen."

I opened the door. She smiled sheepishly and said, "Can Archie play?"

Framed in the doorway, she reminded me of a painting I couldn't quite place. She wore jeans, a simple white blouse under a thin leather coat, no jewelry, and as usual, no makeup. Her hair was down, resting comfortably on the level plane of her shoulders, and although she continued to smile, there was no hiding her fatigue. I said, "Archie would love to play, but he hasn't had his dinner yet. Have you?"

"No, but I—"

I swung an arm in the direction of the stairs. "Great. Then join us."

She shrugged and followed me upstairs, whereupon I poured her a glass of wine and began cooking dinner. With Archie settled in at her feet, she began telling me about the events of her week. There was a pending budget cut from her sponsoring foundation, a rash of emergencies from a bad batch of ecstasy that got loose on the street. Worst of all, she'd lost two staff members so far that week.

"What happened?" I asked.

"Well, Sherry, my best nurse, told me she was going to take some time off, then look for another job. I think the whole Picasso thing kind of freaked her out. Then my janitor, Howard, quit in a huff."

"What's his story?" I asked, peeling the skin from a piece of ginger.

She sighed and shook her head. "Oh, he didn't beat around the bush. He told me I should get rid of Picasso, that he must've killed that restaurant owner."

"Ouch. What'd you say?"

"I, uh, got pretty hot, I'm afraid. I told him Picasso was innocent, that he found that man dead in the swimming pool and pulled him out. He just sneered and said, 'You're a fool to trust that kid.' Then he packed up his stuff and left. Hasn't shown up since."

"Maybe it's just as well."

She managed a laugh. "Yeah, except he was a volunteer, which was a big help to my budget. God, I hope nobody else leaves." Then she leveled her pale blue eyes at me. They were full of concern. "I have this sense of impending doom, Cal. What do you think the police are going to do?"

I stopped mincing the ginger for a moment. "It's hard to say. To be honest, I'm surprised they haven't arrested Picasso by now. Apparently, they're still searching for the murder weapon."

While my rice cooked, I brought her up to speed on what I'd learned so far. By the time I served up dinner—a stir fry of chicken in hoisen sauce and garlic along with sautéed spinach with ginger and red pepper flakes—I had answered most of her questions. She said, "So, this accident-prone lobbyist, how do you propose to smoke him out?"

"I have a private detective investigating the so-called accident. Like I said, I think he got shot on the river but went to a hospital in Tualatin, near his home, to make it look like an accident. But, I'm not sure I'll be able to show that. The trail's very cold."

"Why would he kill Conyers?"

I stroked my mustache with a thumb and forefinger. "That's the fly in the ointment. I don't know. I *do* know Conyers was blackmailing someone. Maybe it was him." I said this, but didn't really believe it. Something was missing, but I didn't know what it was.

I left Anna sitting on the couch while I cleared off the table and straightened up the kitchen. When I returned, she was fast asleep. I sat down and watched her. Her breath was slow and measured, her eyelids down, fringed with blond lashes that gently curled against her cheek. The fatigue I'd seen in her face was gone, replaced with an almost childlike serenity. I couldn't bring myself to wake her, so I read through the paper for a while, stealing glances now and then and wondering about the odd twists and turns that had resulted in this lovely woman sitting here beside me.

I woke Anna an hour later. She was embarrassed and only agreed to a ride when I told her I was going out anyway. I was telling the truth. I'd decided to have a drink at the Happy Angus to see what I could stir up. Jessica Armandy had to know more than she'd told me, which so far had been nothing.

I circumnavigated the restaurant several times but couldn't find a parking spot on the street that night. Finally, I pulled into a dimly lighted lot, part of which was being resurfaced. I weaved my way through some lumber and rebar as I returned from the kiosk to put the parking receipt on my dash. A few late night diners were huddled in the first floor of the restaurant, and I could hear the Thursday night buzz in the bar above.

Armandy was at her usual table in the back of the bar. She saw me enter and followed me with her eyes as I worked my way across the crowded room. When I stopped in front of her table she smiled without mirth, "Well, if it isn't the snake charmer. Is this a business call or are you looking for companionship?"

I returned the smile in kind. "Business. I—"

"Tell me, Claxton," she interrupted, her voice ringing with frustration. "Why haven't they arrested that little shit?"

I sat down across from her and rested my arms on the table. "They don't have enough evidence, that's why. Despite what Larry Vincent tells you, Danny Baxter didn't do it."

"Then who did?"

Before I could answer a man appeared next to Jessica. It took a moment in the bar light to realize it was Conyers' stepbrother, Seth Foster. He was well dressed and younger than Armandy, with a shock of black hair and a shadowy three day growth. He glanced at me, then turned to her. "You okay, Jess?"

"Sure, hon." She handed him her empty glass. "Would you be a dear and top me off?" She shot me a look and added, "And bring him whatever he's drinking."

I looked up at Foster. "A Mirror Pond. Thanks." As he walked away, I said to Armandy, "You asked me who killed your friend. The answer is whoever the hell he was blackmailing." I leaned forward and locked onto her eyes. "You know anything about that?"

She held my gaze, crossed her arms, and drew her mouth in tight. I could almost hear the wheels spinning in her head. "I don't know what in the hell you're talking about."

"Conyers knew Hugo Weiman, didn't he. He's the guy Conyers was squeezing, right?"

"There you go again. It's always about someone else, not your little Snake Boy."

I knew she was baiting me, so I let the comment ride. There was an uncomfortable silence until Foster returned. He stopped next to me and I saw a flicker of recognition in his eyes. Color rose in his face. "You're the douche bag trying to get Mitch's killer off, aren't you?" Before I could say a word he threw the glass of beer in my face and shoved me hard.

The chair and I went over, and I popped up ready to defend myself. Foster pointed at the staircase. "Get the fuck out of my restaurant."

Wiping beer off my face with my handkerchief, I walked out with as much dignity as I could muster. On the way, it occurred to me that Foster's use of the pronoun *my* was interesting. I was nearly to the parking lot when I heard footsteps rushing up behind me. I tensed and spun around.

"Cal, it's me, Bambi. I saw what happened in there. Are you alright?"

"Sure. A little damp, is all. Uh, how have you been?" She was wearing a low cut wife beater, tight jeans, and massive platform shoes. When she drew closer I saw the bruises on the right side of her face, a mosaic of purples and yellows. I took her chin in my hand and gently turned her face for a better look. "Who did this to you?"

"They saw us driving off at the funeral. Don't worry, it didn't hurt." She smiled, and I saw a glint of steel in her eyes. "They told me not to talk to you anymore."

"I'm sorry, Bambi."

"Not your fault." Then she looked back anxiously toward the restaurant. "Can we get out of here? I thought of some more stuff to tell you."

We were halfway through the parking lot when I heard the crunch of gravel underfoot behind us. We turned and saw the shadowy figure of a man approaching. He took several more steps and stopped in the dim pool of an overhead light. Bambi gasped.

It was Jessica Armandy's driver, Semyon, and he was a lot bigger than I remembered him.

Chapter Twenty-two

There was a disquieting eagerness in Semyon's eyes as a cold, reptilian smile spread across his face. He wore black jeans, thick soled shoes, and a tight fitting t-shirt that had "Bikes Babes & Brawls" inscribed in a circle around the words "Portland Cage Fights." A swarm of intricate tattoos on his arms looked like so much smeared ink in the low light. He said, "Jessica's looking for you, Bambi. You'd better get your ass back to the bar."

Bambi said, "Fuck you, Semyon." Not exactly the words I would have chosen under the circumstances.

"Watch your mouth," he said as he came forward. We held our ground and he stopped in front of us. He looked me over and said, "Run along now. This doesn't concern you, asshole."

My saner half screamed for me to de-escalate the situation, but raw anger boiled up in my chest and rose to my head faster than I could contain it. I heard myself saying, "Are you the one who beat her up?"

He chuckled as if I'd cracked a joke. "What if I was?"

"Well, first off, it's called assault and battery, and that's a felony. Second, it makes you a goddamn coward." Again, the words slipped out before I could stop them. To make matters worse, Bambi snorted loudly while trying to stifle a laugh. Maybe she knows something I don't, like Semyon's not as dangerous as he looks? I could only hope.

"Buzz off," he said as he stepped forward and chucked me hard in the chest with the palms of his hands. There was brute power in his arms, and the blow sent me sprawling on the gravel. So much for hope.

Bambi backed up slowly. The color had gone out of her face, but she remained defiant. "Leave us alone, you dumb bastard. Go back to Russia where you belong," she screamed.

Semyon made some guttural sounds, choice epithets in Russian, no doubt, and moved toward her. Scrambling to my feet, I shoved him hard. I might as well have shoved an oak tree, but my effort did get his attention. He spun around, pointed a thick, blunt finger at me and said, "I warned you, motherfucker."

Ignoring Bambi, he clinched his fists and started to move within range of my jaw. I backed up slowly until I bumped into a car. His eyes grew large, telegraphing his first punch. I ducked under it and drove a hard right into his heart. He grunted and lunged for me, but I spun out of his grasp. He came at me again and threw the same punch. I ducked and countered with an uppercut that snapped his mouth shut. He stepped back, spit a mouthful of blood, and said something in Russian again, this time with more feeling.

He moved in a third time, throwing another right, but quicker and straighter this time. I bobbed to duck it and slipped on the gravel. His eyes enlarged again as he launched a left hook that caught me off balance and defenseless. The punch landed flush on the side of my face. Jupiter's rings collided with the aurora borealis and hot, flaming shards rained down on my brain. A second blow, harder than the first, crushed my left ear and sent what was left of my brain crashing into the right side of my skull in the mother of all contrecoups.

I wobbled before dropping to my knees, and with my arms dangling at my sides, waited for the *coup de grace*. Instead of a final blow, however, I heard a loud crunch. I opened my eyes and saw Semyon kneeling in front of me. His eyes were open but they weren't focused on anything. Then they closed and he slumped to the side like a rag doll. Bambi was standing behind him holding a stout chunk of two-by-four. She said, "I hope I killed the bastard."

She helped me up, and when some of the fog lifted, I got back down on one knee and felt for Semyon's pulse. It was strong and even. Then he groaned and moved an arm. "Well, you didn't kill him," I said. "His head's way too hard for that. But you slowed him down pretty good. Thanks."

I searched his pockets, found his cell phone and made an anonymous 911 call, just in case. Then we got in my car and got the hell out of there with Bambi driving.

Bambi alternated between giggling hysterically and moaning about how much trouble she was in. I was fighting back nausea from having the world twist and spin around me, while trying desperately to keep the blood from my ear off my upholstery. She said, "Do you need a doctor, Cal?"

"I'm not sure. I'm more concerned about you. Where do you live?"

"Oh, Jesus, I can't go there. He'll come looking for me."

"It's going to take Semyon a while to sort things out. We'd better go to your place and have you pack up fast."

"Everything?"

"As much as you can."

"Oh, shit. I've really done it now."

Bambi lived in an apartment across the river in Westmoreland. I waited in the car after telling her she had five minutes to pack, a request that got me an incredulous look. My nausea and dizziness had morphed into a pounding headache, as if a wrecking ball was at work inside my head. I examined my ear in the rearview mirror. It looked like an overripe eggplant that had split open. The gash would need stitches, but the blood had slowed to a trickle. Fifteen minutes later Bambi came out with two bulging suitcases and a backpack. I popped the trunk latch and pointed over my shoulder with a thumb. She stashed her bags and hopped in the driver's seat. "What now?"

"Take the Ross Island Bridge. I'm going to call a friend." Anna picked up on the fourth ring. "Yes, Cal," she said after I finished a cursory explanation of the situation. "Bring her here straight away."

Anna's condo was on the edge of Old Town on Northwest Flanders. She took one look at me and got an ice pack for my head and a gauze compress for my ear. While I sat in her darkened living room, she moved Bambi into her spare bedroom. When she returned I said, "How is she?"

"Fine. The adrenaline's worn off, and she's in bed. With luck, she'll get some sleep. Now, let's have a look at that ear." She switched on the lamp, and I groaned, raising my hand to shield my eyes. With the lamp at the lowest setting, she removed the gauze and examined my ear more carefully. "You're going to need stitches, but I'm more concerned about your concussion."

"Concussion?"

She raised her hand in front of my face. "How many fingers?"

"Two."

"Good. Did you lose consciousness when he hit you?"

"Uh, yeah, but only momentarily."

"Headache?"

"You could say that."

She wanted to take me to the ER, but I said, "The clinic's only five minutes away. Can't we go there?" I'd made only one trip to the hospital in my life. That had been enough for me. Ten minutes later, I sat grimacing on a treatment table in the clinic while she cleaned the wound. "Have any bullets?" I asked.

"Sorry. We're fresh out."

When she placed a menacing looking curved needle along with thread, scissors, and bandages on a steel tray, I was beginning to reevaluate my decision to bypass the hospital. My ear was throbbing like a bass drum. "Let me guess," I said. "You're out of anesthetic, too."

Opening a cabinet, she said over her shoulder, "Had to cut somewhere." But when she returned with a syringe and small vial, I breathed a sigh of relief.

As she sutured my torn ear, I sat with my head down, listening to the cadence of her breathing and feeling her warm breath on the side of my face. When she finished, she stood in front of me smiling. Against the sterile white walls of the room, her eyes were bluer than I'd ever seen them. I took her head in my hands and kissed her gently on the forehead. "Thanks, Doc."

Her eyes began to tease. "Are you like the proverbial bear after a thorn's removed, or should I read more into this?"

I took her head in my hands again and started to kiss her on the lips, but when I closed my eyes the room took a nauseating half turn. I pulled back. "Whoa."

She smiled and placed a hand on my cheek. "You're coming back to my place. You need observation tonight." Our eyes met and held for an interval that had no time associated with it.

On the way back to Anna's condo, I said, "What am I going to do about Bambi? I got her into this mess."

"There's a shelter in Beaverton for women trying to get out of the sex trade. I could call them in the morning. I know the people who run it. It's a great place. Low recidivism rate. Do you think she'd be willing to go there?"

"She told me she wanted out. I think she meant it. Will she be safe there?"

"Yes. It's essentially a safe house. The address is kept under tight wraps, so the pimps can't find their wayward girls."

"Bambi saved my life, you know."

"I know."

When we got back to her condo, Anna gave me a fresh ice pack and put me on the couch in her living room. I went out like a light, but an hour later she woke me and checked the dilation of my pupils with a pen light. She did this two or three more times that night. The next morning she shook me awake, handed me a mug of coffee, and said Bambi was all set up at the shelter. She gave me the address and said, "You can take her over there this morning if you're up to it. Ordinarily they don't allow access to someone they don't know, but I convinced them you could be trusted."

"Good. I'll take care of it." I looked down at the coffee. "Uh, my stomach's saying no to this. Do you have any tea? I can make it."

Bambi didn't get up until after Anna had left for the clinic. Her eyes were red and puffy, but with her thick blond hair pulled back and no makeup, she looked like a college coed, a very beautiful one. After I accepted her apology for getting me beat up, and she accepted my thanks for saving my life, I broached the subject of the shelter. She jumped at it, explaining she'd spent a sleepless night making up her mind to return to Boise and face the music with her family. She wiped a tear away, saying, "I just can't show up, you know? I need some time to let people know I'm coming."

"That's what the shelter's there for. I'm sure they'll work with you." I listened while she cried and told me about her family and why she'd left. Most of all, she missed her little sister, who was what, twelve now? When she'd cried herself out, I said, "Bambi, last night you told me there was something else."

She blew her nose. "Oh, yeah, that. Well, I don't know how important this is, but I remembered an argument Seth and Mitch had."

I nodded encouragement.

"It was at the restaurant. Maybe two weeks before Mitch died. I'd been in the restroom—the one used by the staff. It's in the back, down from Mitch's office. I came out and heard them going at it. They both sounded really pissed. I just froze there in the hall and listened."

"What were they arguing about?"

She wrinkled her brow. "Something about the other restaurants, the ones in L.A. and San Francisco. Seth was saying, like, "We do the same gig there. It'll work, I *know* it will.""

"What was he referring to?"

She shrugged. "I don't know."

Hiding a growing sense of disappointment, I said, "Uh, that's it?"

She shook her head vigorously. "No, right after that all hell breaks loose in the office. I can tell they're actually fighting. Then Seth comes out rubbing his cheek and cussing a blue streak under his breath."

"Did he see you?"

"I don't think so. It was dark in the hall, and he went the other way."

"What happened after that?"

"That's the night Mitch told me he loved me, when he said he wanted me out of the life. I told you about that."

"Why didn't you tell me about the fight the first time we talked?"

"I don't know. When I saw how broken up Seth was right after, you know, I just forgot about it."

"What changed?"

"Seth did. It's like, now he's got this attitude. The big man. The other night he told Tiffany to go change. Said her outfit wasn't sexy enough. That's none of his damn business, you know?"

"What did Jessica have to say about that?"

"That's the other thing. She's going along with it. All of a sudden, she's like hot for the guy, well as hot as she could be for any man."

I raised my eyebrows.

She shook her head. "It's not like that. She just likes to be on top. Anyway, it just seems like they're both enjoying Mitch's absence too much." She managed a smile. "So that's what I wanted to tell you. I don't trust Seth or Jessica anymore."

We talked for another twenty minutes, but I didn't learn anything else. I still had a low grade headache and got dizzy if I moved too fast, but I managed to drive Bambi over to the shelter in Beaverton and help her get moved in. I wasn't followed, either. I made sure of that. As I was leaving, I said, "Are you going to be okay?"

She nodded, bit her lip. "Cal, you need to watch your back. Semyon's going to come after you to get to me. I know it."

I patted her cheek. "Don't worry, I can handle Semyon," I said with knee-jerk male bravado.

She smiled sweetly, came up on her toes and kissed me lightly on the mouth. "I'm sure you can."

That makes one of us, I said to myself.

Chapter Twenty-three

When I got back to Caffeine Central I found Picasso waiting outside. He was sitting next to his bike, slouched against the building wearing a black, hooded sweatshirt, cut-off jeans, and his ever present combat boots. When he saw me approaching, he scrambled to his feet. His eyebrow ring was still missing, and the neck of his sweatshirt obscured all but the single red, yellow, and black repeat pattern of his coral snake tattoo. "Are you okay, Cal?" He asked. "Doc told me you got beat up last night. She said it was some Russian cage fighter dude."

"I'll live. Come on up. We can talk."

While Picasso wrestled with Archie, I brewed us both a cup of tea and used mine to wash down three aspirin. Watching me drink my tea, he said, "Thought you were an espresso geek."

"It's tea today. I'm still a little wobbly." I wasn't hungry, but I could tell he was. I made him a three egg omelet with Gruyere cheese, toast, and diced potatoes fried up in red onions, sage, and olive oil. While he ate I brought him up to date. Of course, the first thing he wanted to hear about was my fight with Semyon: "Is the dude really a cage fighter?"

"I don't know. He was a little slow, come to think of it. Maybe he just bought the t-shirt."

"Man, I wish I'd been there."

"To see me get my butt kicked?"

"No, to help you."

I chuckled. "The truth is I got more help than I ever expected."

Picasso laughed. "Yeah, Doc told me about the hooker with the two-by-four." He put his hands together and made a chopping motion. "*Ka-boom*. She must've really nailed him!" We both laughed at the image—his imagined, mine seen through a fog of semiconsciousness. Then Picasso added, "Doc said the hooker had some information about Conyers."

I described what Bambi had overheard. After meeting Bambi, and in view of what she'd done to help me, the term "hooker" seemed unjust, and I didn't use it.

Picasso piled a chunk of omelet on a piece of toast and paused before wolfing it down. "I don't know, Cal. Brothers fight all the time. Maybe that tip wasn't worth getting your ass kicked."

I nodded. "The thought occurred to me. We've been assuming Conyers was killed by the person he was blackmailing. Surely he wasn't blackmailing his stepbrother." I wondered about Jessica Armandy's role in this, but my thoughts were so vague I didn't even bring it up. Picasso sighed, but not before taking another huge bite of egg and potato.

"I've got much better news about your mom's case. I think I've identified her lover."

He lowered his fork to his plate. "Who is it?"

"He doesn't know I know. You can't breathe a word of this to anyone, agreed?"

"Agreed."

"His name's Hugo Weiman. He's a big time lobbyist in the state."

Picasso stopped chewing and narrowed his eyes. "Did he do it? Did he kill her?"

I raised a hand like a traffic cop. "Whoa, I don't know yet. I've got a private investigator digging into it as we speak." Then wagging a finger in his direction, I added, "You need to stay cool." I was glad I'd left out that Weiman was the owner of the property where his mother's remains were found and had suffered a gunshot wound on the day she disappeared. The last thing I needed was for Picasso to go after Weiman.

We fell silent for while until Picasso spoke. "So, Doc stitched your ear up?"

"Yeah, saved me a trip to the ER."

A mischievous smile spread across his face. "She's pretty hot, huh?" When I didn't respond, he added, "You married?"

"Uh, no. My wife passed away three years ago."

He smacked his forehead with his palm. "Sorry." More silence, then, "Mind if I ask what happened?"

I looked down and studied the surface of the table. "She took her own life." It was my dirty little secret, something that still hung over me with a stench of guilt. But there it was, freely admitted with little urging. I was again surprised at my trust in this young man.

"Bummer," was all he replied.

We sat there without speaking. Cars whooshed by down on the street and a jackhammer some blocks away came on intermittently. Finally, I said, "Yeah, it's something I don't talk about much. It wasn't my finest hour. I, uh, missed the warning signs."

He gave his lip ring a couple of tugs and sighed. "It's easy to blame yourself when shit happens, man. It's the *easiest* thing to do, believe me."

I met his eyes and nodded. I could only imagine the blame he'd placed on himself, a kid of twelve, when his mother suddenly vanished. I got up and made us more tea. I told him about my meeting with Cynthia Duncan and how she'd agreed to look into the scandal Larry Vincent had suppressed. When I told him Cynthia had talked to Ronnie Lutz about the broken camera, and it looked favorable, he said, "Man, that's a relief. She did that for *me*?"

"Sure. She's in your corner." I pulled out my phone, scrolled down to her number and wrote it on the back of a card. "Here. Use the phone I gave you to thank her. She'd be thrilled to hear from me." Then it was my turn to look mischievous. "How's Caitlin's algebra coming along?"

He shook his head and his face clouded over. "You don't want to know. She's got a locker over at Twelfth Street, you know, a place to put her stuff. And she's in line to get an apartment, *an apartment!* But every time that fucking family of hers shows up, she forgets all about trying to get off the street. I don't know man, it's frustrating." There was bitterness in his eyes I hadn't seen since that first day in my office. "All they're interested in is her income potential."

He needed to vent, so I let him go. I had little to offer except to urge him to be patient and to remind him how he felt at sixteen. To that, he shot back, "Yeah, but the street's no place for a sixteen-year-old girl." I had to agree. The streets were no place for anyone, boy or girl.

I was still feeling light-headed, so Picasso did me a favor and took Arch out for a short walk before he left. I sat down on the couch with my laptop, caught up on my email, and made a few phone calls. I left a message for Nando to get back to me. I wanted to know if he had any thoughts on what to do about the Russian, Semyon.

I laid my head on the back of the couch with the whole mess swirling around in my mind. I drifted off and dreamed Semyon was at the front door. When my cell went off, it became him ringing a doorbell. I awoke full of anxiety, my head pounding. It was Anna checking in. I told her I'd dropped Bambi at the shelter, and when I mentioned I still had a low grade headache and that my bandage was leaking she told me to stop by the clinic.

My phone rang a second time. It was Nando. "*Hola, amigo. ¿Que tal?*" he barked out in his deep, accent inflected voice.

"*Bien*," I said without enthusiasm.

"I've got some information on the gun accident."

I felt a flutter in my gut. I knew that tone of voice. Nando had something important to tell me, but he wasn't going to share it on the phone. We agreed to meet at the apartment that evening, and I talked him into bringing takeout from Cuba Cuba.

Later that afternoon I sat in a treatment room clenching my jaw and grinding my teeth. Anna had just removed the bloody bandage from my ear and was poking around with a cotton swab. Before starting this torture she'd handed me a small mirror. I took one look at my ear and looked away. It was a pulpy, yellow-purple mass, and the stitched, vertical split looked like the zipper in my jeans. But her warm breath was caressing my cheek again, which helped me cope.

She said, "Hold still. I'm just about done. This looks okay, but I'm worried about a hematoma. If one develops, you'll have a true cauliflower ear."

"Then what, a transplant?"

She laughed, a kind of girlish sound I hadn't heard before. "*No*, but I'll have to drain it so the skin can reattach to the cartilage. We'll keep an eye on it." With that, she rushed off to see another patient.

Outside, it was misting slightly, but not enough to stop Picasso from working and Archie from keeping him company. His mural of rowdy health care agitators was becoming more fully populated. They poured off the flanks of Mt. Hood like ants and crossed Portland's eastern plain like an advancing army before crossing the Morrison Bridge. They carried signs and banners. The life-size lead marchers—Gandhi, King, Lennon, and Mother Teresa—were arm in arm and now fully sketched in. Picasso was busy painting John Lennon. The image caught the pop star in the blush of his youth, and he seemed to burst from the wall in three dimensions. I stopped dead. The image took me back to another time, and a thickness developed in my throat that I couldn't quite explain. I waited a few moments before saying, "It's looking good."

He turned around but didn't smile. He was all business when he worked. "It's a long ways from done."

"How do you decide who to put in?"

He shrugged. "Artist's prerogative, man. It's just based on what I've read about people. John Lennon spoke out on health care way ahead of his time. So did King. I found a great quote from him that I'm thinking about using as the tag line for this mural."

"What'd he say?"

Picasso set his brush down and leafed through his notebook. "Here it is." He cleared his throat. "'Of all the forms of inequality, injustice in health care is the most shocking and inhumane.' Then I'm going to add something like, 'Join the march for universal healthcare.'"

"Nice." I nodded toward the mural. "You really nailed Doc."

He laughed. "Thanks, man. You think she'll like it?"

I glanced at her image then back at him. "I know she will."

Picasso picked up his brush, but before he turned back to his mural, he said, "Did you get a chance to look into Joey's situation?"

I sighed more heavily than I meant to. It had been a long day. "Yeah, I did. I need to talk to him next. I'm tied up tonight, but I'll be around tomorrow."

"Yeah, well things aren't cool. I was in his tent last night. He's got a big, honkin' gun, Cal."

"Hand gun?"

"Yeah, but it looks like a friggin' cannon. He's no danger to the public, but I'm worried what he might do to himself."

"Set something up for tomorrow night and let me know."

Nando arrived at Caffeine Central just after seven with a large white bag filled with food and a six pack of La Tropical. After setting the food and beer down upstairs, he went over to the window and carefully moved the blinds just enough to allow him to look down at the street. My stomach tightened. "What's up?"

He let the blinds slide back into place and turned to face me. "Two guys in an SUV down by the corner are watching you. They look like Russians to me."

"Yeah," I said. "That's one of the things I wanted to talk about."

Chapter Twenty-four

Nando swirled a jumbo shrimp around in a thick garlic sauce, popped it in his mouth, took a swig of his La Tropical, and belched appreciatively. He sat across the table from me wearing a pearl colored blazer over a lime green silk shirt, dark slacks, and hand tooled leather sandals. I'd just finished telling him about my encounter with Semyon. He frowned, shook his head. "It is bad enough that you hurt this Russian in a fight, Calvin, but it is much worse that you caused Jessica Armandy to lose one of her girls. I believe this is called a double whammy."

The beer Nando had opened for me tasted flat and bitter. I set it down and shrugged. "Bambi wanted out. What was I supposed to do?"

"A noble gesture, to be sure, but there may be consequences. I will tell Armandy that your fight with the Russian was unavoidable and that you have no idea where this Bambi has run off to. I doubt she will accept this." He shook his head and made a face. "The sex trade is a nasty business. As for the Russian, there is no use talking to him. We Cubans know some things about Russians. They are a mean, stubborn lot. I could have one of my—"

I waved him off. "I don't need a damn bodyguard. Can't afford it."

Nando shook his head and flashed that knowing smile that never failed to irritate me. "You are as stubborn as a Russian, my friend. Where is the gun I gave you?"

I pointed down the hall. "In the bedroom."

"Good. If you go out at night, take it with you."

I nodded, but wasn't sure what I was going to do. The thought of packing a gun around didn't thrill me, particularly since I didn't have a permit to carry a concealed weapon in the first place. On the other hand, squaring off against Semyon again, unarmed, didn't thrill me either.

Nando must have sensed my ambiguity, because he added, "If this Semyon confronts you again, he will do more than cut up your ear, Calvin."

I raised my hands in mock surrender. "Okay, okay, I get it." Then I pushed the shrimp around on my plate before saying, "Are you going to tell me about Weiman's accident or what?"

Nando ate another shrimp and took a long pull on his Tropical. His face brightened. "Hugo Weiman lives with all the other millionaires on the north side of Lake Oswego. I have befriended his gardener, a Mexican from Oaxaca named Clemente Rodriquez. He has worked for Señor Weiman for eleven years. He remembers when El Patron shot himself. He wasn't there when it happened, but a live-in maid was, a woman named Maria Escobar. She now lives and works in North Portland."

"Did you approach her?"

"No. Rodriquez said she has good English, so I figured you would want the pleasure. But here is the best part—he also told me that the accident did not happen at the house in Lake O."

"I knew it," I blurted.

"Maria told him Weiman came home wounded that night. He arrived in his wife's car with a bloody towel wrapped around his hand. The wife was driving and they were both very upset. Maria said something very bad had happened."

I smiled so hard it hurt my ear. "Nice work, Nando. How can I get hold of her?"

He fished a card out of his shirt pocket and handed it to me. It had a street address and phone number written on the back. "She lives in St. Johns. She owns a taqueria there, Maria's. I have heard the fish tacos are to die for. There's one potential problem. Rodriquez thinks she might be unwilling to talk to you about this matter."

"Why?"

"He said Escobar stopped talking about the incident shortly after it happened and then left Weiman's employ a week later. He thinks Weiman might have paid for her silence."

"There's always a catch," I said, scraping garlic sauce off a shrimp with the shard of a *tostones* before taking a small bite. My headache was nearly gone, but my stomach was still tentative. I pushed my plate toward Nando. "Here. Take the rest of my shrimp. The ones I ate are thrashing around in my stomach."

Before Nando left, he took another look out on the street. The Russians weren't there, but he still made a show of checking his shoulder-holstered revolver. Setting an example, no doubt.

I was in bed reading a James Crumley paperback when Picasso called thirty minutes later. He told me Joey was expecting me the next night, and I told him I'd be there after dinner. I put the book aside and sat propped on a pillow for a while. Archie came over and laid his head on the bed next to me for an ear scratch. Food, an occasional run, and a nightly ear scratch—that's all he required of me in exchange for his unconditional love. I finally turned off the light, and the last thing I remember thinking before slipping off was how many people in Portland seemed to be hurting and in need of help. Too many, by my count.

The next morning I did some more research on the VA policies on PTSD and checked my office voice mail. I returned two calls from prospective clients, proving not everyone in the northern valley listened to *Vincent's View.*

I left for Maria's Taqueria at a quarter past ten. I didn't have a plan except that I wanted to be her first customer for lunch. I took the 405 over to Highway 30 and crossed the St. Johns Bridge. The massive Gothic towers of the structure made it look like something spanning the Thames in London. It was a fine day and people were out on the streets in St. Johns, a rapidly gentrifying neighborhood in North Portland crammed with small shops and two-thousand-square-foot houses.

The taqueria was located in a converted Cape Cod painted green with bright yellow trim and a red door. A sign in a window read Gringos Welcome. It wasn't open yet, so I crossed the street and got a cappuccino to ease the wait. That's one of Portland's finer points—you're never far from a great cup of coffee.

At 10:25, a young, attractive Hispanic woman hurried down Lombard and let herself into the taqueria. She wore white sneakers and a white cotton blouse over cropped pants. She was probably six months pregnant, and her stride was strong and purposeful, reminding me of Anna Eriksen. A few minutes later, two older women in white blouses showed up and were let in. The hired help, I guessed. At eleven, someone inside flipped the closed sign on the door to open.

The place had a warm, spicy smell: tomatoes, cumin, and red peppers. One of the older women was in the kitchen, the other busy placing menus on the tables. The woman I assumed was Maria Escobar was behind the small counter next to the entry, scanning a clipboard, pen in hand. She had a round face, high cheek bones, and a rosebud mouth accentuated with blood red lipstick. She glanced up and smiled. I smiled back and keeping it light, said, "Hi. Maria Escobar?"

She maintained the smile, but her face stiffened slightly. "Yes, I am." Her look was direct, her dark eyes wary.

I found myself wondering if I looked like an immigration officer or something. I handed her a card, introduced myself, and told her I'd like to ask her a few questions about a previous employer, Hugo Weiman.

"What would you like to know?"

I glanced around and said, "Is there someplace we can talk in private?"

She nodded toward the back of the dining room. "We can talk back there, but I don't have much time. We'll be busy soon."

I followed her to a back table, and after we sat down I plunged right in. "I'm investigating an accident Hugo Weiman had back in 2005, on May 18. A gun accident."

Her eyes narrowed. Her posture became more erect. "I know nothing about this accident," she said, her voice not quite defiant. "I'm sorry. I cannot help you."

She started to push away from the table, and I raised a hand. "Wait. I need your help, Ms. Escobar. I know what you told the gardener, Clemente Rodriquez. The accident didn't happen at Weiman's home. It happened someplace else. Weiman lied about it."

Her eyes flashed. "Why are you asking these questions?"

"Because a young man's life hangs in the balance," I shot back. "I'm trying to help him find out who murdered his mother eight years ago." I opened a folder I'd brought with me and handed her two pieces of paper clipped together. "This is a copy of a newspaper article about the murder."

She took the papers and dropped them on the table without looking down. "I am sorry this boy lost his mother, but I know nothing about it."

"I know you don't. What I need from you is the truth about what happened to Hugo Weiman and his wife that night. That's all I'm asking."

She stood up, and I followed. "I'm sorry, Mr. Claxton."

"It's been eight years. Did Weiman pay you to be quiet?"

Her eyes flashed sharp daggers and her mouth quivered. "I did *not* take his money. I decided to work somewhere else. That was all."

"So why not talk to me then?"

She dropped her eyes and rested her hand on the gentle swell of her stomach. "I don't want to get involved. I have others to think about." She turned and walked away.

I followed, and speaking to her back, said, "I understand, Ms. Escobar. I'm just asking you to tell the truth about that night, that's all." Of course, she was right to be wary. If she were illegal, getting entangled in the justice system, even as a witness, would pose serious risks for her. I knew it, and she knew it. I said, "Look, I'll treat everything you tell me as strictly confidential and keep your identity anonymous." This would mean using her only as a source but not as a witness, a tradeoff I was willing to make.

She turned around. "I'm sorry, Mr. Claxton. I cannot help you."

So much for tradeoffs. "You have my number. Think about it. It's the right thing to do."

I left the taqueria feeling thoroughly dejected. The only good news was that Maria Escobar's reluctance to talk seemed to corroborate what the gardener, Clemente Rodriquez, had told Nando. Weiman had tried to buy her silence, but she had refused the money. It seemed certain now that Hugo Weiman had covered up the true circumstances of his gunshot wound on the evening Nicole Baxter disappeared. I only lacked the details. How much did Maria Escobar know?

An east wind from the Gorge buffeted my car as I headed back over the St. Johns Bridge. The river was flecked with glistening white caps. I thought about this young woman turning down easy money offered to her by Hugo Weiman. I'd seen pride as much as anger flash in her eyes. Suddenly I felt a little better about my chances of hearing again from Maria Escobar. Maybe she would do the right thing.

Chapter Twenty-five

A TriMet bus had just dropped off a group of passengers in front of the Columbia River Correctional Institution as I was parking on Sunderland Avenue. It was around 6:30 that evening, and I was on my way to meet with Picasso and his friend Joey at Dignity Village, which was next door to the prison. A man and woman in crisp blue uniforms peeled off from the group and headed for the prison. The rest made for the entrance to the village, located on a flat, treeless chunk of unused city property. I clipped Archie on his leash and fell in behind them.

A woman missing her leg below the knee swung adroitly on a pair of crutches. A short man with tangled, shoulder-length hair held hands with a tall, angular woman carrying a black puppy. Another man in a stained sweatshirt carried a sign on which was scrawled "I'm homeless and need work." They ignored the distant thunder of a 747 taking off at PDX across a wide, empty field from the village. The jet lifting off seemed to accentuate the isolation of the place, and I wondered if the people walking in front of me yearned to be on that plane. People who fly, after all, have jobs, homes, and important destinations.

Picasso and Joey were sitting in front of Picasso's place on a pair of rickety folding chairs. Joey had a plastic bottle of water in his hand and a cigarette dangling from his lips. His full beard looked matted and unkempt, his forearms even bigger than I remembered them. I thought of Popeye. As I approached, Picasso flashed a rare smile, turned to Joey and said, "See? I told you he'd show."

Joey flicked me a half salute, and they both stood up. Archie went up to Picasso for a head pat, then turned to Joey. He dropped to one knee, said, "Hey, buddy," and gave Arch a bear hug.

I laughed. "He doesn't let just anybody hug him like that. You just made a friend."

Joey said, "He reminds me of a Bernese I had once. Best dog I ever had."

I turned to Picasso. "Lots of construction going on around here."

"Yeah," Picasso responded, "Part of the deal with the city is that all these structures in here have to be brought up to code." He put quotes around the word "code" with his fingers. "It's a giant pain in the ass."

"The Man will have his way," Joey chimed in.

"Are you two within code?"

Picasso tugged on his eyebrow ring a couple of times. It was back in place. "I'm okay, I think. My roof leaks, but that's allowed."

Joey laughed. "My place leaks, too, man. I just ran out of duct tape."

I chuckled and set my briefcase down. "Do you have another chair? We can work out here until it gets dark."

I knew Joey had fought in the battle of Fallujah, the bloodiest single battle of the Iraq war. It was intense, often hand to hand combat in the narrow streets of an ancient city. I had him take me back through his experiences while I asked questions and took notes. When he finished, I said, "What you've told me so far is good background, but I could have read about it online. I'm more interested in what happened to you *personally*, Joey. What caused your PTSD? The VA terms it the "stressor," the event that triggered your symptoms. You must have gone through a lot. Is there any one event that stands out?"

Joey combed at his beard with his fingers and shifted in his seat. His eyes were recessed below the thick bone of his forehead like lights in a cave. "It all sucked, man. They told us the civilians had fled, but that wasn't the case. People were caught in the crossfire. Shit, we didn't know the insurgents from the civilians. It was a cluster fuck."

I shook my head. "It must have been brutal."

He smiled ruefully, took a deep drag on his cigarette and didn't respond.

"What stood out, Joey?"

He exhaled the smoke slowly through his nose as he twisted a lock of his beard between his thumb and forefinger. "We were in the Julan district, trying to take this big, honking mosque the insurgents were holed up in. They loved the mosques, man. They were built like brick shithouses. Anyway, I see this woman in a doorway. She's waving her hand. Then I see this kid across the street. Couldn't have been more than twelve. He makes a run for his mother. I think he's gonna make it, but somebody pops him half way across."

Picasso and I gasped in unison. Picasso said, "He got shot?"

"Yeah. Some trigger-happy marine. The dumb fuck."

Joey tapped the long ash from his cigarette, took another drag and exhaled. "The kid was flailing around out there and crying. I put my weapon down and ran out in the street and scooped him up. By the time I got him back to our position, he'd lost a lot of blood and gone limp. I went ape shit, man, screaming at the medic to save the kid." He flicked the cigarette, and it landed with a shower of sparks in the gathering twilight. In a barely audible voice, he added, "He didn't make it."

The three of us sat there for a long time without speaking. I broke the silence after jotting down a few lines. "What happened next?"

Joey put his head in his big hands and without looking up, said, "That's the thing, man. After we took that block, the mother came looking for her son. She finds him under a bloody tarp. I go over to her to try to say something, you know, to console her. She turns around and screams something in Arabic, then she slaps me hard, and starts going for my eyes with her fingernails. By the time I got her off me, we're both crying."

Another long silence. Finally, I asked, "How did you feel after that?"

"Okay for a while, then I started dreaming about the kid. I—"

Joey stopped speaking at the sound of several people approaching on the path from the main gate of the village. Archie, who was lying between Picasso and Joey, stood up and made a low, guttural sound. The three of us looked around. Lieutenant Scott and Detective Jones came striding into view out of the low light. Four uniformed officers followed them. I stood up, and Joey and Picasso followed. I said, "Evening, gentlemen," but got no response.

Scott's face was tight, his mouth a thin line. Jones had an I-told-you-so look on his face. I felt an urge to slap him. They stopped in front of Picasso. Scott said, "Daniel Baxter, you're under arrest for the murder of Mitchell Conyers," then proceeded to read him his rights.

Picasso managed a defiant smile, but even in the low light I could see the fear in his eyes. Jones cuffed his hands behind his back and they started to lead him away. Suddenly Joey appeared in the path. I hadn't noticed he'd slipped away in all the commotion. His bear-like bulk blocked the path completely, and he was holding a large, chrome plated revolver in his right hand. It was pointing toward the ground. Speaking in a level, almost casual voice, he said, "Let my friend go. He didn't kill anybody."

All six cops drew their service weapons in unison. Scott said, "Drop the gun right now, son, and step back."

There was a long pause. I could hear the crickets in the field behind us and the soft murmur of voices in the village. Joey's hand started to move up and Picasso broke from the group and ran toward him screaming, "NO, JOEY, NO!"

I lunged at Picasso, missed him and yelled to everyone with a gun, "NO! DON'T SHOO—"

The shots shredded the stillness of the evening in a staccato pattern that's still etched on my brain—*Bam bam, bam bam*

bam, bam bam, bam. I got to them first. Picasso was sprawled on top of Joey, who was face down in the path. I kicked Joey's revolver away from his outstretched hand and rolled Picasso off of him. Picasso's face had gone white, and it was contorted with pain. Blood was spurting from a wound just above his elbow at a frightening rate. "He's bleeding to death," I yelled.

Scott was right behind me. "Pressure point's just below his armpit. Get on it," he hissed to me as he rolled Joey over to assess his condition. A moment later I heard him say under his breath, "Oh, mother of Christ."

I couldn't get a decent grip on Picasso's arm because it was pulled tight against his body by the handcuffs. Scott was still working on Joey. I turned to Jones, who was standing there, gun in hand, eyes wide with disbelief. "Get the damn cuffs off him," I barked. "I can't get to the pressure point." Picasso moaned, his eyes rolled back in his head and he slumped backward in my arms. Jones slid on one knee and unlocked the handcuffs. I fumbled around frantically for what seemed an eternity before the blood loss slowed. I kept Picasso's artery clamped against his arm bone until a paramedics team arrived from Emanuel Legacy.

I wanted to follow the ambulance to the hospital, but I was a material witness to a double shooting and knew I wasn't going anywhere. The last image I remember of Picasso that night was his head lolling from side to side as they slid him into the ambulance, a uniformed policeman scrambling in behind him. Joey's bullet-riddled, lifeless body remained at the scene—exhibit A.

The rest of that night at the village was a blur of questions and confusion. It wasn't long after they'd taken Picasso away that I realized Archie was missing. I became frantic with worry— thunder and fireworks make him crazy—but they weren't about to cut me loose so I could look for him. I told myself he'd settle down and find his way back to me. I must have told my version of the shootings at least three times. After giving their statements, Scott, Jones, and the four uniforms were whisked from the scene. As Scott was leaving, I managed to corner him for a few moments. "What the hell triggered the arrest?"

He took his glasses off, rubbed his eyes, and kept them averted. In the glare of the klieg lights he looked haggard, older. "We found the murder weapon. It was a big honking screwdriver, and it had your boy's bloody prints all over it. He did the deed, Claxton." Then he added, "I'm sorry about tonight. We did what we had to do."

I didn't speak. He was asking for my understanding, but I couldn't give it to him. I knew he was right, but every fiber in my body was repulsed by the brutality of what I'd just witnessed. Next to the singular horror of that act, the question of justification seemed silly, irrelevant.

When they finally released me that night, I combed the village for Archie. I was really beginning to worry when I heard someone say from behind me, "Hey, mister, this your dog?" I turned around and there he was, standing next to the woman I'd seen on crutches, wagging his stump of a tail. She said, "All those gun shots scared him, I could tell. He's been hanging out with us. He's mellow now."

Archie's ears were down, and he whimpered softly as I kneeled and pulled him in for a hug. I thanked her, clipped his leash on, and headed for the car. Arch jumped into the back seat, lay down, and put his nose between his paws. I got in, and that's when the emotional shock hit me. I sat there in the darkened car. My ears still rang from the gunshots, and the acrid smell of gunpowder lingered in my nostrils. Picasso's blood stained my clothing, my shoes, and my skin. I was all business and efficiency back there, but now I started to shake, the tremors starting in my gut and rippling up through my chest. They seemed to carry the energy from my body, and when I stopped shaking I felt exhausted. Then my eyes filled, and I wept silently. I wept for Joey and for Picasso. I wept for all the desperate, cornered people in this city. And to my surprise, I wept for cops like Scott and Jones, the people we call on when our frayed safety net unravels.

Chapter Twenty-six

"How is he?" Anna asked, rushing into the waiting room at Emanuel Legacy. I'd called her just before leaving Dignity Village for the hospital and told her to meet me there. The waiting room was brightly lit, too bright, and deserted except for a young couple huddled in a corner, speaking Spanish in hushed tones.

"I don't know," I answered. "They won't tell me a damn thing."

"Hold on. I know an ER doc here. I'll see if he's working tonight." She headed for the entry to the emergency room suite.

I sat back down, then got back up. My mind ricocheted between fear about Picasso's wound and the apparent discovery of the weapon used to kill Mitchell Conyers. I got a drink at the water fountain, picked out a six-month-old *Sports Illustrated* from a stack of magazines, and sat back down again. I tossed the magazine aside before even opening it and scratched my head with both hands. The shooting kept playing over and over again in my mind—Joey crumpling face-first in front of me, Picasso falling on top of him. That smug look on Jones' face before the arrest kept coming back, too. I wanted to prove him wrong in the worst way, but like a trickle of oil into a clear pool, doubt had begun to cloud my thoughts. No judgments, I told myself. Wait till you speak to Picasso.

Anna returned ten minutes later looking grim-faced. "The bullet shattered his right humerus and cut his brachial artery," she said. "He's in emergency surgery. They're trying to save his arm."

I sucked a breath involuntarily at the last words. "What are his chances?"

"Fifty-fifty. It's a hideous wound. All bullet wounds are." She eyed my bloodstained clothes. "Who got to his pressure point?"

I dropped my eyes because I couldn't shake a feeling of guilt for reasons I couldn't fathom. "I did, but it took me a long time to find it."

"That saved his life."

"What do we do now?"

"Wait. My friend said he'd update me when Picasso's out of surgery."

We sat down on a couch, and the next thing I knew a cell phone was buzzing some classical music riff. I opened my eyes and realized my head was leaning on Anna's shoulder. I sat up and glanced at my watch as she answered her phone. I'd been out for over an hour. It turned out to be one of Anna's nurses, who called to say she was going to be late in the morning. We wandered over to the cafeteria and got coffee. She asked me a lot of questions about Picasso's new legal reality, and I had very few answers. Truth was, his legal prospects were terrible, but I wasn't about to tell Anna that, nor did I admit to the seed of doubt that had sprouted in my mind.

A second call came in at a little past 1:00 a.m. After several "uh huhs" and "I sees," Anna said, "Thank you, Shawn," snapped the lid of her phone shut and turned to me. "He's out of surgery. He's got a steel bar and eight screws holding his arm together now. It went okay, but he's not out of the woods. He'll probably need more surgery before this is over."

"Can we see him?"

"No. He's in recovery now, under armed guard. We might as well go home, Cal."

I walked Anna to her car and watched her drive away. When I got back to Caffeine Central, I was surprised to see her Volvo parked in front. She rolled down her window as I approached and gave me a sheepish smile. "I was thinking maybe you could use some company tonight."

I said, "I only have one bed."

"That won't be a problem."

We made love that night with an urgency that surprised us both, I think. Afterwards, Anna sat up, pulled a sheet over her breasts, expelled a long breath and said, "God, that was good. Where have you been all my life?"

I sat up next to her and chuckled. "Likewise, I'm sure."

She took my hand in both of hers, pulled it to her mouth and kissed it. Then she sighed deeply. "God, I feel guilty now. The world's so damn conflicted, you know? People suffering at the same time that people are immeasurably happy. I don't get it. Never have."

I turned, kissed her eyes, and placed a finger to her lips. "Shhhh. Don't spoil it, Anna. Happiness is rare. Take it when it comes."

She was gone the next morning before I got out of bed. I called the hospital and was told Picasso was in guarded condition and that visitors were not allowed. I wanted to do something about Joey—like call his family—but I didn't have any information. I decided to wait on that until I talked to Picasso. I leashed up Archie, and we took a long run along the river while I tried to decide what to do next. It was cold that morning with angry gray clouds clumping to the north like wet cotton.

One thing was clear—now that Picasso was arrested, I could no longer represent him. I knew an attorney who might be willing to step in, but money would be an issue. Would he take the case for the publicity? After all, it was going to be a blockbuster when it came to trial. I didn't feel much urgency on this since Picasso wouldn't be arraigned until he was out of the hospital, and I knew Scott and Jones would be placed on administrative leave until the shooting was thoroughly investigated. Portland had had several controversial police shootings in the last couple of years, and I was sure City Hall would be anxious to prove that Joey's was a righteous kill.

Despite the grungy weather, the river walk was jammed with energetic Portlanders. Arch and I threaded our way through long boarders, spandex-clad bikers, and other joggers. What the hell should I do now, I asked myself? I felt stretched between two murders eight years apart with no solid connection between the two. Hired to find Nicole Baxter's murderer, I liked Hugo Weiman for the crime. But without Maria Escobar's cooperation, my case was as leaky as a fishnet.

I'd been sucked into the vortex of Mitch Conyers' killing. Thanks to Bambi, I knew Conyers was blackmailing someone. Who, and for what? My best guess was it had to do with Nicole Baxter's exposé. It was a potential connection between the two crimes, and it had vanished along with her eight years ago.

There was the shock jock, Larry Vincent. Was he Baxter's target? Had Cynthia Duncan dug up anything on that creep yet, I wondered? There was also the fight between Conyers and his stepbrother, Seth Foster, that Bambi told me about. Jessica Armandy had to know about this and probably other things, as well. But she wasn't about to talk to me.

By the time Arch and I turned around at John's Landing, my head felt ready to explode. There was another option, of course—one that had worked its way out of a dark corner in the back of my mind. Simply go home. Cut my losses. After all, I was no longer Picasso's attorney, and this so-called case was costing me money I didn't have. The thought had a certain appeal, but I set it aside, at least for the time being.

I called Central Precinct when I got back to the apartment. Neither Scott nor Jones was available. No surprise there. I wound up with the precinct chief who grudgingly agreed I could see Picasso the next day at ten, provided the hospital cleared it. My voice mail was jammed with calls from reporters asking for statements and interviews. I listened to a few of the messages, then deleted the whole lot. At 9:00, I switched on Larry Vincent, that gun-toting, God-fearing defender of the common man.

He got right to it. "Good morning Portland. I have an exclusive for you today. Last night, Portland's finest stood tall. Six police officers were dispatched to that great bastion of the unwashed, Dignity Village, to arrest Daniel Baxter, better known as Snake Boy. Snake Boy, you will recall, is the prime suspect in the murder of Mitchell Conyers. During the arrest, Snake Boy along with his dirtbag buddy, also a resident of the village, started a gunfight. I'm happy to report they were both cut down in a hail of gunfire. The accomplice is dead, and Baxter's in the hospital. We thank God that none of the officers was injur—" I switched the radio off. Compared to Vincent's voice, fingernails on a blackboard would sound like Mozart.

I called the attorney I had in mind for Picasso and left a message for him to call me, then spent the next two hours trying to do some work—the kind that actually brings money in.

At eleven thirty, I walked over to the *Zenith* headquarters on Ash Street. I blew by the receptionist like I knew what I was doing and found my way back to Cynthia Duncan's office. She looked up from her laptop. "My God, Cal. I just heard about Daniel. Is he alright?" Her eyes dominated her face—big, luminous saucers full of worry and concern.

"He's alive, but his right arm's severely injured. It was touch and go last night, but it looks like he'll be okay."

"Thank God." She noticed the bandage on my ear. "Were you injured, too?"

"No. I banged my ear up, is all. Come on, I'll tell you about what happened last night over lunch. I'm buying." This girl needed some nourishment.

She took me to a little joint on Third called the Bijou, the kind of place you know is good from the friendly buzz of the crowd and the delicious food smells. I ordered the roast beef hash, and Cynthia asked for a side salad. Out of frustration, I said, "Don't you ever eat?" Which, of course, was a big mistake even though I said it with a smile.

She shot me a withering look. "The salads here are *very* filling. You know, Americans eat way too much. It's a national epidemic."

I nodded agreement and began describing last night's events. When I got to the bloody screwdriver with Picasso's prints on it, Cynthia shrugged and said, "I figured Daniel might have done it. That son of a bitch Conyers had it coming, believe me. You're going to get Daniel off, right?" For her, it seemed, the question of guilt or innocence was irrelevant. If Picasso had done it, then he had done society a big favor.

Her comments did nothing to assuage the doubt that had sprung up in my mind, but I kept my mouth shut. I asked her about Larry Vincent. She took a small bite, dabbed her mouth with a napkin and pushed her half-eaten salad away. "Oh, you mean the guy who's given a whole new meaning to the term scumbag?

I smiled and nodded. "I guess so."

"Well, I'm glad you didn't bring this up until I'd finished eating. I was stymied until a source of mine in the legal community tipped me off about a disgruntled paralegal. Turns out she was fired by the attorney who handled the thing for Vincent."

"Who's the attorney?"

"Alan Prescott, you know, of Prescott, Brady, and Brown."

I nodded. I knew Prescott by reputation. A "go-along to get-along" type who handled a lot of old-money clients in and around Portland.

"Anyway, she gave me a sense of what happened. Even she didn't know that much. The Vincent family used a thirteen-year old to babysit the kids occasionally. The girl was brilliant, beautiful, and physically mature beyond her years. Larry Vincent becomes a kind of mentor for the girl, whose family life is in disarray, and you guessed it, he begins to have sex with her. This lasts four or five *years* until the girl's mother finds out. Enter Prescott. A deal is struck, which pays off the mother, pays the girl a monthly sum, and covers her college expenses. In exchange, mother and daughter agree not to press charges and to maintain strict confidentiality."

"Mom agrees so her daughter won't get dragged through the courts."

"That's a charitable view. If it had been my daughter I would have cut off Vincent's balls with a razor."

"I was thinking more along the lines of a shotgun." We had a head-shaking laugh before I added, "Your source didn't give you a name?"

"No. Sorry."

"How do you know she's telling the truth?"

"She told me she did some of the legal research for the case and typed up parts of the agreement. I believe her."

I laid my fork across my plate and leaned back. "Losing your reputation, public humiliation and condemnation, loss of your livelihood—pretty good motives for murder, I'd say."

Cynthia eyes grew wet, and her jaws flexed as if she were grinding her teeth. She'd have used that razor, for sure. "So, you're saying Vincent killed Nicky to silence her, then maybe he killed Conyers, too, because Conyers was blackmailing him all these years?"

"If Nicole really had him in her crosshairs, I'd say you could be right. Trouble is, I don't have a damn thing to connect him to either one of them except an entry in Nicole's planner for a meeting the week after she disappeared."

Cynthia dabbed at her eyes, looked down at the mascara on her napkin and swore, reminding me of Bambi. Then she looked up at me and nodded. "So what else can I do, Cal?"

"You've already done a lot. It would be nice to know the name of the girl Vincent molested."

"Don't worry. I'm on it. I'm going to expose that bastard. If you nail him on a murder charge, that's frosting on the cake."

"Look, Cynthia, I don't need to tell you this could get dangerous. Who knows what you're up to besides your source?"

"Just my boss."

"Good. Be careful who you talk to, and keep me in the loop. I'll do the same."

I walked Cynthia back to her building, then headed for Caffeine Central. I should have felt good about the meeting, but versus the overwhelming case against Picasso, trying to implicate Vincent for either killing looked like a steep climb—Everest, maybe. Would the view be worth the climb? I wasn't sure.

Chapter Twenty-seven

Picasso was asleep when I entered his room. The sight of him caused my chest to tighten. His face was drawn, the skin so pale it had a bluish tint. His lip and eyebrow rings had been removed, and the colorful bands of the coral snake coiled around his neck seemed somehow muted. His right arm was heavily bandaged and elevated in a sling device that held it off the side of the bed. His left arm had an IV drip and pulse monitor attached. He must have sensed my gaze, because his eyes slowly opened. In a weak, raspy voice he said, "Hey, wassup, Cal?"

"Not much. How're you feeling?"

His eyes welled up. "How's Joey, man? I can't get a straight answer around here."

I couldn't believe no one had leveled with him. "He didn't make it. He died at the scene. I'm sorry."

Picasso nodded, and a single tear broke loose and worked its way down his cheek. The tear was on the edge of his jaw when he said, "I knew it. I can still hear the shots. Jesus, how many times did they shoot him?"

"Eight, by my count."

"Trigger happy bastards."

"I'm as angry as you are, but the truth is, Joey made the call. Once he raised the barrel, they had no choice."

"What the hell was he trying to do, anyway?"

"I'm not sure we'll ever know. Talking about his experiences, then seeing you get arrested seemed to push him over the edge. I think it was suicide by cop."

Another tear broke loose. "Suicide?"

"Yeah. I think Joey just couldn't cope, so he baited the cops into killing him."

I pulled a chair up to his bed and sat down. We talked about Joey, and he gave me the name of Joey's wife in San Francisco. I promised to contact her and offer our condolences. Then I glanced at my watch. "They only gave me half an hour. The cops arrested you because they found a screwdriver with your bloody prints on it. I need to know what happened. The truth this time."

Picasso closed his eyes for a few seconds. His dark lashes looked like fine brushes against his pale skin. "Shit, I figured they'd find it all along. After I pulled Conyers out of the pool, I saw the screwdriver on the deck. I recognized it in a heartbeat, man—it was mine! I just stood there for a minute gaping at it. I couldn't believe it, but there it was. My old screwdriver with paint all over the handle, and blood, too. I knew I'd be toast if I just left it lying there. So I pried the cap off one of the gate posts in the back and dropped it in. You showed up right after that."

"Pretty convenient hiding place."

He chuckled, which made him cough. "I knew that hiding place. Conyers used to keep his stash in a bag tied to a string in that post. I saw him take that cap off a bunch of times. Best I could do on short notice. Didn't fool the cops for long, did it?"

I sighed. "You came up with that on the spot?"

He shot me a sideways glance. "Yeah, I came up with it on the spot, just like I said."

"Why didn't you tell me this before?"

"Things were bad enough, man. I was afraid you wouldn't believe a dumb-ass story like that. Maybe you don't now."

"Tell you the truth, I don't know what to believe."

Picasso turned his head to face me. Color pooled in his cheeks. "You *don't* believe me, do you?"

"Should I?" I regretted saying that the moment it left my mouth, but it was too late.

He jerked his face away from me. "Fuck you, Claxton! You're like all the rest. Get the fuck out of here! I don't need you, man."

"Picasso, I'm—"

"No. Spare me. Just get out!"

Alerted by Picasso's yelling, a nurse and the uniformed guard were standing at his door as I slunk past them. I think I said something stupid, like "Excuse me." Mixed feelings churned around in me as I found my way to my car. I hadn't meant for things to get out of hand like that. I felt foolish and ashamed of my actions. After all, I figured it would come to this—the last brick in the wall of his frame-up. On the other hand, the doubt I felt was real. I had to express it, damn it.

I'd reached an impasse with myself.

I drove back to Caffeine Central, leashed up Archie, and headed for the clinic. On the way over, a call came in from Nando. I let it go to voice mail. I was in no mood to talk. A large group of street kids was milling around in front of the mural. Word of the shooting had obviously gotten out. When Arch and I approached, Caitlin rushed up to me and asked about Picasso. The rest followed. I told them what I could and ended by saying Picasso was counting on them to protect the mural. I figured he would have gotten around to that if I hadn't blown up the conversation. Caitlin assured me they would.

Anna was hunched over her computer when I entered her office. "How's he doing?" She aimed her glacial blues at me. I'd called earlier to tell her I was meeting with Picasso.

"Uh, he looked pale and tired. I talked to his nurse before I went in. She assured me he was doing fine."

"Did you discuss the screwdriver situation?"

"Uh, that didn't go so well."

"Why?"

"Well, I, uh, challenged his story a little bit, and he blew up. He decided I didn't believe him, and he told me to get the hell out."

The blue in Anna's eyes seemed to fade. Now they were the color of ice. "*Do* you believe him, Cal?"

"I'm trying to."

She placed her fingertips on the desk as if to rise, but she didn't move. "What does *that* mean?"

I shrugged and tried to smile. "It means I'm not sure. The evidence against him is pretty overwhelming. Maybe he went over there with the screwdriver just to threaten him, and things got out of hand. He lied to me, Anna. Now I'm not sure what to believe."

She stood up and faced me. "Oh, Cal, how could you? If he lied, it was because he felt he had to. He didn't kill that man. I know it."

Irritation washed over me like a wave. How can some people just *know* something? I wasn't built like that. I said, "Well, maybe I lack your faith in human nature," which was my second really poor choice of words that day.

Anna's mouth quivered ever so slightly as she scooped up a sheaf of papers and stood up. "Excuse me, please, I've got patients to see." She brushed by without looking at me and stormed down the hall. I stood there as my cheeks began to burn, wondering if there was any way in hell to start the day over.

Chapter Twenty-eight

A plan was forming in my mind—I would get out of Portland, grab my fly fishing gear at the Aerie, and head for the nearest river with a decent steelhead run. Give myself some time to think. But when I came out of Caffeine Central with my bags packed Nando was just parking his Lincoln Navigator in front of the building.

When he got out of his car I set my bags down and shook my head. "Cuba's going to be a submerged reef in ten years because of people driving cars like that."

He opened his hands and raised his eyebrows. "What? I am buying American. Is it not the patriotic thing to do?" Then he glanced at my bags and added, "Where are you going?"

"Fishing. I need some alone time."

"Ah, a wise thing to do under the circumstances, but, you should eat before such a journey. I want to hear the details of the shooting, and I have some information to share, too."

We ate at a little Mexican joint on Division called Nuestra Cocina. It was painful to relive it, but I took Nando through the events of the night before. When I finished, he said, "I would not want to be a policeman in America. Too many guns. Too many crazy people."

I told him what Picasso had told me about hiding the screwdriver and about our falling out. He shrugged and said, "What does he expect? He lied to you."

"I know that," I snapped back. Then I said something that had suddenly crystallized in the back of my mind, something that surprised me. "He would have taken that screwdriver into Conyers' backyard only if he went there with the intent to kill him. I'm not sure he would have done that. Kill him in a moment of rage, maybe, but premeditated?"

Nando arched his eyebrows and smiled. "So, you still believe him?"

I shrugged. "That's why I'm going fishing, to think it over." Then to cut off any more discussion on that topic, I said, "So, what've you got for *me*?"

"Well, perhaps it is wise you are leaving town. I hear Jessica Armandy is on the path of war."

"Why's that?"

"The young prostitute, Bambi—"

"Ex-prostitute."

"Yes, excuse me. The ex-prostitute, Bambi, has been calling some of the other girls and encouraging them to leave Armandy's employ. Apparently, three young beauties have run away just like she did. Armandy is furious, and she doesn't have any idea where Bambi or the others got off to."

I burst out laughing. "Oh, that's perfect, that's the best news I've heard all day. Armandy may have met her match."

"She may be wondering if you encouraged Bambi in any way, or know where she is."

I smiled. "I'll never tell."

"Have you seen the mad Russian?"

I shook my head. "What else you got?"

"Maria Escobar has contacted the gardener, Clemente Rodriquez."

"About what?"

"Hugo Weiman called her."

My smile evaporated. "When?"

"A few days ago."

"Why didn't she call me?"

"She told Clemente she didn't trust you. She talks to you and the next thing she knows, Weiman is calling and asking to meet with her. She wasn't happy about that."

"When I talked to Weiman, I didn't even know she existed," I shot back. "He must have gotten nervous after I confronted him. He's afraid she'll talk."

"That's what I told Clemente. He went back to her, and now she has agreed to talk to you. She met with Weiman last night."

"*What?* Last night? What the hell happened?"

He shrugged. "I don't know, but I have arranged for you to speak with her."

We spent the rest of the meal speculating on what might have transpired between Maria Escobar and Hugo Weiman. Afterwards, Nando dropped me off at Caffeine Central, and I reluctantly unpacked while Archie watched from the corner with a slightly puzzled expression. There would be no fishing trip now. I spent a restless night and left for St. Johns at nine the next morning.

Whoever said there was no rest for the wicked wasn't kidding.

Maria Escobar was waiting for me at the taqueria and showed me to the same table as before. "Thanks for meeting with me, Maria," I said as we took our seats. The place was empty, the shades drawn. She wore her pregnancy beautifully—her skin tone and dark hair glowed with health and vitality. "When's the big day?"

She smiled demurely, her face like an open book. "Around the first of September." Her eyes were focused on me, clear and direct. "I read the articles you gave me. That poor boy was made an orphan by what happened that night at the cabin. I, ah, couldn't stand by and do nothing. But you must protect me from *la migra* like you promised, Mr. Claxton."

"I'll do everything I can." It was the strongest statement I could give her. I wasn't sure where this was going, now that she'd talked to Weiman.

She fixed my eyes and held them hostage for a few moments. "I know you will, Mr. Claxton."

That simple act sealed it for me. I pledged to myself not to let her down. "I know you met with Hugo Weiman last night, but before you get to that, I'd like you to take me back to that night in 2005 and tell me everything you remember."

She joined her fingertips in the shape of a steeple and tapped them absently for a few moments. "Mr. Weiman was gone that Friday. I was cleaning upstairs and surprised Mrs. Weiman in the master bedroom. She was crying and had just closed the drawer of the side table on Mr. Weiman's side of the bed. She snapped her purse shut and rushed out, telling me she'd be back later that night. After she left I checked the drawer out of curiosity. The gun Mr. Weiman kept there was gone."

"Did you see her take the gun?"

"No, but that gun was always in the drawer. I was afraid something awful might happen. Mrs. Weiman was not a nice person. She was an insanely jealous woman." She cast her eyes down. "Once she even accused *me* of flirting with Mr. Weiman."

"Did you?"

Her dark eyes came up flashing with anger. "No, it was the other way around."

I nodded. "I see. What happened next?"

"Well, it must have been five hours later, around eleven. I was up in my apartment when I heard a car return."

"One car?"

"Yes, her Jaguar. My apartment was above the garage. I looked out and saw her helping Mr. Weiman to the house. He had a bloody towel wrapped around his hand. I rushed down to help them. They told me he'd had an accident, but didn't explain. They were arguing. Mr. Weiman did not want to go to the hospital. Mrs. Weiman told him he must go. When we removed the bloody towel to look at the wound, Mr. Weiman nearly fainted. That's when he agreed to go to the hospital."

"Did you see the gun?"

"No."

"Then what?"

"Two days later Mrs. Weiman asked me to go to the river with her to pick up Mr. Weiman's car. I drove it back. A big Mercedes. On the way there, Mrs. Weiman asked me not to discuss what had happened with anyone."

"But you told your friend Clemente, the gardener?"

She smiled mischievously. "He's Mexican. I figured she meant white people. Anyway, when Mr. Weiman returned from the hospital, he told me I was to tell anyone who asked that the accident happened at home, not at the fishing cabin. Then he told me he was giving me a big raise."

"A lot of people would find it hard to turn down money like that."

She sat back and squared her shoulders. "Being paid to lie? I could not do that. Besides, I didn't want to live with that crazy woman. So, I quit."

She filled in a few more details, answered some questions, and when she finished I thanked her profusely. "Okay, now tell me what happened last night."

"He took me to dinner at an expensive place in Southwest. He wanted to pick me up, but I told him I'd meet him there. He was very interested in the taqueria, you know, how is it going? Am I making a profit? I told him things were very tough, but I was squeaking by. He said he liked small businesses and would be interested in investing in mine, you know, to help me grow."

I nodded. "What did you tell him?"

Her eyes flashed again, with fire this time. "I told him I wanted to own my business outright. No loans. He said, 'Well, then maybe I can just make a contribution to your baby's college fund, no repayment necessary.'" She closed her eyes and shook her head. "That's when I decided to just tell him what I was feeling."

My stomach started to dive, and I came forward in my chair. "Uh, what was that?"

"I told him I did not want his money, that I knew why he was offering it to me. I said what happened at the fishing cabin eight years ago was wrong. A mother was killed, a young boy orphaned. The boy became homeless because of what happened there. I told him he should be on his knees begging God to forgive him, not trying to buy me off."

Nearly speechless, I managed to say, "How did he react?"

She shook her head slowly and met my eyes. "He just sat there, and his eyes filled with tears. I said, 'Mr. Weiman, I do not think you killed that woman. You are a good man, not a murderer. You must tell the police what really happened that night. The boy has been suffering all these years.'"

She paused, her eyes burning with conviction. "He sat there for the longest time staring at his plate. Then he got up and said, 'Maria, please forgive me,' and left. That was it. He left me with the bill, too."

I drove back to Old Town with my mind spinning like a wheel in a rat's cage. Maria had told Weiman that she believed he was involved in a murder. What would he do now? Maria didn't think he was a killer and the truth was, I didn't either. I glanced at my watch. It was almost eleven, a Saturday. I decided to pay Hugo Weiman a visit.

Lake Oswego is a posh town south of Portland that takes its name from a man-made lake stretching like a skinny finger between the Willamette River and Interstate 5. Weiman's house was on the north rim of the lake, and like all the other million-dollar homes in the neighborhood, was unimpressive from street level—a three car garage and a massive wooden gate to the left of the garage with a call box mounted in it. I parked and got out of the car, thinking of Nando's Glock, which was sitting in my bedroom at the apartment. Why had I been in such a damn hurry? I should have swung by and picked it up. But Maria was right, I told myself. Weiman was no killer. Or was he?

I almost turned back, but the gate was ajar. I had the weirdest feeling that he had left it that way for me. In any case, I let myself in like I knew what I was doing. The gate opened to a steep, narrow staircase that led straight down to a dock and boathouse on the lake. The house was at my immediate right, a large structure that rambled down to the lake in three stories. A landing midway marked the entrance. The top story was curtained off and when I reached the landing, I caught glimpses of a well-appointed living and dining area through narrow windows on either side of a hand carved, wooden door. I didn't see anyone inside. I was almost to the base of the stairs when a side window afforded a diagonal view through a large bay window facing the lake. Weiman was sitting at a table on a deck cantilevered out over the lake. When I reached the level of the deck, I said, "Good morning, Mr. Weiman. It's Cal Claxton. I was hoping we could talk."

He turned and squinted as he looked me over. "Oh, it's you. Claxton. I thought you might show up." He wore a blue corduroy bathrobe over what looked like yellow silk pajamas. His face was pinched from apparent lack of sleep, his silver hair disheveled. A half full bottle of Grey Goose sat at his elbow next to a tumbler of liquid and ice and a pen and paper.

He didn't invite me to join him, but I moved across the deck and stood in front of him anyway. He looked at me and smiled. "Should be a good caddis fly hatch going on at the Deschutes about now. I was thinking about packing up my four weight and heading on over." He looked down and shook his head. "But I can't go there. Too many ghosts." He made a sweeping gesture with his arm. "Too many damn ghosts here, too."

I sat down. "I know you didn't kill Nicole Baxter. Your wife shot her and then she tried to kill you. She came to her senses after she wounded you, right?"

Weiman took a long pull on his vodka, squinted at me and didn't respond.

"If you come forward, I think the courts would be lenient. You were in shock. It's understandable that you initially went along with the cover up, and then it was too late."

He grew wistful and looked out over the water. "Why is it everyone loves salmon flies? Like goddamn celebrities. I caught my biggest redsides with the lowly caddis fly. Doesn't seem fair, does it?"

I nodded. "Look, I can help you get this matter off your chest."

My words seemed to cut through his fog, and he snapped to attention, like some gears in his addled brain had finally meshed. I tensed up at the mood shift, and when he smiled a chill rippled down my spine. He said, "Oh, I think I've had about all the help from you I can stand, Claxton." He reached into the pocket of his bathrobe and pulled out a long barreled pistol. It was a small caliber gun, probably a twenty-two, but it looked like a howitzer to me.

I stood up and backed away from the table, upending the chair behind me. "I've talked to the police," I lied. "Lots of people know I'm here. You need to put that thing down."

"You're just the messenger, Claxton. I wouldn't dream of shooting you." With that, Hugo Weiman turned the gun around, placed the barrel in his mouth, and pulled the trigger.

Chapter Twenty-nine

I took a deep breath of cool air and let it out slowly. The water pushed playfully at my thighs, and a bald eagle I'd been watching launched itself from the top of a sun-bleached snag, made a lazy one-eighty, and hitched a ride on a spiraling updraft. I was doing what I should have been doing yesterday—fishing. Hugo Weiman's suicide was stuck on replay in my head, and I'd gone fishing to erase it or at least come to terms with it. That, and to decide if I should ever go back to Portland again. It had been a hell of a summer already, and it was only July.

This time of year most of the steelhead move on, but one particularly big fellow hadn't gotten the memo. I was swinging a gaudy black and white fly with a chartreuse tail—aptly named a green butt skunk—through a nice little riffle when the fish hit. The strike started Archie barking on the bank behind me in that high pitch that signaled he was also spinning in circles. I battled the fish the better part of ten minutes, and when I finally brought it up to me, near the bank, Arch stepped into the river for a closer look. Its adipose fin was clipped, signifying a hatchery fish, and it glittered like a newly minted silver coin. When I released it, Archie howled with delight. That dog of mine loves fishing as much as I do.

I didn't get another bite that morning, but it didn't matter. The sun had burned off the marine layer and a light breeze rippled the green water. The tasks of executing a forty-foot cast, retrieving the expended line drifting back at me, and then picking my way upstream before doing it all again mercifully demanded my full attention. This was my yoga, my meditation, and by the time I scrambled up the bank for a break, my mind had cleared considerably.

I had just poured a cup of steaming coffee from my thermos when my cell chirped.

"Cal? It's Anna. I just read what happened yesterday. Are you alright?"

"I'm fine."

"Where are you?"

"I'm on the Clackamas River, above the North Fork."

"You're fishing?"

"Yeah. The water's still pretty high, so I thought there might be a few steelies left in here." I paused, leaving nothing but the busy sounds of the river.

Finally, Anna said, "Cal, I, uh, I'm sorry about the way I acted. You hardly know Picasso, and I had no right to expect you to just fall in line with my opinion after what happened. My God, I must have sounded like the thought police."

I felt a lump in my throat. The surge of emotion caught me off guard. I cleared my throat. "It's sorry all around then, because I'm not proud of the way I acted, either. My left brain gets in my way a lot." The call started breaking up, so I added hastily, "Look, Anna, I'll call you when I get off the river." The line went dead. Anna. I thought of the fine line of her neck, the perfect arc of her cheek and the lock of hair that seems always across her forehead. And the glacial blue eyes, especially those. Somehow, she made me feel grounded, like I had some purpose, or at least that I *should* have. Being around her was like an awakening, and I realized at that moment how much I liked that feeling.

My thoughts drifted to Picasso. Did he take the screwdriver with him? Only if he planned to murder Conyers, and I just couldn't buy that. And there was the fact that he was left-handed, too. As I told Nando, there's no way someone uses his off hand or tries some fancy backhand stroke when he's committing premeditated murder with a screwdriver. I had lost sight of these arguments in the face of Picasso's deception about the murder weapon. But there it was for me, plain and simple—Picasso didn't kill Mitchell Conyers. Of course, convincing a *jury* of that would be another problem altogether. After all, he had the perfect trifecta going against him—the means, the motive, and the opportunity.

I leaned back against a warm boulder and took a sip of coffee. The eagle had returned to its snag and seemed to be watching me. I felt crappy about Weiman. I knew it wasn't my doing, but I still felt like I had blood on my hands. I thought about his suicide note. What a joke that was. The death of Nicole Baxter was a tragic accident, he explained. He had shot himself in the hand accidentally and then, in the confusion that ensued, his wife somehow discharged the gun a second time, killing Baxter. Sure.

He and his wife panicked and hid the body in the reservoir above the cabin. For this act he begged forgiveness from the Baxter family, his friends and colleagues, and a married daughter I didn't know he had. He never explained what the three of them were doing at the cabin to begin with—an evening of target practice, perhaps?—or why, exactly, the incident was worth blowing his brains out over. My guess was that the media circus he knew was coming had unhinged him. Better to die by his own hand, he figured, than from a thousand humiliating cuts from the media. The man had a point.

The eagle took off again, swooped low over the river this time, and snatched a trout that had surfaced beneath a cloud of caddis flies. The fish struggled furiously unlike Weiman, who gave up without a fight, his body going slack instantly, relieved, it seemed, to be unshackled from the burdens of living.

His suicide would close the case on Nicole Baxter's death. After all, the three principals were dead. There would be no disputing that she was shot by one of the Weimans. It was clear, as well, that he was having an affair with Baxter, giving his wife a strong motive. But only Maria Escobar's testimony would point the finger firmly at the wife. When I was interviewed after the shooting, I kept quiet about Escobar, as I'd promised. There was no need to take it any further. Weiman had withered in the face of Maria's moral courage, but even so, she cried when I called to tell her that Weiman had killed himself. She said she would beg God for forgiveness and pray for his soul.

I returned to the Aerie that afternoon, a Sunday, and spent the next two days catching up in my office in Dundee. Scott and Jones were still on paid administrative leave, and Picasso was still not strong enough to be arraigned. My lawyer friend had told me he was too busy to defend Picasso, which didn't surprise me. That left a public defender, who turned out to be an inexperienced attorney named Alicia Cole. Cole called and we chatted about the case. She was gung ho about preparing for his defense. I liked her and didn't have the heart to tell her she couldn't win the case no matter how good her defense was. It looked to me like the only way to save Picasso was to catch Conyers' real killer.

I called Cynthia Duncan that Sunday to tell her who had killed her best friend, Nicole Baxter. I held the phone while she cried and then answered a thousand questions that only a newspaper reporter could ask. Finally, I said, "How's your investigation of Larry Vincent going?"

She made a sound half way between a sigh and a groan. "I knew you'd ask me about that. God, I'm so frustrated I could scream and run naked. People in this town either don't know what happened or aren't talking. I don't get it. Vincent's such an asshole. Why are they protecting him?"

"Who have you approached?"

"Well, I went straight to his ex-wife. She lives in Beaverton. It was clear she took money to keep her mouth shut. Wouldn't tell me anything at first, but finally I got her to give me a list of other people I might talk to, you know, some friends who took her side after the divorce, a couple of guys who had business dealings with Vincent. You'd think one of them would have known about the babysitter, or whatever she was, but I didn't get a damn thing. I've got a couple more to talk to, but I'm not optimistic."

I told her to stay at it, and I knew she would.

On Wednesday morning I headed into Portland to mend another fence. I went straight to Legacy Emanuel Hospital to see Picasso. Cole had gotten me in to see him. He was just coming through a rough several days of high fever owing to an infection and had not been told about Weiman's suicide. When I walked in, he took one look at me and rolled on his side to face the wall.

I said, "How're you feeling?"

"Shitty."

"You look better. More color."

"It's the fever. Let me guess, you came to drop off your bill."

"Is that what you want?" He didn't answer. Except for the whirring of Picasso's IV pump, the room fell silent. I let out a long breath. "Look, Picasso, I still believe in you, but I'm not going to apologize for being pissed off. You lied to me."

"Like I had a fucking choice."

"Okay. I get that. You did what you had to do. Why don't we call it even and move on?"

He rolled gingerly on to his back, looked up at the ceiling, and massaged his forehead with his left hand. Finally he said, "So, when are they going to hang me?"

"We're not going to let that happen. I've got some good news. Your mom's case is solved."

He lifted his shoulders off the bed, winced, and lay back down. He waited for me to speak, his big, liquid eyes unblinking.

"Remember the hotshot lobbyist I told you about, Hugo Weiman?"

"Mom's secret lover?"

"Right. His wife followed your mom and him to the fishing cabin that night and shot your mom. The wife's name was Eleanor, Eleanor Weiman. She died of cancer five years ago. She also shot Weiman in the hand that night, and that's what finally led me to him."

Picasso closed his eyes, but no tears came. "The woman's dead, huh? Cancer. Is Weiman going to jail?"

I shook my head. "No. He didn't want to face the music, so he shot himself Saturday morning. It's all over now." I handed him a newspaper. "You can read about it in here."

The room fell silent again. A gurney squeaked its way past the room and down the hallway. He looked up at me, his eyes now bright with moisture. "I dreamed about this moment for a long time, but I don't feel a damn thing. Closure. What the hell is that, anyway?

"Closure's knowing the truth. Give it a chance."

Picasso raised his good hand and clamped on to mine. "Thanks, man. Thanks for coming back." He glanced in the direction of my ear. It was angry looking and the stitches were still in place, but I'd stopped bandaging it. "What's Doc say about the ear?"

I shrugged. "I'm going to stop by to see her today."

"Good. Maybe she knows a good plastic surgeon." We both laughed and then he added, "Well, one thing's for sure."

"What's that?"

"I'm glad I didn't kill that son of a bitch Conyers like I wanted to. Wrong guy." We laughed again and then he grew serious. "You told me you thought my mom's and Conyers' murders were related. You still believe that?"

"Weiman used the prostitution ring running out of Conyers' restaurant, but I wasn't able to find any other connection between them. It's true he covered up your mom's murder, but he did that to protect his wife. And that act eventually caught up with him. No, I don't think he was a murderer."

"In other words, I'm still screwed, blued, and tattooed."

"No you're not," I shot back. "Conyers' killer made a mistake somewhere along the way. We'll find it."

"*We*? Who's *we*? I can't even pay this hospital bill. How in the hell can I afford to pay you?"

"We'll worry about the money later," I heard myself say once again. "Right now I have a couple of good leads I want to chase down. Sit tight and behave yourself."

That's what I told him. Of course, in truth, money was still an issue, and I didn't really have any good leads. Other than that, things were just great.

I stopped at Whole Foods and dropped a bundle on groceries again before going to Caffeine Central. It was warm that day, and the apartment was stuffy, so I opened the windows over the street. If I stayed much longer in the apartment, I decided, that floral print wall paper would have to go. I leashed Arch up and we walked over to the clinic. Caitlin was there with a small group of street kids. The mural was in good shape. Caitlin made a fuss over Archie. She looked strung out to me, hair unwashed, face drawn, her eyes perhaps a bit too dilated. "Are you in your apartment now?" I asked.

She examined her boots for a while and ran a hand through tangled hair. "Uh, it hasn't happened yet. Maybe next week." Looking up as if remembering something, she added, "A couple of guys were asking about you the other night. I think they were Russians."

My stomach did a half twist. "What did they say, exactly?"

"They wanted to know where they could find you, you know, where you hung out."

"What did you tell them?"

She shot me a look. She was streetwise, after all. "Nothing."

Caitlin asked me about Picasso, and I filled her in on his condition and the fact that his mother's killer had been identified. We talked for a while with the other kids huddled around us, and after thanking them for guarding the mural I went into the clinic to find Anna. Archie stayed behind to catch up with Caitlin.

I caught her in her office, leaned in the doorway and said, "Hi."

She looked up, took off her glasses and set them down. Her hair was up, accentuating her slender neck and her eyes were that deeper blue that seemed to come and go mysteriously. Without saying a word, she came across the room, pulled me in, shut the door, and kissed me. Long and soft and tender.

"You're back," she said when we came up for air.

"Yeah. I guess I am."

She took my hand. "Come on. Let's get those stitches out of your ear."

Chapter Thirty

Although I was a bit nervous, I had to suppress a chuckle as I parked across from the KPOC parking lot that afternoon. I was about to play private eye like some character in a paperback, and I even had a pair of horn-rim glasses I'd picked up to give myself a different look. After all, my picture had been in the paper again. So far, Cynthia Duncan had struck out trying to get information about Larry Vincent's young victim through his ex-wife. Apparently, those in the know had been bought off and then silenced with some kind of confidentiality agreement. But what if the source of Nicole Baxter's story was one of his colleagues at KPOC, the person known to me only as X-Man? It was a risky play, but if I ever had any patience about this case, it was long gone. And who knows—it just might be easier to find the source of the story than the victim.

Vincent's spiffy BMW convertible was still in the lot, and when he came out of the station and drove away in it, I made my move. There are no receptionists anymore, just someone who juggles a phone, a computer, and annoying walk-ins like me. This particular multitasker was a woman with tightly curled auburn hair, robin's egg eyes, and machine-tanned legs that seemed to go on forever below a very short skirt. The plaque on her desk told me her name was Shelly. I waited for her to finish talking and for her eyes to come off the computer screen in front of her, but neither happened. I shifted on my feet. Still nothing. I cleared my throat softly. Finally, she said, "I'll call you back, okay?" into her mouth piece, then looked up at me. "Can I help you?"

"Uh, yeah, Shelly, my name's Syd Walker," I said in a bright, chamber of commerce tone. "I'm a writer doing some research on small, independently owned AM radio stations. I was wondering if you might be able to help me?"

She smiled, revealing a set of unnaturally white teeth. "Do I get my name in your book?"

"Sure. And when it becomes a bestseller, I'll put your picture in, too."

The gleaming smile again. "What do you need?"

"I'm interested in the history of some of the local stations, like KPOC, going back a decade or two. Who would be the best source of that kind of information? I don't want to talk to the on-air personalities. I want the behind-the-scenes story."

"Damn, there goes my fifteen minutes of fame. I've only been here six months," she replied. "You need to talk to Arnie Katz. He was the general manager for ages. He retired last year, but I'm sure he'd be glad to talk to you."

Katz's place, a meticulously restored Craftsman, was on a quiet street across from Laurelhurst Park in southeast Portland. No one answered the bell, but I followed the keening of a power saw down the driveway and found Katz in his garage. Birdhouses of every size and shape hung from the rafters like exotic fruit. Katz saw me approaching through a cloud of sawdust and shut off the saw, which powered down with a moan. A small man with a full beard and eyes magnified by thick glasses, he wore a forest green t-shirt with a huge yellow O on it, the ubiquitous University of Oregon logo.

Katz bought my cover story, and with notebook and pen at the ready I launched into a series of questions about KPOC. I covered the station's core staff and some of the other programs first before working my way around to Larry Vincent's show, *Vincent's View.* I said, "Vincent's program really took off in the last decade. Do you remember some of the personnel he had around then?"

Katz gave me a pained look and shook his head. "Larry's show rose alright, like a hot air balloon. Apparently you can build an audience on bigotry and racism, even in Portland. But he did have some good people back then." He ticked through them while I made notes. I was about to ask him if anyone used the nickname X-Man, when he said, "Oh, I almost forgot Bidarte, the researcher."

"Remember his first name?"

"Xavier, Xavier Bidarte. He's a Basque. Smart as a whip with computers."

I almost punched a hole in my note paper. I said, "Uh, tell me a little bit more about him. Is he still around?"

"No. He worked the show for maybe five years and left, let's see, around the middle of 2005. Damn good research man. That was back when Vincent stuck to facts once in a while. Left abruptly, as I recall. I always figured he'd had enough of Vincent's bullshit."

"I see. Is he, uh, still working somewhere in the area?"

Katz shrugged. "I don't know what happened to him."

I asked several more questions about other topics to cover my interest in Bidarte and left Katz a believer, as far as I could tell. On the way back to Caffeine Central, I mulled over the X-Man question. Picasso had told me he was crazy about the movie back then, so maybe his mom chose that name for her source—X-Man for Xavier Bidarte, or perhaps he chose it for himself. It didn't matter. I liked the fit. And I liked the timing of his departure from Vincent's staff, too, and wondered why it had been "abrupt."

Only one Xavier Bidarte lived in the Northwest, according to the online white pages. The listing was in Tacoma, Washington, but no address or phone number was given. I called Nando and left a message for him to see what he could find on this guy ASAP.

Anna came over that night, and after dinner we drank wine and took turns scraping off the ugly wall paper with a kitchen spatula. The bare plaster walls, with bits of paper, patches of glue and gouges, were a vast improvement over the floral pattern that predated my grandparents. I saw a new side to her that night. She was giggly, funny, and spontaneous. We tried to make it to my tiny bedroom, but wound up making love on the floor in the hallway.

Before she went home that night, I asked about Caitlin. As if I'd thrown a switch, her face darkened, and the blue seemed to drain from her eyes. She sighed and shook her head. "Caitlin failed her last drug test, and now the apartment offer's on hold. She claimed it was second-hand smoke, but nobody's buying that. I think they're going to put her on probation. Oh, Cal, I wish Picasso could talk to her. He's the only person she listens to."

I held her a long time, and neither of us spoke. Finally, she said in a husky voice, "I don't know how much more of this I can take. These kids are ripping my heart out."

"You've got to maintain some distance, Anna. You can't carry the weight of the world directly on your shoulders. It'll crush you." The corner of my brain housing my sense of irony began laughing hysterically, as if to say, *Look who's giving advice.* But I had been there, damn it, and knew what she was feeling.

She gently untangled herself from my embrace and left without saying anything. I let her go. I understood.

Nando called the next morning with information on the Xavier Bidarte living in Tacoma. The quick turn-around meant he'd used an expensive online search service. I didn't even want to *think* about the bill I was running up. Bidarte was the right guy since his job history showed he'd worked at KPOC until June of 2005. Nicole Baxter had disappeared on May 18 of that year. He was now on the support staff at the University of Puget Sound, a small liberal arts college in Tacoma. Nando gave me an address and phone number.

I called Cynthia Duncan and told her what I'd found. We agreed to drive up together and talk to Bidarte. To make sure he was home Cynthia would call and make an appointment, using a cover story similar to mine. We figured he'd be more receptive to a cold call from a woman.

That afternoon, I met with Picasso's attorney, Alicia Cole, to go back over what I'd witnessed at the Conyers' crime scene, and to discuss my theories—they were nothing more than that—about who really killed Conyers. I didn't tell her I'd located X-Man. I didn't want to jinx it. I did tell her to be sure to depose Seth Foster and Jessica Armandy. It would be interesting to know what they stood to gain by Conyers' death. According to Bambi, Foster was now acting like he owned the Happy Angus. Did he? And what, exactly, was Conyers' business relationship with Armandy?

Cynthia swung by after rush hour the next morning to pick me up. I intended to take Archie with us, but Anna convinced me to leave him at the clinic. Picasso's posse would take good care of him, she assured me. I agreed after telling her not to let them take Arch off the property. We headed north on the I-5. At Cynthia's insistence we took her car, a late model Toyota. Better gas mileage, she explained. She wore a short skirt, black tights, boots, and a conservative white blouse. A full bottle of raspberry-flavored water stood at the ready in her cup holder. "In case she got the munchies." We sped through North Portland toward the Columbia River Bridge at eighty-five miles an hour. So much for gas mileage. Her hands gripped the steering wheel like she was strangling a snake.

She said, "God, my boss is such a wimp. He keeps saying, 'Now, go slow on this Vincent thing, Cynthia. Keep me in the loop.'" She laughed sharply and the car speed nudged over eighty five. "I didn't even tell him about what we're up to today. I'm not sure he really wants me to work on this, but he doesn't have the balls to tell me no. I think he's hoping I'll just give up."

Fat chance, I thought to myself. To get my mind off my personal safety, I switched on the radio and tuned into KPOC just in time to hear, "gun-toting, God-fearing, pro-life warrior, Larry Vincent."

Cynthia groaned. "Oh, God, give me a break. It's too early in the morning for *him*."

I laughed. "Let's hear what he has to say."

Vincent started off the program by combing through the news for items to comment on. There was the high cost of the state government pension plan and the proposed new bridge across the Columbia River, both monuments to the stupidity and greed of the local politicians. A bill in the Oregon legislature barring teens from tanning salons was ridiculed as anti-business. There was the serial rapist operating in and around Forest Park. About this, Vincent said, "You wait, folks, when they catch this guy, we'll find out he's one of those homeless creeps camping out in the park. Mark my words."

Cynthia reached across and turned off the radio. "That racist, hypocritical bastard. He's triggering my gag reflex."

I laughed. "Tell me how you really feel."

Gray clouds spit rainy mist most of the way, but just before the turnoff to Olympia, the clouds parted and Mt. Rainier loomed out of the east, a white bearded behemoth peering down on the thousands upon thousands of homes and businesses scattered on its western flanks. I found myself wondering what will happen when it decides to blow like its sister, Mt. St. Helens.

We met Bidarte in front of the student union on the Puget Sound campus, which looked like a movie set with rich green lawns dotted with old growth cedars and ivy-covered brick buildings. We followed him into a small coffee shop adjacent to the dining hall. I was relieved that the place was nearly empty. We could talk without the risk of being overheard. Bidarte had sharp features, a quick smile, and eyes that were darker than his black hair. He had the build of a runner, and his clothes—an open collar button down tucked into crisply pressed jeans and low cut hiking boots—draped his slender frame with casual elegance. Cynthia said something under her breath that included the words "so hot." I missed the rest but caught her drift.

Cynthia nursed her flavored water, and by the time Bidarte's and my coffees arrived, it was clear I was odd man out. Their eyes were locked together and the space across the table so charged I felt that if I put my hand between them I'd get zapped. After some small talk about the scene in Portland, Bidarte said, "So, tell me about this project you and Cal are working on."

Cynthia moved her eyes from Bidarte to me. We had agreed that I would be the one to break the ice, as it were. By this time, I was having my inevitable second thoughts. What's the chance this guy's X-Man? What was I thinking, anyway? But I barged ahead. "Xavier, we're really not researching the history of radio in the Northwest. I'm an attorney and Cynthia here is a newspaper reporter. We think you were the source of a story another reporter was working on eight years ago, in the spring of 2005. The reporter was Nicole Baxter, and the story concerned Larry Vincent, your boss at KPOC."

The words hung between us, solid, palpable—a wall or a bridge, I couldn't tell which. Except for the muscles that flexed along his jaw line, Xavier held a neutral expression. He looked at me, then Cynthia, set his coffee down and got up. Cynthia sprang to her feet before I could move. "Don't go," she said. "We need your help, Xavier. Talk to us."

Looking directly at Cynthia, he said, "I don't appreciate being set up."

A blue vein appeared in Cynthia's neck. "We just want to talk to you. Hear us out."

"Why should I? There's nothing in this for me except trouble."

I didn't dare move or speak. This was between the two of them.

Color filled Cynthia's cheeks, and she leaned forward with both hands on the table. "You're wrong, Xavier. You have a chance to do the right thing. I think you've been waiting for this chance. Now sit down. *Please.*"

An eternity passed while they stood glaring at each other. Finally he exhaled a breath, shook his head, and sat back down.

"So, what do you want to know?"

Chapter Thirty-one

"Oh my God, I thought he was going to walk for sure," Cynthia said, her hands clamped on the steering wheel as we tore onto the I-5 heading back to Portland.

I laughed. "Not a chance. He was hopelessly smitten by you, but I'm sure you didn't notice."

She shot me a faux indignant look. "I wasn't using him, Cal. I'd say it worked out pretty well all the way around. He's coming down to Portland next weekend."

It had worked out well indeed. Xavier Bidarte was hesitant at first, but once he started to talk he told us everything. He was X-Man—his name choice—and Larry Vincent was the target of Nicole Baxter's exposé. Vincent's victim was a beautiful young girl named Sherrill Blanchard. She wasn't a baby sitter, as the rumors had it, but a high school intern at the station. Bidarte had seen Vincent with her too many times. His suspicions were confirmed when he saw her late one night in Vincent's car, at least until Vincent's hand came up and pushed her head down. He went to the girl's mother, then the police, and was first astonished and then angered when nothing happened.

Cynthia shook her head. "I'll bet Nicky was surprised when Xavier walked in and handed her a story like that on a platter. I can't believe she didn't tell me about it."

"Yeah," I responded, "but she wouldn't have had much if Xavier hadn't hacked Vincent's email. Those puppy-love notes from the girl and Vincent's explicit responses back to her, compounded by the beginnings of the negotiations with the mother, gave her the makings of a bombshell with a lot of shrapnel."

"I can understand why Xavier left Portland," Cynthia went on. "I mean, suddenly Nicky disappears along with all the evidence he'd supplied her, and nobody else seemed to give a shit about the situation, including the girl's mother." Cynthia squeezed the steering wheel until her knuckles turned white. The speedometer nudged over ninety. "I can't believe Xavier didn't keep a copy of those files. We can't prove a damn thing unless the girl's willing to talk after all this time."

We discussed various strategies for approaching Sherrill Blanchard, who was now a young woman of twenty-two or three. Bidarte had no idea what had become of her. The best approach, we decided, was a direct one. Cynthia would make the contact, provided we could locate Blanchard, which we didn't think would be that hard.

This was good as far as it went. Cynthia had a shot at resurrecting the blockbuster story that her friend was working on when she was killed. The story would take down a man who richly deserved it. But none of this helped Picasso. Sure, I now knew that Baxter had damaging information about Larry Vincent. When she vanished, it wasn't a stretch to believe that Mitch Conyers found the files and used them to blackmail Larry Vincent, who in turn killed him for it. Trouble is, I couldn't prove it. Not yet, anyway.

Cynthia let me off at the clinic. A couple of kids hanging out on the vacant lot next to the mural told me Caitlin had taken Archie down to the Burnside Bridge. I felt a twinge of anger at this. I was feeling less sanguine about Caitlin and didn't want Archie out and about in the city without close supervision. I found them with a group of kids lounging in Ankeny Square. Arch yelped when he saw me and pulled her out of the group by his leash to meet me. The oily herb smell of marijuana hung in the still air. The tall, blond kid I'd seen over at the clinic stood up, shot me an annoyed look, and said, "Well, *finally.* Come on, Snuggles, let's get out of here."

I said to Caitlin, "Snuggles?"

She dropped her eyes and looked embarrassed. "Yeah, well, it's what my family calls me."

I said, "Didn't Anna tell you not to bring Archie down here?"

"Uh, yeah, she did." She glanced at the group, then back at me. "They wanted to come down here. I didn't think it would hurt."

I nodded. "I can smell the pot, Caitlin. I know you're on probation. You sure you want to hang with these kids?"

"Come on, Snuggles, let's go," one of the girls in the group called out.

She shuffled her feet for a few moments, then patted Archie on the head and turned to join them.

"Thanks for watching my dog," I said to her as she walked away. She hesitated a moment as if she were going to turn and say something, but apparently thought better of it. Archie whimpered softly as she hurried off to join the group.

That night I had dinner with Nando at a Vietnamese joint over on Division called Pok Pok. He wore linen slacks and a salmon colored silk golf shirt stretched taut by his ample girth. After our beers had arrived and he had finished ordering for us—prawns grilled over charcoal, boar collar meat rubbed with garlic, and a noodle dish served with minced pineapple, ginger, and green mango—I said, "Putting on some weight, I see."

He took a long pull on his beer, then smiled and patted his stomach. "It is probably true, although I do not own a scale." He wagged a finger at me. "Eating well can never hurt you."

I laughed. "I know a woman who would argue that point," and went on to tell him what Cynthia Duncan and I had learned from Xavier Bidarte.

After I'd finished and answered his questions, he said, "The blackmail theory is admirable, Calvin, but we have no evidence that Conyers was blackmailing *anybody*, let alone this ball of sleeze, Vincent."

"Tell me about it. I need to talk to Jessica Armandy again. If Conyers was blackmailing somebody, she would know about it. No doubt in my mind."

Nando arched his thick eyebrows. "The last time you talked to her it did not go so well."

"Look, she thinks I have some leverage with Bambi, right?"

He popped another shrimp in his mouth and nodded. "She would probably like you to speak to the young girl, get her to leave the other girls alone. Bambi has been bad for her business."

"Well, I wouldn't do that even if I could, but Armandy doesn't know that. Suppose you told her I wanted to talk about a deal?"

"A deal you have no intention of honoring?"

"She wouldn't know that," I answered, and when Nando shot me a judgmental look, I snapped back, "Damn it, a young man's life is on the line here. Give me a break."

He shook his head and made a face. "This is very risky, my friend. And the Russian who dislikes you, you will have to worry about him, too."

"I know that. Just set it up, Nando. Please."

As it turned out, the problem of the Russian who disliked me came to a head sooner than I thought it would. Nando had just pulled away after dropping me off at Caffeine Central. I know, I should have had my guard up, but nothing looked out of place on the deserted street. I was fumbling for my keys in the dim glow of the streetlight when someone, a large someone, stepped around the corner of the building. It was Semyon, and he was too close to me to make ducking into the building or running an option, not that my male ego would have allowed that.

I turned to face him, tucking my keys into my fist for a little extra clout as the adrenaline floodgates opened. Where was the Glock when I needed it? Up in the apartment, of course. And I took no comfort in the fact that he was alone. That was just a reflection of his confidence that he could take care of me single-handedly.

The streetlight lit enough of his face for me to make out that same anticipatory glee I'd seen before. His thick arms hung at his sides slightly bowed, gunfighter style. He wore tight jeans, the same shit-kicker shoes, and a dark t-shirt that covered his upper body like a second layer of skin. No weapon. But then, why would he need one? He said, "Hello, asshole. We've got a score to settle."

I locked my knees so they wouldn't begin shaking and prayed for a passing car, a bicycle, *anything*, but the street was deserted. He stepped forward, and I took a step back. "I'm not looking for any trouble, Semyon. This isn't a goddamn schoolyard. We're grown men, for Christ's sake." I knew the words were futile, but they were all I could come up with.

He pointed a bratwurst-sized finger at me. "If that little bitch Bambi hadn't cold-cocked me, I would have finished this the first time."

The image of Bambi's bruised and puffy face rushed back to me. I felt my gorge rise involuntarily and heard myself say, "Well, at least you're going to beat a man this time instead of a defenseless young girl." *Jesus,* I said to myself, *there you go again!*

Semyon eyes flared at my words. He was a slow learner, because he lunged at me and threw the same roundhouse right I'd seen before. I ducked under the clumsy punch, slammed the fist holding my keys into his gut, and then spun out of his range. He hardly noticed the punch. I dropped the keys, which had done more damage to my hand than to his stomach. He moved in and loosed an awkward left hook. I brought my right forearm up and deflected the punch, then countered with a straight left that caught him flush on the nose. He staggered back and crashed into the front door, which set Archie into a barking rage inside. I instantly regretted jettisoning my keys. With Archie's help, I might have a chance. But the keys were well out of reach.

Semyon wiped the blood trickling from his nose with his thumb, looked down at it, then back at me. Archie was going crazy on the other side of the door.

I turned my head, pointed to the jagged scar on my ear and said, "You did this. We could call it even, you know." What the hell, I figured, it's never too late to negotiate.

Semyon gave me an incredulous look, said something in Russian, and came at me again. I was watching his hammer-like fists, so, of course, he kicked me. I twisted just enough that the blow skidded off my shin, but I lost my balance in the process. He lunged at me, and I ducked under his grasp, came up behind him and pushed him hard as I could. He was off-balance, and when he thudded against the building wall, Archie went wild.

Semyon turned around, put a hand on the fresh abrasion on his forehead, and smiled. I said, "Had enough?" It never hurts to ask.

He didn't seem to appreciate my little joke. Instead, he snorted again in Russian and charged me with both arms outstretched like a mad Russian bear. I knew that once he got his hands on me, I was finished. I stood upright as if I were going to take his charge, then at the last moment, ducked under his grasp, crouched down low and came up with everything I had in my quadriceps. It was definitely not a Marquess of Queensbury maneuver. My dad, who'd taught me to box, would have been ashamed, but I really didn't want to die in some stupid fight on the street.

I heard a sickening crunch as my head met the underside of his chin and saw a brilliant flash of light before everything went black. Again.

I don't know how long I was out, but the next thing I heard was Archie barking and scratching on the other side of the door. I sat up and gingerly touched the growing lump on the top of my head. The sidewalk I was sitting on took a familiar, nauseating half turn.

Semyon was sitting next to me, holding his jaw and groaning. He looked at me, focused his eyes, and said through clamped, bloody teeth, "Yew roke ma ja. Yew roke ma ja."

"Yeah, well, you broke my skull. We should definitely call it even now."

He doubled up in pain. "Aw, shi, dis hurts like a son ofa bitch."

I clawed my cell phone out of my front pocket. "You probably need to get to a hospital, man. Hold on. I know somebody who might be able to help us."

Chapter Thirty-two

I called Anna, and she picked up on the eighth or ninth ring. She'd dozed off reading a book, she explained. I told her we had a little medical situation that needed attention and wondered if she could drop by Caffeine Central. She wanted more information, but I told her it was a long story. I was in no shape to chit chat. I turned to Semyon. "I have a friend who's a doctor. She's coming right over to take a look at you."

Still holding his jaw and moaning, Semyon used the door knob to pull himself up. This set Archie off again. I gathered up my keys, which were lying next to me on the sidewalk, held them out to him and said, "Here, let my dog out, would you? He's giving me a headache."

He shook his head, refusing to take the keys. Archie broke out in another chorus of barks.

"It's okay," I insisted. "He won't hurt you." I extended the keys again. "Go ahead, let him out."

Semyon took the keys and cautiously opened the door, then quickly stepped back. Archie looked at me first, then at Semyon, and as he did, lowered his ears, bared his fangs, and growled with such menace that it even scared me. He wasn't an aggressive dog, but it was clear he meant business. Semyon shot me a shouldn't-have-listened-to-you look, made a guttural throat sound and took a couple more steps back.

I looked at Arch and shot a hand up like a traffic cop. "It's okay, Archie. It's okay. Come here, boy." My dog raised his ears and came over to me with his tail wagging tentatively, looked me over, and tried to lick my bloody head. I struggled to get up. Semyon came over, extended a hand, and pulled me to my feet. Archie positioned himself between us, but it was clear the hostilities were over. We were like a couple of gladiators who'd fought to a draw, but I'm sure the Romans would have given us both a thumbs down for our performance.

We stood there in awkward silence until Semyon met my eyes. "I'm sori bou Bambi. Jessca tol me to rufer up alil. I didn't mean ta hurter like dat. I never it a woman bafor."

"Bambi would be glad to hear that. You should tell her in person. Maybe one day she'll be able to forgive you."

Semyon nodded, and something shifted in that moment. I won't say we became friends, but at least we were no longer enemies.

Anna pulled up in her Volvo and got out, straining to see in the dim light. "Cal, is that you? Oh, my God, what's happened now?"

"Anna, this is Semyon. He's, uh, got a problem with his jaw. Maybe you could look at it?"

She looked at Semyon, then back at me. "Is he the Russ—"

"Yeah, but it's okay now. We've declared a truce."

Anna gave Semyon's jaw a cursory examination. The right side along the jawline looked like he had a roll of quarters inside his cheek. The bulge was already turning a cloudy purple. She had him try to open his mouth, and he made a strange, wounded bird sound. Anna said, "Your mandible's badly broken, and you've chipped a couple of teeth. You need to go to the ER immediately." Then she turned to me. "Are you okay?"

I pointed at the top of my head, accidentally touching the lump, which caused me to flinch. "Bumped my head."

She took my head in her hands and gently bowed it. "Oh, that's a nasty bump, Cal. And the gash is going to need stitches. So, your head hit his chin? Is that what happened?"

I nodded. "Accident."

She rolled her eyes and shook her head. "How do you feel?"

"Whoozy."

She went to her car and returned with a flashlight from her glove compartment. After checking my response, she said, "You might be mildly concussed. Who do you think you are, an NFL quarterback?"

I chuckled, and Semyon chimed in with a couple of clinch-jawed grunts.

Semyon wanted to drive himself to the hospital, and I offered to drive him, but Anna was having none of it. She drove us both to the Good Samaritan Hospital over on Twenty-second at the base of the West Hills. I'd been back in the waiting room for an hour, sporting five new stitches, when Semyon emerged with his jaw wired shut and the prospect of a liquid diet for the next several weeks.

There wasn't a lot of small talk on the way back from the hospital, but Semyon and my truce seemed to be holding. However, when I finally walked him to his car near Caffeine Central, he declined to shake my offered hand. That was okay with me. If we couldn't be friends, I'd settle for being his non-enemy.

When I returned, Anna was still in the driver's seat of her Volvo. "Get in. You'll need close observation tonight."

"Lucky me," I replied.

On the way back to her condo, Anna said, "Two fights with this guy, Cal? There was no way to avoid this? He could have killed you."

I exhaled a breath and shook my head. "Nando had just dropped me off. Semyon came out from the side of the building. I wasn't expecting it. I tried to talk him down, but he wasn't listening."

"So, you stood and fought. You're a male. It's in your DNA, I guess." She fell silent for several moments, seeming to mull her statement over. "I wonder what I would have done in a situation like that? Sometimes, I wonder whether I'm principled or just a physical coward."

"The survival instinct's built into everyone's DNA. You might surprise yourself," I replied.

I had no idea how prophetic that statement would be.

The next morning, Anna dropped me off at Caffeine Central on her way to the clinic. Once again, I was given strict orders to take it easy, although I felt a hell of a lot better than after the last time I encountered Semyon. I spent most of the morning on the phone with clients and also my bookkeeper, Gertrude Johnson, who called to tell me she needed to move some cash from my savings account to my business account to cover the bills. "All this publicity about that homeless kid and the suicide of that lobbyist could kill your business, Cal. When are you going to wrap things up in Portland and get back to focusing on your clients in Dundee?"

"It's going well here, Gertie. I should have things wrapped up in no time." I didn't want to worry her, and I didn't need the lecture I was sure to get if I told her the truth.

She paused for a long time before saying, "Uh huh. Well, I hope you're not shining me on, Cal. You can't afford it."

That bit of news did nothing for my appetite, but sometime after one that afternoon I went into the kitchen, sliced an apple along with a chunk of Gruyere cheese, added a handful of walnuts, and poured myself a chilled glass of Argyle chardonnay. I had just sat down with *The Oregonian* spread out on the table when Nando called.

"The madam has deigned to grant you an audience tonight. You are to present yourself at the Happy Angus around ten to discuss issues of mutual interest."

"Thank you, Nando. You can tell the madam I'll be there."

"Done. By the way, I did not raise the issue of the mad Russian with her, but I am concerned he might try something when you leave the restaurant, even if you and she come to some sort of arrangement."

I laughed. "I don't think he'll pose a threat." I went on to explain what happened the previous night.

After I finished, he chuckled. "Speak low but carry a large club. That is you, my friend." His voice grew serious. "But even though you say the Russian carries no grudge, which I find difficult to believe, you must be careful tonight. Perhaps it would be wise if I dropped in for a drink to even up the odds?"

"Yeah, I'd feel better if you did. But don't crowd me. I want Armandy to feel free to talk."

At 10:10 that night, I climbed the broad spiral staircase to the bar at the Happy Angus. A silver haired man in banker's pinstripe was coming down the stairs with a young beauty draped on his arm. The man was jingling his keys, and the girl was laughing at something he'd said.

It seemed a quieter crowd that night. A soft buzz of conversation lubricated by expensive booze floated up from tight knots of couples, mostly men with women who could be their daughters, but they weren't. The women belonged to Jessica Armandy, perched at her corner table like a general observing a field of battle. She wore a tight, flaming red dress with a scoop neck that revealed an ample portion of cleavage decorated with a multistrand gold necklace. Her face was air-brushed perfection.

We exchanged greetings, and when I sat down she noticed the shaved, bandaged patch on top of my head. She wrinkled her brow and raised an eyebrow. "I see you've banged yourself up. Funny thing, my driver Semyon has a shattered jaw. Said it happened while he was sparring. You didn't happen to be his sparring partner, did you, Claxton?

I shook my head. "Had a squamous removed. Too much sun up here in the Northwest."

She gave me a thin smile and took a sip of her drink without offering me anything. "Well, you've become quite the celebrity here in Portland. I hope you're not investigating any more of my clients. I can't afford to lose another one."

I looked around the room. "Business seems to be pretty good."

"It could be better, but it's hard to get good help these days. You know how it is."

My turn to smile.

She narrowed her eyes and leaned into the table, her cheeks filling with color. "Goddamn it, Claxton, have Bambi call me.

She's got a good business head, and I've got a great offer for her. We're planning to expand."

I shrugged. "I could pass the message on, I suppose, but there's no guarantee what she'll do. Bambi thinks for herself."

She flicked her hand dismissively and shot me an annoyed look. "I know that, damn it, that's why I like her. Just ask her to call me. Tell her I want to discuss a business opportunity."

"Okay, I'll do it, but I need something from you first."

The annoyed look returned as she drained her drink. She raised a finger and a waiter appeared. "Fill me up and bring him a Mirror Pond," She glanced at me. "That's your beer, right?"

"It is, provided I get to drink it, not wear it."

She laughed, a kind of lusty bark. "Not to worry. Seth's not here tonight. I made sure of that. He's a bit of a hot head, but who could blame him? He worshipped his stepbrother. Now, tell me, what is it you want from me?"

I leaned in, placing both arms on the table. "You and most of this town are rushing to judgment about who killed Mitch Conyers. I'm here to tell you you've got it wrong. Danny Baxter didn't do it."

"Oh, please. Not that happy horseshit again. If Snake Boy didn't do it, then who the hell did?"

"Think about it. It was someone who wanted him dead, someone who saw the perfect opportunity to blame it on a young homeless man."

She shrugged. "I don't know of anyone else. All I know is that kid hated Mitch's guts."

"Oh, so Conyers was Mr. Congeniality. Come on, Jessica, you can do better than that. Let me spell it out for you. Who was Conyers *blackmailing*?"

She tried to look indignant but didn't quite pull it off. "Oh, *that* again. If he was blackmailing someone, he sure as hell didn't tell me about it."

I straightened up in my chair. "You don't seem so sure. Maybe you thought of something after we talked last time, something you didn't think was important? I don't blame you for not wanting to talk about it. It doesn't put your friend in a very good light."

She paused for several beats. "Why should I talk to you about this?"

"For openers, I'm not a cop. Sure, I'm trying to keep an innocent kid from being thrown under the bus, but I'm trying to find out who killed your friend, too. It's a package deal."

She sighed heavily and took a sip of her cognac. "Well, Mitch always seemed to have more cash than I thought he should, especially around the end of the month." She laughed. "At one point, I thought he might be skimming from my operation, so I had a client of mine who's an accountant go through the books. Didn't find anything out of line, so I dropped it. But I always wondered."

"Let me guess. You started noticing this around June or July of 2005, right after Nicole Baxter disappeared."

She turned her head slightly, as if in thought, then turned back. Her eyes narrowed and a blood vein in her neck appeared like a faint purple river. "What if I did?"

The lawyer in me screamed *don't tell her too much!* But I had to get her talking. I said, "When Nicole Baxter disappeared that May, she was working on a damaging exposé about a well known man in Portland. Conyers was practically living with Baxter at the time. I believe he found the article and all the supporting evidence after she disappeared and used it to extract hush money from that man. Conyers had plenty of leverage. The exposé would have ruined the man's reputation and sent him to jail."

"You talking about Weiman?"

"No, it wasn't Hugo Weiman." Her question disappointed me. She apparently didn't know the person being blackmailed.

"Then who the hell is it?"

"I was hoping you could tell me."

"Then you don't know shit," she scoffed.

I took a swig of beer to give myself time to think. Should I give Vincent up? I decided it was worth the gamble, that if she heard the name, she might make a connection. I said, "I know who the exposé was being written about, but I can't link him to Conyers yet."

"Who is it?"

"Larry Vincent, your favorite radio personality."

She sat very still for a moment. The color in her cheeks seemed to bleed away. "You're sure of this? Vincent?"

"I'm sure Vincent was Baxter's target. I need you to help me link him to Conyers. That would give him a whopping motive for murder."

She nodded her head slowly, as if in deep thought. "Okay, I get the picture. Now, suppose I can help you. Then what happens?"

"The guy who brutally murdered your friend and business partner gets put away, and a young man gets his life back."

"But it also comes out my friend and business partner was a lowly blackmailer. That, too. Right?"

I shrugged. "Small price to pay from where I sit."

She smiled, and I was reminded of an arctic winter. "I'm going to talk this over with Seth. I'll get back to you, *after* I hear from Bambi."

Chapter Thirty-three

As I walked by the bar, I nodded to Nando, who'd come in twenty minutes earlier. He laid a bill on the counter and followed me out.

"How did it go?" he asked when we reached the street.

"I definitely got her attention, but I don't think she knew exactly who Conyers was blackmailing. She's going to talk to Seth Foster. I have a feeling Foster might know, or that between them they can connect the dots. I told her more than I wanted to, but I decided to risk it."

"Then this is good, yes?"

I shrugged. "I don't know. Maybe they'd just as well have Picasso take the fall, so it doesn't come out that Conyers was a low life blackmailer."

"Or maybe *they* killed Conyers. I'm sure you've thought of that possibility."

"Yeah, I thought of that. But I like Vincent for it better. I'll take the chance." Then I laughed. "Armandy's dying to get Bambi back. They're planning to expand the escort service, and apparently Bambi has management potential."

Nando chuckled. "Will you talk to her?"

"I guess I'll have to. Otherwise, I won't get anything back from Armandy. But I don't know what I'm going to say to her."

When I got back to Caffeine Central that night, I leashed up Archie and headed for the river. I left the Glock behind since I no longer had a beef with Semyon. The moon was a dull silver coin behind a gauze of thin clouds. Not a breath of wind stirred.

The lights on the piers of the Morrison Bridge—a rainbow of primary colors—shimmered on the river in perfect reflection. I'd heard somewhere that you could select a color scheme and have it displayed on the bridge for a hundred bucks a night. The city was always looking for new sources of revenue. I sat on a bench next to the river imagining what colors I'd choose. Archie sat on the ground next to me, sniffing the cool air as I absently stroked his fur.

I wondered how Picasso was feeling and whether my thrashing about was going to do him any good. I knew one thing. The moment he was well enough, he would be hauled in front of a judge and arraigned for first degree murder. I could already hear the crowing from Larry Vincent and see the smug look on Detective Jones' face. Was I right to seek Jessica Armandy's help, or had I made a big mistake? I was feeling less and less sure about that. What if Nando was right? What if the murder had been an inside job?

My thoughts turned to Anna. I could walk over to her place right now and tell her I needed more "close observation." The thought stirred me, but I decided against it. She was an amazing woman, and I felt the pull of her, but at the same time was wary of becoming too involved. I worried about where I would eventually fall in the pecking order of her life, which seemed to be built around the guilt of her brother's death more than anything else. That guilt, I knew all too well, could act like an addictive drug. Of course, I wanted to believe that I could show her a better way, but the call of martyrdom is strong.

Take it slow, I told myself. Feet on the ground, hopes well in check.

The next day I met Cynthia Duncan for a quick lunch. We picked up Thai at the food carts on Ninth and went across the street to the park to eat. Sherrill Blanchard, she told me, lived in Seattle with her mother and was *not* returning her phone calls. "I'm driving up there to see her. Don't worry, Cal, I'll get her to talk."

I stopped by the clinic that afternoon, and Anna put a fresh bandage on my head wound. She invited me over for dinner, and I offered to cook, which pleased her no end. But the evening didn't go so well. Anna had just found out that Caitlin had been dropped from the program that was to provide her with a ticket off the street. And, as I had observed, Caitlin was spending more time with her so called family. There was no light in Anna's eyes that night, and when I mentioned something about trying to keep perspective, she got angry. I cooked, we ate in silence, and I went home early.

I awoke the next morning and groaned when I realized I was out of coffee beans. I got dressed, leashed up Archie, and walked down the street to the Starbucks. Armed with a double cappuccino, I grabbed a paper and took a seat out on the sidewalk. Before I could open the paper, a thin, graying woman in baggy sweatpants and a flannel shirt stopped her overloaded grocery cart in front of me and said, "Can you spare some change? I'm hungry." Her eyes were a bright blue, like the sky that morning, and the grime on her face only accentuated their beauty.

I pulled the last of the meal vouchers I'd bought at the Sisters of the Road Café from my wallet and extended them to her. "My name's Cal. What's yours?"

She took the vouchers and dropped her eyes. "Evelyn, but everyone calls me Evie."

"How long have you been pushing that cart, Evie?"

"Too long."

"What happened?"

She brought her eyes back up and appraised me, wondering, no doubt, what my angle was. "Oh, it was real simple. My husband died and left me with a mountain of medical bills. I got a job but still lost the house. Got tired of being harassed by collection agencies, so I changed my address." She giggled. "Can't find me now. Don't have an address."

She needed a bath, and all her worldly possessions were piled in that shopping cart, but I heard a faint note of liberation in her words. She answered to no one, had zero expectations placed on her, and the possessions she had to maintain were circumscribed within a three foot radius. I felt a twinge of envy along with the guilt I always felt when I encountered a homeless person.

She thanked me and started off before I got the next question out. She was probably thinking about a warm breakfast and a hot cup of coffee now. I pulled a ten out of my wallet, got up, and handed it to her. What a pushover.

That morning I finally got around to finishing a brief that argued for dismissal of a lawsuit against a client of mine. Feeling productive, I set up an afternoon meeting with Picasso's lawyer, Alicia Cole. I had begun to trust her, so I laid out the blackmail theory and what Cynthia Duncan and I were doing to flush out Larry Vincent. For the first time, I allowed myself a speck of hope that we could extricate Picasso from this mess. She told me Picasso's arraignment was set for Friday of that week.

While checking my office voicemail that evening, a message came up that brought me out of my chair—"This is Larry Vincent. I hear you and some little bitch reporter have been nosing around in my personal business. Call me, or you're going to be looking down the barrel of a very nasty lawsuit…"

I called the number he left on the recording. "This is Larry."

"Cal Claxton. I had a message to call you."

"Well, well, Calvin Claxton, bleeding heart defender of the homeless."

"What can I do for you, Vincent?"

"We need to talk."

"We do?"

"Unless you prefer my lawyers in the morning. It's up to you."

"What do you have in mind?"

"Well, I'm tied up for the next hour or so. Meet me here at my place at, say, nine. I live on Hayden Island…"

I agreed to the meeting. The first thing I did when I hung up was call Nando. I didn't want to go to Vincent's place without backup. He didn't answer, so I left him a message. I fetched the Glock he'd given me and checked the clip, putting the loaded revolver in my belt at the small of my back. I put on my leather jacket and checked myself out in the full length mirror on the closet door. The gun wasn't visible.

Hayden Island's a narrow spit of land running for six miles in the Columbia River directly north of Portland. I'd be looking for the houseboat in slip twenty-three at the Columbia River Marina, he told me—the houseboat flying the big American flag.

I arrived at 8:50 and parked in the marina lot, well away from the dock area.

Nando still wasn't picking up.

I got out of the car and, staying in the shadows, worked my way over to the river, down from slip twenty-three. The river was high, and I had a clear view of his place, two stories of burnished teak, steel, and glass floating on a massive barge. An expansive deck surrounded brightly lit bay windows on the second story. I saw no movement inside or on the deck except for the promised American flag, which fluttered gently from a high mast. Some of the windows on the first floor were lighted as well, but they were all curtained, and the first floor deck was bathed in shadow. I stared into the darkness a long time and saw no movement, but it did look like the door facing the gang plank was partially open. That struck me as odd.

I called Nando one more time. Still no answer. I adjusted the Glock tucked at the small of my back and started toward the houseboat, trying hard to shake an inexplicable feeling of *déjà vu*.

The front door *was* open, about half way. I rang the bell and waited. There was no sound except the slosh of river water against the hull of the houseboat. I knocked loudly on the door and hollered, "Vincent? It's Cal Claxton." I pushed the door gently, and it swung into a hallway lit only by the light spilling from a room down and to the right. I saw something move and tensed up. A small dog with a fox-like face and poufy tail came out of the room and trotted up to me. It rolled on its back, exposing a fuzzy belly. His ears were down, and he was shaking and whimpering. "What's the matter fella?" I asked before calling out to Vincent again.

No answer.

I noticed two objects lying in the hallway in the half shadows. They didn't look like they belonged there. I flipped a couple of switches just inside the door and both the hall light and an outside light came on. In the hall, the broken base of a large, ornate lamp lay next to a half crushed lampshade in a spray of broken glass.

The little fox got up, trotted down the hall, and looked back at me before disappearing into the room on the right. I followed and found him licking the face of someone sprawled on the floor. The weak chin, the receding hairline—it was Larry Vincent, no question about it. His face was bloated and purple, his neck visibly bruised. He'd lost a considerable amount of blood from a gash in his forehead. I checked for a pulse, but knew he was dead.

"Not again!" I groaned as I got back up. Judging from the condition of the room, Vincent had put up a hell of a fight. A glass coffee table was overturned, a chair lay on its side below a shattered flat-screen TV, and a mahogany bookcase rested on a jumble of bestselling hardbacks and broken china.

I retraced my steps out of the room and down the hallway, trying not to disturb or touch anything. I looked back and saw I was leaving a trail of bloody footprints. "Wonderful." Having no ear for sarcasm, the little fox glanced up and seemed to smile as he trotted next to me like a pony.

When we cleared the front door, a tall young man in dark slacks and a crisply pressed shirt with a badge on it stood at the top of the gangplank. He pointed a revolver at me and said, "This is Columbia River Marina security. Put your hands up and don't move."

Chapter Thirty-four

The little fox started yapping at the security guard. I shushed the dog and raised my hands.

The guard said, "What were you doing in Mr. Vincent's houseboat?"

"I had an appointment with him at nine o'clock."

"Is he in there now?"

"Uh, yes he is. But there's a problem. He's dead. It looks like someone strangled him."

The guard's eyes widened, and his body stiffened. He came down the gangplank and joined me on the deck of the houseboat. The little fox had replaced his yapping with a surprisingly menacing growl. The barrel of the guard's gun was shaking noticeably. Before he spoke again, I said, "What's your name, son?"

"Jim, Jim Stanfield."

"Listen, Jim. I've got a Glock 19 tucked in my belt. I'm going to raise my coat and show it to you. I want you to remove it, but for God's sake, don't shoot me. Okay?"

I turned around, lowered my hands and pulled my coat up very slowly. Stanfield took the Glock and tucked it into his belt. I breathed a sigh of relief. He swallowed hard and motioned with his head. "Show me Mr. Vincent."

Twenty minutes later I sat in my stocking feet in the hallway of Larry Vincent's houseboat with handcuffs on. I was being questioned by two detectives dispatched from the North

Portland Precinct. My shoes were already in plastic evidence bags. Needless to say, I was a little annoyed.

The detectives were acting like it was Christmas morning and I was their present. Apparently, it had been a while since they'd cleared a murder case, and I looked like a slam dunk. The one with the pinched features and stained teeth was the most aggressive. He said, "So, let's go over this one more time, Mr. Claxton."

"I told you, detective, I had an appointment with Vincent at nine. When I arrived, his front door was open, and I could see the broken lamp and glass in the hallway. Then the little mutt came up to me, whimpering and carrying on. He was obviously upset about something, so—"

"So you read the dog's mind?" pinched face interrupted, glancing at his partner, then back at me.

"No, but when the mutt trotted off my instincts said to follow."

The quiet partner grunted a laugh. "Dog whisperer, huh?"

I rolled my eyes and spread my arms out in front of the detectives. "Look. Do you see any bruises or defensive wounds on me? There was obviously a ferocious fight in there, and I don't have a scratch on me. And you won't find my fingerprints in there either."

"But we have your shoe prints. In blood," pinched face shot back.

"I told you, I walked into the goddamn room and out again."

Quiet one said, "Maybe you trashed the place *after* you strangled him, to make it look like a fight."

Before I could respond, pinched face added, "And you were carrying a concealed weapon to this meeting. How do you explain that?"

It was futile to argue, and besides, I wasn't sure how much to tell them about Larry Vincent's potential involvement in the Conyers murder, so I shut up. I was transported to Central Precinct later that night and held on suspicion of murder. At least I rated a solitary cell. Murder suspects are afforded that luxury.

I called Nando that first night. "*Madre de Dios! No me digas eso. Este caso es una maldicion, Calvin,*" he responded when I broke the news.

"My sentiments exactly."

"What do you want me to do?"

"First off, call Anna Eriksen for me. Tell her Archie's at Caffeine Central. Give her a key and ask her to take care of him for me. And tell her not to worry, I'll be okay." I gave him Anna's cell number.

"What else?"

"Vincent told me he'd be tied up for an hour or so before he was to meet me at nine. See if you can find out anything about what he was doing. Maybe he was meeting someone."

"Like Jessica Armandy or Seth Foster?"

"*Exactly.* Start there. The coincidence sticks out like a sore thumb. But this was no planned hit. It looks like a crime of passion. When you strangle someone, it's very personal."

"True, but we cannot rule out a burglary gone to the south, either."

"Yeah, anything's possible, I suppose. In any case, I walked in at exactly the wrong time. This seems to be a newly acquired trait of mine."

I didn't get much sleep that night. A sporadic chorus of groans, profanity, and laughter from my jail mates echoed up and down the hall, even after the lights went out. I lay staring up at the ceiling on a rock hard mattress, vacillating between planning to sue the city of Portland for false arrest and breaking out in a cold sweat over how screwed I was. Vincent had said nasty things about me over the radio, giving me good reason to want to wring his scrawny neck. But then again, they didn't have anything but motive, opportunity, and means, did they?

The next day went by in a blur of frustration and boredom. My car was impounded and searched, and when informed they had a warrant to search Caffeine Central I was allowed to call Nando so he could meet them there and let them in. I was informed my arraignment was scheduled for 3:30 the next afternoon. I told the police I would act as my own lawyer at the hearing.

Even if the food in the city jail had been good, which it wasn't, I still would have passed on breakfast after I read *The Oregonian* the next morning. The headline screamed "Radio celebrity Larry Vincent brutally slain." When the article got around to me, I broke out in another cold sweat.

> Attorney Calvin Claxton III from Dundee was arrested at the scene on suspicion of murder. Police spokesperson Andrea Clark pointed out there was apparently bad blood between Claxton and Vincent, who had criticized Claxton on his radio program for his defense of Daniel Baxter, the accused killer of restaurateur Mitchell Conyers. Claxton is a material witness in that murder case. Clark said Claxton was also a witness in the death of lobbyist Hugo Weiman, which had been declared a suicide. She said the police were investigating a possible connection between these incidents and the murder of Vincent. Claxton is being held at the Multnomah County Jail and could not be reached for comment.

Well, I told myself, the Portland police had done their homework on me, I'll give them that. There was a connection all right, I said to myself, but it wasn't *me*. I felt a sense of utter despair. How could I ever untangle this mess and clear my name if I was taken off the street? And what about Picasso? What would happen to him? Larry Vincent was our ace in the hole for blowing up the case against him. And now Vincent was dead.

It was a dark night of the soul, and it was first thing in the damn morning.

After lunch two guards came to escort me to an interview room. I was a little surprised when they didn't place me in manacles. I sat alone in the room for ten minutes or so, and then in walked pinched face—his name was Handras—followed by my old buddy, Lieutenant Scott. We exchanged greetings and after clearing his throat, Scott said, "There have been some developments in the Vincent murder case."

There was something about the look on Handras' face—like his best friend just died—that caused my pulse to tick up a beat.

Scott went on, "We received an anonymous tip this morning. The caller said he knew who had killed Larry Vincent, and it wasn't you. Said it was a guy named Seth Foster. Foster's Mitch Conyers' stepbrother, it turns out."

I stiffened involuntarily and nodded. "Right. I met him once at the Happy Angus."

"Anyway, the call came into the central precinct, so me and Jones went over to talk to Foster, you know just a routine chat, doing Handras here a favor. But the guy was bruised and scratched up. Claimed his business partner could vouch for his whereabouts the night before. He seemed a little squirrelly, so we took him in for a few more questions and to get a set of prints. We matched his prints to the prints in Vincent's houseboat in a New York minute. They were all over that room, nice bloody ones."

I tried to maintain professional decorum, but broke into a big, stupid grin instead.

"So we confronted Foster with what we had, and he cracked like an egg. Gave us a full confession. Said it was self-defense, that Vincent attacked him and he fought back."

"We'll see about that," Handras chimed in.

"So, you're dropping the charges against me?"

"Yes, and on behalf of the Portland Police Bureau, I'd like to apologize for what we put you through. We hope there're no hard feelings." Scott stuck out his hand, and I shook it. Handras didn't offer a hand. Taking a lawyer down on a murder rap was probably close to a wet dream for him, and Seth Foster had screwed it all up.

Oh, enjoy this, I said to myself. *The police just formally apologized to you. This is what they do when they mistakenly arrest a lawyer.* I said, "Does that include the concealed weapon charge?" What the hell, might as well go for a clean sweep. I didn't have a permit to carry the Glock, afterall.

Handras started to say something, but Scott waved him off. "We need to talk about that, but not now." He turned to Handras. "Will you give us a few moments, detective?"

After Handras left the room Scott took his glasses off and rubbed his temples, before cleaning them on his sleeve and putting them back on. The lines in his forehead looked like crevasses on an ice field in the harsh overhead light, and the only color in his face was from the tiny blood vessels cross-hatching his nose. "So, here you are again, right in the middle of a crime scene. What is it with you?"

I shrugged. "What can I say? I'm having a bad summer."

"Why do I have the feeling you know more about this case than you told Handras? What was the beef between Vincent and Foster anyway? Foster clammed up after he admitted to killing Vincent."

I was caught. If I talked, I'd give away the defense that was starting to form around Picasso. On the other hand, I could sow some seeds of doubt in the mind of the lead detective on the case. Scott was a tough bastard, but I sensed he might listen. I said, "Foster confronted Vincent because he suspected that Vincent had killed his stepbrother, Mitch Conyers."

Scott sat back in his chair like I'd slapped him. He eyed me through thick lenses. "Why would he think that?"

"Because Conyers was blackmailing Vincent, that's why. I think Foster went to confront him, and things got out of hand. Foster's got a nasty temper."

"How would he know about this blackmail?"

"I'm not sure," I answered, which wasn't a complete lie. "He was close to Conyers and must have put two and two together."

"How do *you* know about this?"

"I have reason to believe Conyers had information that would be very damaging to Larry Vincent if it became public."

"What information?"

I smiled and shook my head. "I can't reveal that. Attorney-client privilege."

"Why didn't Foster tell any of this to Handras?"

"My guess is he didn't want to sully his stepbrother's reputation, although I think his attorneys will talk him out of such a display of loyalty."

"Is there any hard evidence to back this up?"

"I have no idea what Foster knows." I didn't have any idea, and I feared whatever he knew was not enough to directly link Vincent to Conyers' death. More dots needed connecting, and this wouldn't be easy now that Vincent was dead.

"What about *you*? What do you know?"

I shrugged. "Not as much as I'd like. Do you ever listen to Larry Vincent's show on KPOC?"

Scott waived a hand dismissively. "Nah, I don't listen to that right-wing crap."

"Yeah, but you know Vincent had been on a one man crusade to convict Danny Baxter without a trial. In light of what's just happened, I'd say that's pretty interesting."

Scott said, "Well, we'll see how this all plays out with Foster. Meantime, your boy Baxter is still looking good for Conyers' murder as far as I'm concerned. It's gonna take a boatload of contrary evidence to turn that case around."

A hot flower of anger bloomed in my gut and rose to my chest. It wasn't directed at Scott so much. Hell, he was just doing his job. It was directed at this whole, frustrating situation. All I could think to say was, "We'll see about that."

Chapter Thirty-five

Two days after I walked out of jail Picasso was arraigned for the first degree murder of Mitchell Conyers and ordered held without bail.

"What happened to you?" Picasso asked. It was a week later, and I was visiting him in an interview room at the Multnomah County Jail. A faint scent of body odor left by the previous occupants hung in the air, and one of the overhead fluorescent bulbs flickered annoyingly. Alicia Cole was scheduled to meet with us but had a conflict at the last minute.

I sat down across from him, put my briefcase down and pointed at the bare spot on my head. "You mean this? I, uh, went another round with the Russian cage fighter."

"You're kidding!" He exclaimed with a grin he couldn't force back. "Are you okay? What the hell happened?"

I told him about the second fight. When I described how Semyon and I had somehow made peace, Picasso shook his head at me, "Don't be too sure, Cal. He might change his mind about you after trying to eat through a straw for a month."

I shrugged. "How are you feeling?" His right arm was in a thick cast and sling, and his skin looked pale against a bright orange jump suit that sagged on his thin frame. But his eyes were clear and alert.

"Like Joey used to say, 'Everyday's a holiday.' Any luck with the art supplies?"

I took a small sketch pad and a special issue ballpoint mounted on a pliable plastic shaft from my briefcase and handed them to him. "That's the biggest pad they permit, and the only kind of pen you're allowed to have."

He bent the shaft back and forth playfully. "Too bad. I was planning to use a pen to break out of here, but thanks anyway." He shot the flickering fluorescent light an annoyed look, opened the pad and put pen to paper. "If I can't draw I'm going to go nuts," he added without looking up. "And I'm worried about my mural. Is it okay?"

"It's fine. Your posse's taking good care of it." I handed him a photo. "Here, they wanted me to give you this." It was a picture of them kneeling in front of the mural, clowning around in various poses.

He laughed. "Where's Caitlin?"

"She wasn't around that day. She lost the apartment, you know. She's, uh, hanging around a lot more with her old family, I hear."

He dropped the pen and massaged his forehead with his free hand. "Shit, that figures. She's probably using again and God knows what else." He closed his eyes and sighed. "She had a shot," he said, more to himself than me.

"I know. I guess some people have to hit bottom hard before they figure things out. But don't worry, Doc's not giving up on her." What I didn't tell him, of course, was what Doc had told me—that Picasso was probably the only person Caitlin ever listened to outside her "family."

We both fell silent. People shuffled by in the hall outside the room, and we heard a string of expletives followed by a loud, "Pipe down." Picasso focused on something on the wall behind me for the longest time. "Well," he said, finally, "at least she's free to go wherever she wants."

"Hey," I said, "don't get down. We're going to get you out of here."

"But that dude killing the shock jock's a big setback, right?"

I nodded. "Yeah, it's harder to prove a dead man did something, but not impossible."

"What the hell happened?"

"From what Jessica Armandy was willing to tell me, Seth Foster went storming over to Vincent's houseboat after she told him about the blackmail plot. He was going to get some answers, he told her. She said, 'I knew he had a temper, but I never dreamed he'd kill the guy.'"

"How did Armandy find out about Vincent?"

I must have looked pretty sheepish as I paused to put an answer together. By this time, he was sketching again. "I, uh, told her about him. I was hoping she could link him directly with Conyers somehow. It didn't quite work out that way."

He looked up from his sketch pad. "Jesus, Cal. You set the whole thing off."

I nodded. "I know. I screwed up. Should've kept my mouth shut."

He brushed my comments off with his free hand. "Don't beat yourself up, man. If Armandy didn't know what that dude was going to do, how the hell were you supposed to know?"

"There's more to the story," I went on. "Turns out Vincent had an airtight alibi the day Conyers was killed. He was in Seattle doing a guest appearance. Lieutenant Scott called me last night to break that cheery bit of news."

Picasso's face clouded over. "Oh, man. Vincent getting killed is one thing, but having an alibi. That's a clincher. I'm toast."

I put a cautionary hand up. "Yeah, that was my first reaction, too, but then it hit me—Vincent didn't have the *cajones* to kill anyone himself. He hired people to do his dirty work. Just look at how he handled the scandal with Sherrill Blanchard. And that alibi seems way too convenient. He's out of town exactly one day, the day Conyers was killed."

"So, you think he used a hit man or something?"

"Yeah, that's exactly what I think." I shook my head and made a face. "I should have thought of it a long time ago."

"But the hit man's probably long gone by now."

"Not necessarily. He doesn't know we've figured this out. That gives us an advantage."

I tried to leave him with some hope, but when time was up, I could see the concern lingering in Picasso's eyes. Who could blame him? After all, the existence of a hit man was mostly conjecture at this point, and he knew that as well as I.

When I was in my car I looked again at the sketch he'd torn off and handed to me as I was leaving the interview room. "Here," he said, "this is for you. No extra charge." It was a deft rendering of me, and he'd caught me looking sheepish. I could only laugh and shake my head.

That afternoon I had a meeting with Cynthia Duncan and Alicia Cole in Cole's office. The news from Cynthia wasn't good. Sherrill Blanchard wasn't willing to talk about what had happened between her and Larry Vincent. Cole asked, "Now that Vincent's dead, do you think she'll change her mind?"

"I don't know," Cynthia answered. "At the moment, she's still not returning my phone calls."

"Blanchard's cooperation would be useful in Picasso's defense," Cole continued. "It'll bolster the blackmail claim, which provides an alternative theory for Conyers' murder." As she said this, both Cole and I looked at Cynthia.

Cynthia's jaw flexed. "Don't worry. I'll get her to talk. The truth needs to be told about this creep. Right now, he's being treated like some martyred hero. It's disgusting."

The conversation swung to Seth Foster next. I asked Alicia, "When are they going to let you depose him?"

"I'm getting the run around on that," she answered. "He's not talking except to claim self-defense and the DA's still not sure whether to charge him with manslaughter or murder one. In any case, I haven't heard a whiff of anything to suggest he's saying he killed Vincent to avenge his stepbrother's murder. That would be great for us, but I'm not sure we can count on it."

That evening I was supposed to have dinner with Anna. She'd promised to cook. But at about 5:30 she called and said she was snowed under with a report due to her board the next morning. I told her she still had to eat, and that Archie and I would bring something to her office.

At 6:30 that evening I stood in front of the clinic with a hot pizza balanced on my palm, the box radiating warmth and smells that had Archie salivating despite the fact that I'd just fed him. When Anna opened the door, I handed her a cold six-pack of Mirror Pond. "Here. A couple of these will enhance your report writing ability. Guaranteed."

She took the beer and laughed, eyeing the pizza. "Sizzle Pie, my favorite order out, how did you know?" She kissed me on the cheek and patted Arch on the head. "Come in, I'm starving." Strands of gold-streaked hair lay looped across her forehead, and her eyes shone like translucent blue ice above darkened half-moons of weariness.

"That's enough! I've got to stay awake tonight." I was pouring a Mirror Pond into a plastic cup for her. Archie had settled in at her feet.

I handed her a slice of pizza on a paper plate. "Can't your board cut you some slack? I mean, you're head doc and head administrator at the same time. Something's gotta give."

She rolled her beautiful, tired eyes. "The board members are all busy people. Rescheduling is *not* an option."

She nibbled some cheese off the pizza and took a sip of beer. "How're your plumbing skills?"

I eyed her warily. "Uh, severely limited. What's the problem?"

"Oh, we've got a u-trap under the sink in the examining room that's leaking. And the toilet in the back keeps running. A plumber will charge me two hundred bucks just to walk across the threshold. I'd rather spend that money on my patients. God, I miss Howard, even if he was a pain in the backside. That man could fix anything."

"Huh," I said. "I forgot about him. Krebbs, wasn't it? Howard Krebbs?"

Anna nodded.

"He never came around again after you had that falling out?"

"Never saw him again. You know, he was all pissed off that I was standing by Picasso. It was funny, he worked around here as a volunteer, but I never had the feeling he had any empathy or compassion for the kids we serve. He always seemed kind of put off by them."

I set the slice of pizza that was halfway to my mouth back on the plate and leaned forward. A couple of gears in my head meshed. "When did he start working here?"

"Around mid June, I guess. He just showed up one day. Said he was from Seattle and between jobs, that he just wanted to help out. I offered to pay him minimum wage, but he told me he would donate his time. I couldn't believe my luck. He was a gift from the economic gods."

"Mid-June. That would be, what, three weeks or so after Nicole Baxter's memorial service, right?"

She nodded, her eyes widening. "Yes, and about the same amount of time before Conyers was killed. You don't think he had anything —"

"I don't know, but my latest theory is Larry Vincent hired someone to kill Conyers. Howard was on the inside here, and the timing's pretty good. He could have easily had Milo Hartung deliver the fake note to Picasso, taken the screwdriver from Picasso's backpack, and killed Conyers with it. Was he around the day of the murder? That would be June 26."

Anna turned her chair around and pulled her calendar up on her computer screen. "Let's see. Oh, of course, I remember now. I asked him to come in that morning to replace some fluorescent bulbs in the examination room. I was anxious to get that done because I was expecting guests from the mayor's office and planning a brief tour."

"Was he around that afternoon?"

She paused for a moment, tapping a folded index finger on her lips. "No. He left right after he changed the bulbs. That would have been 10:30, maybe, no later than eleven."

I nodded. "That fits. Conyers was killed that afternoon."

Her eyes enlarged again. "And Milo? You think he killed Milo that night?"

"It would have been pretty easy, given Milo's drug habit."

"But it seems so bizarre," Anna said. "I mean, why didn't Vincent just hire someone to go out and shoot Conyers, if he wanted to get rid of him? Why go to all the trouble of a frame-up?"

I smiled and nodded. "I've asked myself the same question a dozen times. Look, Vincent wanted to get rid of Conyers, because he was tired of paying blackmail, right? He knew that he'd run the risk of becoming a prime suspect if the cops found out about that, and Vincent had no way of knowing who else might know. So, he would need a foolproof set up and a rock-solid alibi. Along comes a young, scary looking homeless man who attacks Conyers, threatens to kill him, and it all lands on the front page of *The Oregonian*. Voila. Vincent saw his chance and jumped on it."

Anna said, "Oh, my God. And he couldn't do it alone, because he needed an alibi."

"Right. He was conveniently out of town that day. Plus, he could use the bully pulpit of his radio show to put pressure on the justice system to rush to judgment on Picasso." I picked up a lined yellow pad and a pen from her desk and said, "Now, tell me everything you can remember about this guy."

We went back over Howard Krebb's activities at the clinic, his comings and goings, including the exact date he started work and when he left, and his relationships with her staff. There were none to speak of, except that she had seen him talking to Milo Hartung a couple of times. He hadn't revealed anything whatsoever about his personal life either, nor had he left any personal items behind except for a single deck of well worn playing cards. On a few occasions, Anna had seen him playing solitaire when things were slow.

"Did you run a background check on him?" I asked next.

Anna looked embarrassed for a moment. "No. I should have, but I didn't. He was a volunteer, and I didn't want to go through the time and expense. I needed him right away. Background checks take weeks."

"What about an address?"

She pulled up a file on her computer screen. "Uh, I have an address, no phone number." She wrote it down on a note pad, tore the sheet off and handed it to me. "Are you going to talk to him?"

"Not at the moment, but I'm going to check him out, see if he's still in town."

Anna's face showed concern. "What if he finds out you're investigating him?"

I smiled. "Well, right now he's just a gleam in my eye. Don't worry, I'll be careful."

Right.

Chapter Thirty-six

"Are you sure you gave me the right address for Krebbs?" I was sitting in my car talking to Anna at the address she'd given me in Gresham, a blue collar town just east of Portland. "Archie and I got a little restless, so we drove over to have a look at his place, you know, just to scope it out. It's a motel. The kind you rent by the hour. It cost me twenty bucks to get the attendant to tell me Krebbs isn't staying there."

I read the address back to her.

A few moments later, she came back on the phone. "Yes, that's the address I gave you. Maybe he's moved."

"That's a possibility. I asked the attendant to look back in June, and he just laughed. I don't think they're real big on record keeping at this place."

Back at my apartment still later that night, I called Anna again. "It's me again. I know you're busy, but are you sure it's Krebbs with a double b? I'm not finding a Howard Krebbs spelled that way anywhere in Oregon. There's a Millard Krebbs in La Grande, but he's eighty-nine years old. There are a couple of Krebs with one b, but no Howards, and none in the Portland metropolitan area."

"Yes, I'm sure that's how he spelled it," she answered. "How about looking in Seattle? He said he'd moved down from there. Maybe he's staying with a friend or relative now, so he hasn't established an address yet."

"There's a handful of Krebs with one b, but none with a double b in Seattle. I checked."

"That's strange. Maybe your friend Nando can locate him. I imagine a PI like him has a better database than the computer white pages."

"Yeah, I can do that," I answered. What I didn't say was that Nando's searches cost money. But after I hung up, I reluctantly called him and explained the situation.

"So, here's what we've got," Nando said after I finished— "Howard K-r-e-b-b-s with no middle initial, white male, approximate age forty to forty-five, previous address, somewhere in Seattle, no phone number, no Social Security number, no known place of employment, no photograph, right?"

"That's it." I exhaled a breath. "Here's the thing, Nando. If this guy's really a hit man hired by Vincent, then you can bet his name isn't Howard Krebbs, and he doesn't live in Gresham. So, who I really need to find is the guy who *said* he was Howard Krebbs when he worked at the clinic. How in the hell do I do that?"

There was a long pause. "If he used the name, he probably knew it was reasonably safe to do so, and since he was volunteering to work, he would have had a Social Security number, just in case the doctor asked for one. Do you agree?"

"Yeah, you're right, although the Doc didn't ask for his Social Security number."

"Did the police interview him after the murder?"

"Yes, briefly, I think. There was no reason to suspect him of anything."

"Then I think this person purchased his identity from someone, an identity that would stand up to a certain amount of scrutiny. It is not difficult to buy such an identity in this town."

"Do you know who's in the business?" I asked, my pulse quickening.

Nando sighed like the weight of the world just landed on his shoulders. "Yes, I know these people, but they have the highest business ethics."

I suppressed a laugh. "Meaning?"

"Meaning they do not divulge information about their clients."

"It's nice to know there's still honor among thieves. You can't do anything?"

He sighed again. "I do have a contact in the industry who owes me a favor. Perhaps I could prevail upon him, but it could be expensive."

My turn to sigh. "Can you just find out if we're on the right track without breaking me?"

"I will do my best, my friend. It would help if I had a picture of this man."

I paused for a moment. "You know, I think I can solve that problem. Give me a day to come up with something."

I called Alicia Cole next. She told me she was visiting Picasso the next morning to go over his account of the day of the murder one more time. I explained the situation surrounding Howard Krebbs and the fact that Anna didn't have a photo of him. I told her Picasso could undoubtedly make an accurate sketch of the man from memory, and she agreed to ask him.

I picked up the sketch around noon the next day. It looked dead-on to me, but I'd only seen the man a couple of times. I stopped by the clinic to show it to Anna. She laughed and said, "That looks more like Howard than Howard. What are you going to do with this?"

"First, I'm going to borrow your scanner and shoot a copy to Nando. And there are other people I want to show it to, people connected to Larry Vincent."

It turned out that Xavier Bidarte—Nicole Baxter's source for the Vincent exposé—happened to be in Portland that night visiting his new steady girlfriend, Cynthia Duncan. I stopped by her apartment and showed him Picasso's sketch. Dead end there. He told me he'd never seen the man.

The next day Archie and I drove over to see the retired KPOC station manager, Arnie Katz. I found him in his garage again, painting the trim on an intricate birdhouse that had a familiar profile. "Looks like 1600 Pennsylvania Avenue to me," I said as I entered the garage.

He looked up and smiled, but his expression changed abruptly when he recognized who I was. He said, "You're the guy that found Vincent's body. I saw your picture in the paper. You're not a writer, you're an *attorney.*" He spat the last word out like it was a bad clam or something. "What the hell do you want now?"

I apologized for not being completely honest and tried to show him the sketch of Krebbs, but he told me to get the hell off his property. I tried to argue, but he was having none of it. As I was leaving, I set a copy of the sketch on his workbench along with one of my cards. "Please take a look at this sketch, Mr. Katz. If you recognize this man, contact me. It's a matter of life and death."

I took the Ross Island Bridge back over to the west side of Portland, stopped at a market on Macadam and bought two bottles of water, a turkey sandwich, and a twelve ounce black coffee. Out in the parking lot I poured Archie some water in a dish I kept in the car, and he eagerly lapped it up before hopping in the back seat. I found a parking space on Macadam that afforded me a clear view of the KPOC parking lot across the street. I began eating the sandwich, but it was barely edible. I pulled the turkey from the second half of it and gave it to Archie. He loved it.

Several people exited the station around noon, but not the person I was looking for. I groaned, thinking maybe she didn't go out for lunch. One thing was certain. I wasn't going to show my face inside the station for fear of another reaction like Katz's. To my relief, Shelly—the receptionist with the very long legs—came out at 12:25 and got into a white Honda Civic. I followed her to a sub shop, and when she got out of her car I got close enough to call out to her. "Hi, Shelly. We meet again."

She looked puzzled for a moment before recognizing me. Her hand went to her mouth. "Oh, my God, you're the writer, the guy they thought killed Larry. Then they found out some other person did it."

I nodded, relieved she apparently didn't read the newspaper very carefully. "Yes, it was a terrible experience, and I'm sorry about the loss of your friend and colleague."

Her expression hardened like stone. "I don't wish a dead man any ill will, but he was no friend of mine. Couldn't keep his hands to himself, if you know what I mean."

I nodded. "Yeah, I heard he was like that." I pulled out the sketch, and showed it to her. "I'm wondering if Larry Vincent knew this man or if you ever saw him around the station?"

She examined the sketch then looked back at me a little more skeptically. "Is this guy wanted for something?"

I laughed. "No, I'm just trying to identify him for background purposes."

She scrunched up her nose, little girl fashion, "Well, sorry, I don't know who he is." Then she added, "If you want, I'll put the sketch up on the bulletin board at the station for you. What's his name?"

"Uh, no thanks. I'd rather you keep this to yourself. You know, confidentiality and all that."

"We have photographs of all our former and current employees. I could look for him in the files, if you want."

I hesitated for a moment, but I had a feeling I could trust her. "Okay, I'd appreciate that, but please don't show the sketch around, and don't say anything about what you're doing for me. This kind of research is highly confidential."

She nodded solemnly.

I fished a card out of my wallet and jotted my cell phone number on the back. "If you find anything, give me a call."

She batted her mascara-laden eyelashes at me and smiled. Her eyes were a pretty periwinkle blue, and one was slightly larger than the other. "And what if I *don't* find anything?"

I gave her a puzzled look.

"Can I still call you?"

I chuckled and even might've blushed a little. "I'm very flattered, Shelly, but I'm, uh, sort of seeing someone." It sounded a little strange when I said it, but, yeah, it was the truth. I *was* seeing someone. Sort of.

Nando called just as I got back to Caffeine Central. "I had to twist someone's arm *very* hard, but I believe I have made a bingo for you. The man in the sketch you sent me purchased the Howard Krebbs identity package."

"When?"

"In June. I do not have an exact date."

I felt a rush of excitement. "That's a bingo alright! Did you get a name?"

"Unfortunately, no. The man paid in cash and did not give a name. They seldom do."

"Nando, you're a Cuban miracle!"

He chuckled, a deep baritone resonance. "I don't think the person who gave me that information would necessarily agree with you, but I accept the compliment nonetheless."

I knew the answer to the next question, but I asked it anyway. "This is good enough to go to the cops with. I don't suppose you have or could imagine getting any hard evidence to support the claim?"

Nando's tone turned brittle, almost hard. "Calvin, I already crossed the line here to save you money and will have to watch my back for some time. There is nothing more I can do."

"Okay. Understood. And thanks, Nando."

In the immortal words of Mark Knopfler—"Sometimes you're the windshield, sometimes you're the bug." Well, I was feeling like the windshield when I leashed up Archie and headed for the clinic. I was anxious to tell Anna what Nando had told me.

We caught her in her office, and before I could say a word she said, "Cal, I've found something."

She handed me a small datebook. "I was cleaning out a cabinet in the records room when I found this. It was in a mangy old sweater that Milo used to wear. I know the datebook is his because I gave it to him. He kept screwing up his schedule. I thought it might help him."

I glanced down at the book but kept quiet, knowing she had more to tell me.

"Look at this, she said, taking the book back and opening it to the month of June. She pointed to an entry on June 26. In a bold, legible hand, it read—9:00 HK-DND.

I smiled broadly. "Nice work. Looks like Milo was meeting with Howard Krebbs and someone else just two nights before the murder. Who's DND?"

Anna shrugged. "I don't have a clue."

"You think Picasso might know?"

"Maybe. It would be worth asking him."

"For sure," I replied. We went back over everything we knew about Howard Krebbs one more time, but nothing else surfaced.

That night Anna *did* cook dinner, which was a good thing, because I was tapped out. Actually, I supplied most of the directions, and she did the heavy lifting, all the while telling me cooking was not her forté. She had brought a couple of nice steaks, baking potatoes, fresh mushrooms, asparagus, and a bottle of reserve Carabella pinot noir.

When she finished trimming the mushrooms, I said, "Make sure the butter's nice and hot when you sauté those 'rooms. It'll sear the juices in. And if you want a dynamite sauce for the asparagus, try some Dijon, a little mayo, juice from half a lemon, and salt and pepper. Simple, but delicious."

She smiled and shook her head. "How did you learn to cook like this, anyway?"

"It was either learn to cook or eat out all the time. I couldn't afford the latter. Plus, there aren't that many restaurants I want to eat at. Call me picky."

She chuckled as she put the mushrooms in the skillet and began stirring them. Without looking up, she said, "Picasso told me about your wife. I'm so sorry, Cal."

I squirmed in my chair. "Uh, thanks. I'm, uh, it was a long time ago."

She looked up then, her face almost pleading. "How did you do it?"

"Do what?"

She turned to face me. "How did you put it behind you?"

I dropped my eyes and studied the pattern on the linoleum floor for a few moments, then looked up. "The truth is, you never put it behind you. Not completely. Time's your best friend. You have to find a way to forgive yourself, Anna. That's the key."

She nodded, and I watched helplessly as her eyes welled up. "Time's no friend of mine," she said in a thick voice. "It's like everything happened yesterday, you know? Every time I get up in the morning, it's there to greet me."

"You have to let it go. What happened to your brother was tragic and unfair and horrible, but it wasn't your fault. Your brother would want you to move on."

I got up and took her in my arms, and she cried until my shirtsleeve was wet. She finally pulled her head up, laughed and said, "Shit, I burned the damn mushrooms."

The dinner was still delicious, and we ate in fine spirits thanks to Anna's emotion-clearing cry. After dinner, she looked at me with wide, expectant eyes and asked, "How would you like to come to Norway with me?"

It was close to the last thing in the world I expected her to say. "*Norway?*"

Her eyes burned like a couple of blue flames. "Yes. I haven't been back in a decade. I want to show you the fjords. The Geirangerfjord's so beautiful, Cal. It'll bring you to your knees."

I smiled at the thought. "You, uh, can get away?"

"Yes, I think so. My contract covers a stand-in for two weeks a year, but I've never taken any time off."

I shuddered at what it would cost with the weak dollar and all, but there was no way I was turning that invitation down. "Sure. Wonderful." Two weeks with Anna and no other distractions was almost more than I could imagine. I picked up my wine glass and said, "As soon as we get Picasso out of jail." Our glasses met over the table with a soft clink of crystal.

"And his mural is finished," she added with a smile that lifted my heart.

Was it the company, the wine? Suddenly everything seemed possible, a feeling I hadn't experienced in a very long time. I was wondering if perhaps Anna felt the same way. But I also wondered how long it would last. After all, when things start to go well, that's when I begin to worry.

Anna stayed the night and was up early. Without lifting my slightly hungover head from the pillow, I said, "Where are you going?"

"Home," she said. "I have a busy day planned, and I want to get a jog in before work."

I groaned. "Wait, I'll go with you."

"That's not necessary," she answered, predictably.

I sat up and scratched my head with both hands. Anna was stubborn as hell, and sometimes it irked me. "Yes, it is," I countered with some irritation in my voice. "It's dark out there, and you walked over from the clinic last night, right?"

She smiled and said, "Oh, come on, Cal. I walk around Old Town all the time when it's dark."

"I know, but work with me here. I spent yesterday afternoon showing Howard Krebbs' sketch around Portland. Word could have somehow gotten back to him."

She looked at me, her smile fading rapidly. "You think he might try to do something?"

I shrugged. "I doubt it. He probably left town a long time ago. But I'll drive you anyway." I looked at Archie and said, "You up for a ride, big boy?"

The parking lot adjacent to Anna's condo was well lit and deserted. I parked and before I could get out, she moved her body against mine and kissed me. "Remind me," she said with a teasing gleam in her eye, "Why did we get out of bed so fast?"

I brushed a lock of hair from her eye and smiled. "I believe it was your idea. Something about the busy day you have planned."

"Oh, you're right." She kissed me again and pushed me away playfully. Then she added, "Tonight I want you to dream of fjords."

"What would Freud say about that?"

She laughed as she got out of the car. "He would say you have repressed your libido long enough, that you need intense, one-on-one therapy with a trained professional."

We laughed together. "Oh, and who might this trained professional be?"

"Me. Of course."

We joined hands and started off toward her condo. Birds in the maple trees along the path cheered the sunrise, and the thin cloud cover glowed in the east like lavender smoke.

If I had to chose the happiest hour of my life that morning with Anna Eriksen would rank right up there.

Chapter Thirty-seven

Alicia Cole managed to get me in to see Picasso two days later. The overhead fluorescent light still flickered, and the air in the interview room still smelled of body odor. Picasso was brought in by a burly guard with thick forearms and a tiny island of dark whiskers below his lip. The coral snake tattooed on Picasso's neck stood out in bold relief against his pale skin, and he looked like a scarecrow in his jump suit. "Are you okay? You look like you're starving," I blurted out.

He rolled his eyes, which seemed to have retreated noticeably into their sockets. "It's the institutional food," he said, his voice lacking energy, "that's code for it tastes like shit."

"Well, you have to eat," I shot back. "Your body's still on the mend, you know."

He slowly shook his head. "I don't know, man. I'm not sure how long I can take it in this dump. The food's not the worst part. There's no *color* in here, and nothing's growing. It's just shades of fucking gray. That's all there is."

His eyes were flat, his sense of defeat palpable. He was just a boy, after all, a boy on the cusp of manhood, and his optimism had been tempered, if not crushed, long ago. Life could be unremittingly cruel, he knew that, and he had no illusions about his chances of beating the crime he was accused of. He was hated and feared in a town that was supposedly proud of its tolerant nature. What would the prospect of indefinite incarceration do to him? Hell, how would I act, facing something like that?

The thought of it gripped my gut like a cold hand and at the same time strengthened my resolve. I hadn't made a mistake. This is what I should be doing.

I opened my briefcase and handed him another small sketch pad. "Here. I figured you'd need another one of these. I've got good news. That sketch you made of Howard Krebbs really helped us." I went on to tell him what we discovered about the man posing as Krebbs and what we were doing to find him. This revived his spirits.

"Howard, or whatever his name is, is a weird dude," he said when I'd finished. "Pretty much kept to himself around the clinic. I always got a bad vibe from him, judgmental, you know, like he didn't approve of my lifestyle." Picasso laughed. "Shit, that would include half the people in Portland, come to think of it. But he was no stranger to the streets. He'd been around."

"How do you mean?"

"I don't know. He had an edge to him. I could sense it. The dude always wore long sleeve shirts. I figured nasty tats or needle marks, something he didn't want people to see."

"Did he ever say anything about his background, about being from Seattle or anything like that?"

"Nah, not to me." He chuckled. "Seattle? I doubt it."

I raised my eyebrows in a question.

"He came in one day out of the rain with an umbrella. Nobody in the Northwest uses an umbrella, man."

I nodded and smiled. It was true, umbrellas were a sign of weakness around here. I'd learned that lesson not long after I arrived from sunny California. "Well, if he is who we think he is, then you're probably right. He wouldn't be telling anyone where he was really from. What about Milo? Did they have any interaction?"

"Yeah, Milo was about the only one he talked to at the clinic besides Doc. You think he killed Milo, too?"

"Yeah, that's what I think happened. Let me ask you something. Doc found Milo's calendar the other day. On June 26—that would be two days before Conyers' murder—Milo had written down the initials HK and DND at 9:00 p.m. It looks like he was meeting Krebbs and someone with the initials DND that night. Any idea who that might be?"

Picasso looked up from the doodle on his sketch pad and considered the question. "DND? Doesn't mean anything to me."

I felt a stab of disappointment. "You're sure?"

"Yeah, but I don't know many of Milo's friends. You know, if you can find her you might ask Caitlin. There's a guy named Fish in her family. He hung with Milo back when he was dealing smack. Maybe Fish knows who DND is.

"Is Fish his real name?"

"Nah, I don't think so. I heard he came from the coast—Astoria, I think. He used to fish with his dad all the time, or some shit like that. Caitlin can find him."

I left that day disappointed Picasso didn't know anything about DND, but at least some energy had crept back in his voice, and I'd managed to extract a promise that he would eat more.

I drove back to Caffeine Central and picked up Archie, who did an excited little dance when he saw me. We walked over to the clinic and caught Anna in her office. "Got time for a walk?"

She glanced at her watch. "I've got forty-five minutes. What's up?"

I told her about my meeting with Picasso while Archie led us down Burnside toward the bridge, our best guess as to where Caitlin might be. We took the stairs to the underside of the structure and walked over to Ankeny Square. A group of kids were lounging next to Skidmore Fountain among a jumble of backpacks, sleeping bags, and assorted trash. We saw a couple of familiar faces but not Caitlin or any of her family members. Finally, Anna spotted one of the kids who guarded Picasso's mural, a thin boy with reddish dreadlocks and a baby face bearing wisps of an amber beard. He patted Arch on the head and said, "How's Picasso?"

Anna said, "He's doing fine, and he said to tell everyone guarding the mural that they rock."

The boy nodded then looked at me. "You gonna get him off?"

"We're working on it."

He spit between his teeth. "Yeah, well, good luck with that."

Anna said, "Have you seen Snuggles around?"

"She split, man. Took off with some old dude."

"Where'd she go?" Anna persisted.

He spit again. "L.A., I heard." He laughed with a coldness that belied his innocent looking features. "Thinks she's ready for prime time, but she isn't."

Anna shot a look at me, her eyes filled with pain, then back at the boy. "Are you sure she's gone?"

He laughed again. "Yep. Got herself a brand new pimp."

Anna turned away, her eyes filling with tears. I said, "Is Fish around?" The news about Caitlin hit me hard, too, but I needed answers.

He nodded back toward the bridge. "He's back there, man. Sleepin' off a bad trip."

We found the kid called Fish—at least he mumbled that was his name when I shook him awake. But I couldn't get anything else out of him. Anna gave me a concerned look, and kneeling down beside him took his pulse and felt his brow. His cheeks were sunken, his complexion sallow—the kind of kid you knew had been on the streets too long. His eyes opened to slits, and he snarled, "Go away, goddamn it," before turning his head away from us.

Anna got up, shaking her head. "Well, at least he hasn't overdosed. He's okay, but we're wasting our time. We'll have to come back."

As we were leaving the kid with dreadlocks said, "Told you Fish was out of it."

I turned to him. "We're looking for a guy named DND. Do you know him?"

The kid scrunched his brow and shook his head. "Can't help you."

Anna said, "The initials D-N-D, do they mean anything to you?"

He scratched his ear and furrowed his forehead. "Uh, yeah, maybe. There's a poker club over on the east side called the

DND. I think it stands for the Down n' Dirty, or something like that." He chuckled. "Cards are just a sideline there. Drugs are the main business."

Anna and I walked back to the clinic in silence. A part of me was excited that at least I had a lead to follow up. The Down n' Dirty could be where Krebbs had met Milo that night. The deck of cards Krebbs left behind at the clinic lent some credence to that. Maybe somebody there would know him. At the same time, I was sick about Caitlin. Worse yet, I knew that the news devastated Anna. I tried to get her to talk about it on the way back, but she remained silent. I asked her to join me for dinner that night, and she told me she wanted to be alone.

My heart ached when I left the clinic that afternoon. This kind of stuff shouldn't be happening to young kids, I told myself for the umpteenth time.

I ate in, an uninspired meal of a blackened salmon steak, roasted red potatoes, and a green salad. Over a second glass of wine, I thought about going to the cops with what I had. After all, it wouldn't take them very long to discover what I already knew—that the name Howard Krebbs was a fake identity—and they had the resources to find the man behind the name and pull him in. But, on the other hand, I had no proof at all, and what's more, I'd established no connection between this man and Larry Vincent. Going to the cops was premature to say the least.

A visit to the Down n' Dirty Poker Club, on the other hand, struck me as a much better idea. I knew such an impulsive act entailed risk, but how else was I going to find this guy?

I decided to go there that night.

Chapter Thirty-eight

The Down n' Dirty Poker Club was in southeast Portland, smack in the middle of Felony Flats, one of the few neighborhoods in the city where the bars and clubs outnumber the espresso joints. If you crave a grande, half caf, soy milk frappuccino, Felony Flats is not your neighborhood. I parked in front of a closed bakery that had a sign in the window that said, "I am the Bread of Life…John 6:35." The poker club was directly across the street, a low, brick structure with a freshly painted exterior trim and a sign on the roof that was blinking Texas Hold'em in red neon.

Two young guys in skinny jeans and hooded sweatshirts arrived at the club about the same time I did. I waited and fell in behind them for a bit of cover, just in case Krebbs was in the house. But this was a serious poker-playing crowd; hardly anyone looked up to see who was coming in. I counted ten card tables as I worked my way to the back of the club where a fully stocked bar, a couple of giant flat screens, and two pool tables were located. I took a seat at the corner of the bar, next to where the waiters picked up their drink orders. This allowed me to view the entire room without being obtrusive.

I ordered a Mirror Pond and scanned the crowd for Krebbs, my memory of his facial features reinforced by Picasso's sketch. He had short-cropped black hair, a face that tapered to a sharp chin, and eyes made to look even paler by a beard so heavy it shadowed his face even after a close morning shave. I strained to remember the rest of him—a little shorter than me, stocky build, and, oh yeah, the tufts of black, wiry hair nested in his ears. I didn't expect Krebbs to be there, and as far as I could tell, he wasn't.

What now? The truth was, I really didn't have a plan.

I turned my attention to the doings at the bar. The short-haired, tattoo-less bartender wore a single gold loop in his right ear, but otherwise looked more like a college kid than a Felony Flats homie. Two working girls sitting across the bar eyed me momentarily as I took my seat, then continued their animated conversation with each other. Business was slow. Sorely lacking the nubile qualities so sought after by Jessica Armandy, the girls were in little danger of being recruited by her.

Two waiters covered the poker tables, a gangly kid with spiky hair and tattoos on his arms like the flames of hell, and a tall woman with short, dirty blond hair and a face that had been pretty once but had hardened with age like petrified wood. The bartender was an outgoing type and seemed to know an awful lot of the customers. When he brought my beer, he said, "Waiting for a table to open up?"

I nodded. "First time. Just getting the feel of the place." Then I added, "You seem to know a lot of people. Worked here long?"

"A year and a half. Saving up to go to college."

"Where?"

"Portland State. It's all I can afford. No college loans for me."

I nodded. "Smart man," then asked, "Is this mainly a local crowd?"

"Pretty much." He chuckled. "Not many people from other neighborhoods come into the Flats at night. They think we're a bunch of badasses, you know, urban rednecks."

It took me most of a beer to decide whether to chance showing Picasso's sketch of Krebbs to the bartender. I finally decided it was worth a try, and when business ebbed at the bar, I made my move. "I'm wondering if you could help me try to locate someone."

He took a fresh look at me. "You're not a cop, are you?"

I raised my hands, palms out, smiled, and shook my head. "No. I just want to talk to someone, a witness in a legal case. It's important to me. I could, uh, donate to your college fund."

His face brightened. "Okay, whataya got?"

I took the sketch of Krebbs from my coat pocket, unfolded it and slid it across the bar to him. He studied it for a few moments. I saw his Adam's apple bob as he swallowed. He looked up at me with an expression that had turned wary, and then his eyes shifted to someone behind me. He turned the sketch face down and pushed it back to me. "Sorry, can't help you," he responded with finality.

The blond waitress with the hard face stepped up to the bar from behind me and said to the bartender, "Two vodka martinis and an IPA, hon." I wondered if she'd seen the sketch. I couldn't be sure. In any case, I *was* sure the young bartender recognized the person in the sketch and had decided to keep his mouth shut. The waitress stood next to me, drumming her fingers as she waited for her order. I folded the sketch up and put it back in my pocket.

I finished my beer, left a twenty dollar bill on the counter, and got the hell out of there. My gamble had backfired, and I felt pretty damn foolish. Had I been compromised? For sure, if the bartender tells Krebbs I was looking for him. What was the chance my generous tip would persuade him not to? Slim to none, I figured.

But instead of heading back to Caffeine Central I drove my car behind the club and parked in the far corner of the small lot. What the hell, I decided, it was worth taking another crack at the bartender in a more private setting. While I waited, I stewed about how much money I'd be willing to part with for Krebbs' real name.

By 2:40 the parking lot was empty except for four cars and a Yamaha motorcycle that was tucked in against the building. At 2:50, it was down to one car and the motorcycle. The young bartender came out the back with the tall blond waitress. She got in the remaining car, and he got on the Yamaha. I followed him to a shabby apartment building off of Eighty-Second. He was locking up his motorcycle when I approached. It was pissing rain.

"It's me again. I'm pretty sure you know the guy in the picture I showed you. I'm still anxious to help you go to college."

He straightened up, peering at me though the half-pipe of a Blazers ball cap that was dripping rain water. "I told you, man, I don't know the guy."

"You sure? I could, uh, provide a scholarship, say two hundred dollars. All I need is a name."

He smiled in exasperation, shook his head, and wagged an open palm at me. "I could use the money, man, but there's no fucking way. What I can tell you is that you shouldn't mess around with certain people, if you get my drift. Now, leave me the fuck alone."

As he turned to leave, I said, "Do me a favor. Keep this to yourself." It never hurts to ask.

I had to return to my office in Dundee the next morning to meet with a client and then make a court appearance on a divorce case that afternoon. I had just cleared the Terwilliger curves on the I-5 when Nando returned an earlier call of mine. He listened patiently while I described my foray into Felony Flats and the poker club. When I finished, he said, "Hmm, this is not good, Calvin. If Krebbs hears of this, he will go further underground." There was another action he might take, of course, but Nando didn't mention it, and neither did I.

"I realize that. What can I say? It was a gamble."

"And you didn't show the picture to anyone else?"

I thought about the blond waitress for a moment, but I didn't think she saw anything. "Nah, just the bartender. I don't think he'll say anything, but who the hell knows? My guess is our guy came to Portland just to make the hit on Conyers. He hung out at the club for something to do at night. The word got around about him being a nasty dude."

"And the bartender would not talk."

"Right, not even for cold cash. Look, Nando, you think you could sniff around at the Down n' Dirty? Someone else must remember this guy."

"It is not a part of town that I have a great deal of contacts in. I will see what I can do. Meanwhile, you should exercise caution, Calvin. Perhaps you can stay at your Aerie for a while?"

"Nah, I'm not going to do that. I'm coming back to Portland tomorrow night. We're close to nailing this guy, Nando. I can feel it."

"You can?" was all he answered.

I had another reason for returning to Portland. I didn't want Anna to be alone, worrying about the disappearance of Caitlin. It was a painful blow, and I wanted to be there to support her any way I could. In fact, I realized, I liked being with Anna no matter what the reason.

I took it as a positive sign when she told me she was attending a lecture the next evening at the Schnitzer Concert Hall—on nano solar technology, of all things. We agreed to meet after the talk and grab a bite at a little joint on the South Park blocks, a long swath of majestic elms, fountains, and statues running through the heart of downtown. It was a balmy night, and the blocks were teaming with people. While we walked from the Schnitzer to the restaurant, I told her about my misadventure at the poker club.

"Howard a hired murderer?" she said when I finished. "I still can't get used to the idea. It gives me the creeps. What happens now?"

"We wait. Nando's going to make some inquiries at the Down n' Dirty."

She was excited by the lecture, and during dinner she described how nano particles were going to reduce the cost of solar panels and save the world from frying in greenhouse gases. Afterwards, we walked back to Caffeine Central for a nightcap. It wasn't until we were settled on the couch with glasses of wine that she broached the topic I'd stayed away from all night. "I found out the name of the man Caitlin left with," she said.

"You did?"

"Yes. His name's Derek Lewis, and he's probably twenty-nine or thirty years old. A real bottom feeder." She hesitated for a moment. "And I did something terrible."

"What?"

"One of her friends told me his name. I told her I wouldn't tell anybody, but I lied."

I waited for her to continue.

"I went to the police with the information. If they pick them up, Lewis is going to be in a lot of trouble." She looked at me, her eyes pleading. "I just want her back, Cal. I don't care about my street cred."

I held her eyes, thinking of the deception I used to get Armandy to meet with me. "I don't know, but I suspect the truth doesn't mind being sacrificed for the greater good once in a while, especially when kids are involved."

She leaned her head on my shoulder and sighed heavily. "You're such a pragmatist. Thanks. I needed that." The room fell silent except for the sound of Archie breathing in the corner. A car passed by down on Couch and we could hear the thump, thump of a bass speaker.

I said, "It hurts to see a sweet kid like her screw up so badly. Doesn't make a lot of sense to me."

Anna sat back up. "It's not surprising she's not making rational choices. She's only sixteen and had to leave home because her mother was a meth addict and her stepfather was abusing her."

I sat there for a long time, chewing on that. Finally, I said, "Yeah, like Picasso says, 'Everybody on the street's got a story.'"

We talked about Caitlin and Picasso and all the kids out there on the streets. It was a conversation we'd had many times before, and we both knew there were no quick fixes and few happy endings. It was that night that I realized I had undergone a change. I came into this thing focused on Picasso, and now my concern had expanded to include *all* these lost kids. I had the good doctor to thank for that.

After a second glass of wine, Anna yawned, looked at her watch, and announced she was going home. I wanted her to stay, but I knew better than to argue. I checked my watch. It was nearly one. I said, "I'll drive you, no arguments." I walked over to the window and moved the blinds just enough to check the street. I saw no cars and nothing moved.

Anna raised her eyebrows and said, "You're taking this security thing more seriously."

I nodded. "I don't think Krebbs knows we're looking for him, but just in case." I excused myself and retrieved Nando's Glock from the bedroom. I tucked it in my belt so Anna couldn't see it. I knew how she felt about guns. Archie got up and stood by the door, wagging his stump of a tail and whimpering softly. I grabbed his leash. "Okay, Arch, you're in."

We hadn't gone more than two blocks when two cars fell in behind us. The first car turned onto Sixth from Davis, and I didn't see where the second car came from. When the first car followed us into the parking lot adjacent to Anna's condo, I tensed up. The car parked down from us, and when Anna unbuckled her seat belt, I extended my arm in front of her and said, "Wait a second."

A man got out with a ball cap on and carrying a thick briefcase. He hurried over to the path that led to Anna's building and disappeared into the shadows. I said, "Do you know that guy?"

Anna laughed. "Yeah, that's my neighbor Murray. He works weird hours."

I breathed a sigh of relief. Anna kissed me and said, "Thanks for the ride. Call me tomorrow."

"I'll walk you to your door," I insisted. She made a face but didn't argue.

It was past Archie's bedtime, so we left him dozing in the backseat. The gravel path that connected the lot to the building was lined on either side with trees and dense bushes, and owing to the spacing of the light poles, a short section of the path lay in deep shadow.

I didn't see anything in the shadowy section—not surprising since my eyes didn't fully adjust until we'd traversed it. I relaxed a little, that is, until I heard the crunch of gravel underfoot behind us. "Okay, folks," a calm male voice said, "I have a gun trained on your backs. Raise your hands where I can see them and keep your mouths shut."

He approached us, I felt the barrel of his gun against my neck, and then, just like that, he found the Glock and slipped it from my belt. So much for the protection of a handgun, at least in the hands of an amateur like me.

Anna said, "Is that you, Howard?"

Chapter Thirty-nine

The man came around to face us in the dim light. Anna sucked a breath. He wore a black knit cap, and his eyes were shadowed in their sockets, but I recognized that angular face and sharp chin. Howard Krebbs grinned out at us, light reflecting off the barrel of his gun.

He said, "Okay, we're going to go back to the parking lot. Just turn around slowly and walk. And keep your mouths *shut*. If you try anything, I'll shoot you both." He stepped in behind Anna. "Starting with Doc here."

Fear tightened around my throat like a noose. I tried to push down the sense of panic and think clearly. There's no question why we're being kidnapped, I told myself. The only question is—when will he kill us? If it's when we reach the parking lot, then I should make a desperate, probably suicidal, move right now. But if he wants to know how much we know, then we just might buy some time. I decided to wait, hoping against hope for the latter.

As we started toward the lot, I thought about Archie. If Krebbs marched us past my car, I might be able to call him out and create a distraction. Were the windows down? I wasn't sure. But that's stupid, I told myself. He's no attack dog and wouldn't go after Krebbs on my command. And by the time he figured out what was going on, it would be too late for him and us.

Krebbs took us to the opposite end of the lot, so the opportunity never presented itself. I was filled with fear but felt a sharp stab of sadness. What would become of my dog?

We stopped at a weather-beaten Chevy Malibu parked in the shadows. I was sure it was the second car I'd spotted that had been following us on our way here. Someone in the car must have been watching my apartment while Krebbs waited here in ambush. The door opened, and the tall blond waitress with the tough demeanor from the poker club got out, carrying a roll of duct tape. Her face was pulled into a kind of eerie half-smile, and when she glanced at me her eyes seemed glazed, like she was high on something. They exchanged the revolver and the tape, and while she held the gun on us, Krebbs crossed my wrists behind my back and taped them tightly before shoving me toward the Malibu.

The blond woman muttered, "Cell phones and keys." Apparently, she wasn't that whacked out.

"Right," Krebbs said. He patted us down, and after taking both phones and sets of keys, popped the trunk, looked at me and said, "Get in."

Anna said, "No, Howard! He can't breathe in there."

"Shut the fuck up," he shot back, glaring at her. Then he pushed me again. "Get in the trunk, or I'll hurt her. And listen, Claxton, Doc will be riding in the backseat with a gun in her side. If you make as much as a peep in there, she'll pay for it. Are we clear?"

I nodded, lifted one leg tentatively, then balanced a foot on the lip of the trunk and leaned forward. From behind, Krebbs lifted then shoved me hard with an audible grunt. I tumbled in face-first with my hands locked behind my back. The trunk lid came down with a thud. My face wound up jammed against the wiry carpet covering the floor of the trunk. It smelled like grease and dust, and it chafed my skin. Anna was right—I couldn't breathe, at least at first. Fighting to control the panic of near asphyxiation, I turned my head just enough to free up one nostril. Breath rhythmically, I told myself. Calm yourself.

I was terrified at this point, but anger dwarfed my fear.

The Malibu eased out of the parking lot and turned left, which meant we were headed north on Sixth Avenue. Desperate to control my fear, I tried to concentrate on where the car was taking us. We took another quick left, which must have been onto Glisan, then went ten or twelve blocks before heading north again. This had to put us on the west side of the 405. After another long stretch, we turned left and pulled into what felt like a driveway, made a right turn and stopped. I guessed we were somewhere in the light industrial area near the far corner of Northwest Portland, where the 405 intersects Route 30.

The car rocked slightly as the doors opened and thumped shut. I tensed up, waiting for the trunk lid to open, but nothing happened. I strained to hear what was going on outside but didn't pick up anything except perhaps the closing of another door. More time passed. It seemed an eternity. Bent at an awkward angle, my neck began to scream with pain. Sweat streamed into my eyes. I feared they would leave me locked in that tomb. Then my fear shifted to Anna. Now she was alone with that bastard. I felt a wave of shame. How could I have been so careless?

Anger and frustration seethed in me, and I narrowly beat back an urge to start flailing and kicking in rage and panic. Breathe! I told myself. Stay centered!

Another eternity passed. The pain in my neck was close to unbearable, my breathing more ragged with each breath. Hot tears of pain mingled with sweat and dripped from my eyes. Suddenly I heard the scraping of feet. The trunk lid popped open and cool, fresh air rushed in. Krebbs yanked me up and helped me out of the trunk while the blond held the gun on me.

They hustled me into the back door of a brick building, some kind of industrial site. A tattered sign at the door read, Bridgetown Roasters. Deliveries Only. I was pushed into a large room with two high windows on each exterior wall. The room was bare except for a small table and several chairs. I could see the outline of where machines of some kind had been bolted to the floor. The aroma of stale coffee hung in the room like a fog.

Anna was sitting in one of the chairs. Her hands were pulled back and taped to the chair stiles, and her feet were taped together, as well. Our eyes found each other, and I mouthed, "I'm sorry," as Krebbs slammed me down in a chair facing her. I expected to see fear in her eyes, but what I saw, instead, was cold Viking anger.

Krebbs taped me to the chair like Anna. Our two captors left the room and locked the door.

I looked at Anna, then closed my eyes, scowled, and shook my head in a gesture of self-directed anger and apology. She said, "Cal, this wasn't your fault. Howard, or whatever his name is, seems deranged, and that woman, my God, she's high on something."

We heard Krebbs' voice in the hall. Anna put a finger to her lips. "Shhh. Sounds like he's talking to someone on the phone," she whispered. We both strained to hear the barely audible words that followed.

"…okay, okay, but now what?" There was a long pause followed by, "Alright, I've got his keys. I'll go there and get his computer and anything else that looks interesting. Yeah, you already told me about the dog. If it makes trouble, I'll kill the fucker. Yeah, I hear you. I'm as anxious to get this over with as you are."

A chill rippled down my spine. Anna gasped and lost some color in her face. It was pretty clear to both of us what he meant. I whispered, "At least Archie's not in the apartment." Anna nodded and managed a weak smile.

We sat in stunned silence for a while. Finally, Anna whispered, "Who do you think he was talking to?"

I shook my head. "I don't know. I thought he was working for Vincent, but he's dead. Someone else must be involved, too." I had my suspicions but didn't say anything to Anna. We'd know soon enough, I figured.

The Chevy started up and backed out of the driveway. I said, "He's going to search my apartment, yours too, maybe. He'll be back."

"What should we tell him?" Anna asked.

I shrugged. "We don't know anything except that his real name's not Howard Krebbs. So, I guess we just tell the truth." Not that it matters, I told myself as a sense of utter futility washed over me. They had kidnapped us. There would be no letting us go, no matter what we knew or didn't know.

Chapter Forty

The room fell silent. My hands and feet were bound so tightly to the chair that I had lost all feeling. I wiggled in the chair, trying to use what little movement I could generate to loosen the tape. Anna looked at me expectantly. I rocked and strained as hard as I could, turning, I'm sure, several shades of red and triggering a dull ache above my right eye. Finally, I slumped in the chair, defeated. I looked up at Anna. "Try yours." She struggled for a few moments, but she was taped as tightly as I was.

We sat there for a while in that awful silence. Anna's head was cast downward. The overhead lights played off the gold streaks running through her hair. I felt a catch in my throat as the memory of the first time I saw her rushed back to me, lifting for a moment, at least, the threat hanging over us. Something about her hair. So damned endearing. No, not really her hair, which was beautiful, but her careless disregard for how it looked. That strand that always seemed draped across her forehead said something about her; a woman with physical beauty but without a trace of vanity. The doubts I'd felt about Anna fell away, and sadness came over me as I glimpsed what could have been. I said, "Tell me about the fjords in Norway."

She raised her head. The blue in her eyes deepened in that mysterious way, then closing her eyes, she smiled wistfully. "Think of the Gorge, but on a grander scale. Sheer mountains diving down, straight into the water. You get a sense there's no bottom to it, the depth is infinite, the water, the color of the ocean far out to sea." She smiled more fully, losing herself in memory. "The views. Oh, God, the *views*. They go on forever. And the air, it's like crystal. The grandeur of the place, it's... it's just so humbling. All the petty things in your life just drop away." She shook her head slowly, holding the smile. "That's what it's like."

I nodded and smiled. For a short period of time I was there, in Norway, with Anna. I met her eyes and held them. "I can't think of any place I'd rather be than there with you."

We fell silent again. Time passed like the slow drip of water torture. Every time we heard a noise we jumped to attention. Later—I honestly don't know how long—we heard one, possibly two, cars drive in and park behind the building. The back door of the building opened and closed, followed by conversation out in the hall too low to be understood.

A key rattled in our door. It swung open, and Jessica Armandy sauntered in. She was followed by Semyon. He took up a position in the corner of the room, crossed his arms and looked straight ahead with no expression. The right side of his face was still slightly swollen and discolored, and his jaw looked rigid, suggesting it was still wired shut.

I wasn't that shocked to see Armandy and Semyon. After all, very few people in Portland knew I had a dog. But Semyon certainly did. I guess Picasso was right about Semyon, I told myself.

With no makeup, Armandy looked at least ten years older in the harsh fluorescent light. Her colorless, collagen-packed lips were drawn up in a tight line, and patches of finely etched wrinkles nested at the corners of her eyes and mouth. She wore a thin leather jacket over a t-shirt, tight jeans, and high black boots.

She sighed theatrically, looked at Anna, then at me, and shook her head. "I should be getting my beauty rest right now," she said, gesturing toward us, "But no, I have to deal with this freaking mess." Her eyes narrowed, boring in on me. "You just had to keep poking around in my business, didn't you, Claxton? Saving that homeless kid was all you could think about." Her look turned genuinely puzzled. "You know, I just can't understand why you would stick your neck out for someone like him." She gestured with her hands, palms up. "I mean, what's a drugged-out, homeless punk to you, anyway?"

Anna said, "You could *never* understand that."

Armandy swung her gaze to Anna and smiled coldly. "I'll tell you what I can't understand—I can't understand you imitating Mother Teresa. What a waste of a good body."

Color rose in Anna's neck and into her face. She glanced at me and started to speak. I gave a quick shake of my head to stop her. This conversation wasn't going to help us at all. I said, "You're jumping the gun here, Jessica. We don't know what this is all about. I was just trying to locate Krebbs as part of my investigation. Let us walk now, and we'll forget this ever happened. We don't want any trouble with you."

She pulled her mouth into an ugly sneer, "Oh, sure you'll forget this ever happened. Fat chance. You're like the goddamn Energizer Bunny, Claxton. I can't afford to let you back on the street." She turned back to Anna and added, "And as for you, Doctor, you're just collateral damage. It's too bad. You'd go far in my line of work."

In a strong, even voice, Anna said, "I pity you."

Jessica attempted a smile, but it turned bitter and her right eye twitched. "Well, don't."

I said, "Look, Jessica, we don't know anything. As far as I'm concerned, Vincent killed Conyers, and he's dead now. Let's just leave it at that. No harm, no foul."

Her eyes narrowed. She looked at Anna, then back to me. "Well, judging from your computer and the papers in your briefcase, I agree you don't know much." She laughed, and it came out bitter again. "But, you know I can't take that chance, Claxton. You crossed the line.

"At least let Dr. Eriksen go. She's had nothing to do with this."

She swung her gaze back to Anna and shook her head. "You picked the wrong lover, honey. Don't blame me."

Anna glared back at her with a fierceness I didn't know she possessed. "You won't get away with this."

Jessica turned to leave. Desperate to keep her talking, I said, "What do you hope to gain from all this?"

She spun back around to face us, her eyes blazing. She smiled, successfully this time, clearly pleased I'd asked the question. "Ownership of all three restaurants, for starters, and a free hand to expand my escort business up and down the west coast. See, Mitch was a shitty businessman, and I wound up loaning him a lot of money and owning a good chunk of his holdings. Then he went all soft for Bambi and wanted to dump me and get out of the escort business. Well, I couldn't let that happen. Hell, my escort business makes more money than his lousy restaurants."

"So, you had him murdered," Anna said.

Jessica looked at Anna, then me, opened her hands and shook her head. "I really didn't have a choice. I had too much invested. And when your snake boy threw that tantrum at his mom's memorial service, the perfect way to do it just came to me. I love it when that happens."

I said, "Then all you had was Seth Foster to worry about."

Jessica laughed and shook her head again. "Oh, so true. I thought I was going to have to marry him to get the whole package." She paused and looked directly at me. "But then you showed me the way out of that little dilemma. I had no idea Mitch was blackmailing Larry Vincent, so thank you for that. You see, Seth has serious anger issues, so all I had to do was convince him Vincent killed his stepbrother."

Anna gasped. "My God, you have no shame."

She put her hands on her hips, glared back at Anna, smiling triumphantly. "*Shame?* It was my finest hour, dear. And don't think it was easy. Hell, I should get an Oscar for my performance. I cried. I sobbed. I told Seth that if he was a real man, he'd do something about it. It worked out rather well, I think. Men are wonderful. I do love manipulating them."

I said, "You've been very clever, and it would be hard to prove any of that, but if you kill us, you run the risk of being caught for sure. Think about it, doubling down may not be your best option. You don't have to do this." By this time, I was just throwing words at her, hoping something would stick.

Ignoring me, she turned toward the door and said in a breezy tone, "Well, I've got to run along now." As Semyon followed her out, she said over her shoulder, "You know what needs to be done, Semyon. Make sure they don't screw it up."

I tried to make eye contact with Semyon just as he shut the door and locked it.

Chapter Forty-one

I couldn't look at Anna. I was ashamed of what I'd gotten her into. All I could think to say was, "I'm so sorry."

"Don't. Don't say that," she tried to smile.

We fell into silence again, lost in our own thoughts, but only briefly. The key rattled and the door swung open. Krebbs came in carrying two brand new, neatly folded blue plastic tarps. Anna gasped when she realized what he was carrying. Apparently, our executioners were determined to make a tidy job of it.

His eyes were little beads of excitement, and it was clear from the smile on his face that he was setting about an enjoyable task. His shirtsleeves were rolled up now, revealing a patchwork of crudely rendered tattoos. I glimpsed a couple of swastikas and the clenched fist salute of the white power movement. Picasso was right again. Krebbs wore long sleeves at the clinic to mask his choice of tattoos.

The hard blonde came in next, followed by Semyon. She must've shot up again, because her watery pupils were like full moons, and she had an excited look on her face that mirrored Krebbs' expression.

Semyon's face held no expression at all.

Krebbs handed the blonde the tarps and said, "Here. Spread these out, baby." She took them and set about the task. Semyon walked over to me, pulled a small pen knife from his pocket and opened it with a fingernail. Anna gasped again, and although the knife seemed too small to be a murder weapon, I pressed back against the chair reflexively. But instead of cutting me, he started on the tape on my hands and as he leaned in, I saw something in his eyes I couldn't read.

Krebbs had his revolver trained on me. "That's right, Semyon," he said. "No traces of that tape. Jessica said this can't look like a kidnapping." The blonde was spreading the second tarp next to the first. She looked up, failing to suppress a giggle. When my hands and feet were free, Krebbs said, "Stay right where you are." Semyon began removing Anna's tape.

When he finished, he folded the knife, put it back in his pocket, and turned to Krebbs. "I can't do dis." Then he hit Krebbs flush on the jaw. It was a vicious blow that sent him sprawling.

Krebbs hit the floor, and the gun skittered off across the concrete, stopping midway between Anna and the blonde. There was a moment when everyone in the room froze, then Anna screamed and lunged for the gun, but the blonde got there first. As she brought the gun up, Anna grabbed her wrist with both hands and the weapon swung in a wild arc as they fought for control. The muzzle of the pistol flashed twice, and Semyon and I hit the floor simultaneously. The stray bullets thudded into the cinder block wall to our right, the sound reverberating like thunder in the closed room.

Anna held fast to her wrist, but it was the blonde who had her finger on the trigger. Her other hand was in Anna's face.

I leaped up to help Anna, but the gun swung around and discharged again. The round hit a foot in front of me, sending up a spray of concrete chips. I dove to the left just as the blonde squeezed off another round that punched a hole in the door directly behind where I'd been standing.

Crouched low, Semyon moved in from another angle. I saw movement out of the corner of my eye where Krebbs had fallen. "Behind you, Semyon!" I yelled, "Look out!"

It was too late. Krebbs came in fast behind Semyon. I saw a glint of steel from the shaft of a switchblade. His arm thrust forward. Semyon made a strange guttural sound from deep in his chest and frantically reached behind his back with one arm. Krebbs pulled the blade out and stepped back.

Semyon dropped to his knees, met my eyes for an instant, then slumped forward.

Krebbs quickly took stock. Me first, then Anna, he must have concluded, because he started toward me with the knife.

Anna and the blonde were locked in a death struggle. The gun swung in my direction again, and another round tore into the wall, spraying my face and eyes with cement particles. Krebbs raised the knife and moved toward me cautiously. Without taking his eyes off me, he said to the blonde, "For Christ's sake, Twila, hold your fire. Let me take care of him first." I took a step back, wiping the grit from my eyes. The corner of the room was only another step behind me.

But Anna wasn't through. With the blonde's hand jammed in her face, she began to twist her body and pull with her outstretched arms. The gun started to swing back toward Krebbs, inch by grudging inch. Krebbs was focused on me, assuming, I'm sure, Twila would quickly prevail. He stepped toward me, the knife held low in his hand, light reflecting off the eight inch blade. The gun continued to move until the alignment between it and Krebbs was complete.

Twila suddenly screamed, "Ahhhhh! Stop!" Two shots rang out in quick succession. Both bullets slammed into Krebbs. He pirouetted like a clumsy ballerina and fell face-first onto the concrete. The knife dropped from his hand as he hit the floor.

Anna and the blonde were frozen there, motionless, like a couple of tango dancers, their arms extended, the gun pointing in the direction where Krebbs had been standing. Twila's shoulders slumped, and she screamed, "No! No!"

A moment later Anna had the gun, and Twila was sobbing next to Krebbs' lifeless body. Anna handed me the gun, and I kicked away the switchblade lying next to Krebbs' outstretched hand.

Just like that, it was over.

Anna rushed over to help Semyon. She checked for a pulse, then looked up at me. "He's still alive!" Pointing at the switch-blade, she said, "Give me that knife, quick." She used it to cut off a swath of Semyon's shirt, which she folded and pressed against his wound to staunch the bleeding. He moaned when she touched him. "Stay with us, Semyon" she told him. "You're going to make it. We're calling an ambulance for you."

I could still see Semyon's eyes before he pitched forward. I think he tried to say something to me with that look, something like, "See, I'm not the coward you thought I was."

I told Twila to get up, and when she did, she turned to Anna and held her up her hand. It was bloody with a deep gash in the middle finger. She said, "You bitch, this is *your* fault. You made me shoot him."

Anna cast her eyes down and said in a voice I could barely hear, "I had no choice."

While Anna worked on Semyon, I marched Twila out of the room, recovered my cell phone, and called 911. I found the duct tape down the hall and after marching her back into the room, taped her firmly to one of the chairs while Anna held the gun. Then I called Nando, and quickly filled him in. "Do me a favor, my friend. Go over to Anna's condo"—I gave him the address—"and rescue Archie. He's shut up in my car in the parking lot on the east side of the building." Then I added, "If you wouldn't mind, take him over to Caffeine Central and give him a couple of scoops of kibbles and take him for a walk. I have a feeling I'll be here for a while."

As we waited for the police, Anna was quiet and withdrawn. I said, "You okay?"

She nodded and made a brave face.

"You didn't kill him, Anna," I said. "She had her finger on the trigger, not you."

She looked up at me, held my eyes for a moment, then looked down without speaking.

About the time we heard the wail of police sirens, it dawned on me what Twila had meant when she accused Anna of making her shoot Krebbs. The finger with the bloody gash was on the blonde's *left* hand—the one she had jammed in Anna's face—not her right, which held the trigger. Anna had forced the gun around until it was trained on Krebbs, then she bit down hard on Twila's left middle finger.

It was something Anna never spoke of afterwards and something I knew never to bring up.

Chapter Forty-two

Two Months Later

In Oregon, summer makes up for all the winter rain and then some. The Coast Range and the Cascades were tinged in violet that day, and the floor of the Willamette Valley was a familiar checker board of greens, yellows, and ocher. Clouds that had scaled the Coast Range scudded from west to east against a cobalt sky. We were out on my deck having lunch—Anna, Nando, Picasso, and me. I had made a salade Niçoise with seared Ahi tuna and served it with a baguette and chilled bottles of Sancerre. Archie, of course, was lying next to Anna's chair, and she was stroking his fur with one of her bare feet.

I was breathing a little easier financially, owing to the deep pockets of one of my clients, a wealthy Dundee vintner who was anxious to shed his current wife. I'd waived Picasso's fee, since he was applying to art school, and used the money to pay Nando what I owed him. Despite this, the business discussion we were having had turned a little testy. Nando speared a couple of green beans along with a slab of fish and held the fork above his plate. "So why would I want to make my building available for a law office? It is not good business. I have big plans for that property. I am in business to make money, after all. I am a capitalist."

Anna said, "It would be a charitable donation, Nando. You can take a big tax deduction."

I said, "Look, Nando, like I said, I'll cover the first floor renovations, but paying rent at the outset is going to be tough. I'd only use it a couple of days a week, you know, for pro bono work. Maybe over time I could take on some paying customers and *then* pay some rent."

Anna said, "Homeless kids need all kinds of legal support, Nando. This would be the first of its kind in Portland. Cal's making a big commitment here, but he can't do it alone."

Nando popped the forkful in his mouth, closed his eyes and chewed with obvious relish. "The dressing on this salad is magnificent."

"The secret's fresh herbs," I said, pointing to the pots of oregano, thyme, and three different kinds of basil standing in the sun at the edge of my deck.

Nando speared another forkful and sighed. "I don't know. A tax deduction is a one-time thing. This building could generate a nice cash flow." He shook his head. "I think that perhaps you are asking too much of me."

Picasso had finished eating and was sitting outside the group busily sketching the view of the valley. He had been a free man for seven weeks and gotten his arm out of the cast the week before. The arm was pale, thin, and deeply scarred, but it was fully functional. "Tell you what, Nando," he said, looking up with a playful grin on his face, "if you do this deal, I'll put you in my mural."

Nando's gaze swung around to Picasso, his eyes registering surprise, then delight. "You would do this? You would put me in your mural?"

Picasso nodded. "Cuba has one of the best health care systems in the world."

"How would you manage it? The mural is nearly complete. The public showing is next week."

"The mayor and the city council are going to be there," Anna chimed in.

Picasso said, "I take somebody out, I put somebody in. No big deal."

"Would I be toward the front of the march?" Nando asked, smiling slyly.

"How about a whole body shot? I'll even slim you down a bit," Picasso answered, winking at Anna and me.

"Put him next to Semyon," I added. "He's right up near the front."

"I can do that," Picasso answered.

So it was that Nando became immortalized in Picasso's mural, and Caffeine Central became my Portland law office.

The week before, *The Oregonian* had reported that Twila Burgess—the woman I'd dubbed "the hard blonde"—had agreed to fully cooperate in the prosecution of Jessica Armandy in exchange for a plea bargain. Armandy was charged with the first degree murder of Mitchell Conyers and Milo Dorfman and the kidnapping of Anna and me. Burgess' lawyer stated that she had detailed knowledge of all the alleged crimes. So far, Semyon Lebedev, who had also been cooperating, had not been charged with anything.

And just the day before, Cynthia Duncan called to tell me Sherrill Blanchard had agreed to talk about the sexual abuse she had suffered at the hands of Larry Vincent. So, it looked like Cynthia would get to break her exclusive story after all. The timing would prove unfortunate for a group of citizens who had planned to erect a statue of Vincent in one of the city's parks.

Oh, and by the way, Cynthia told me she and Xavier Bidarte are now engaged to be married.

As for Anna and me? Well, we plan to attend the unveiling of Picasso's mural next week, and then we have to rush off to PDX. We've got a flight to Bergen, Norway, to catch.

I can't wait to see those fjords.

To receive a free catalog of Poisoned Pen Press titles, please contact us in one of the following ways:

Phone: 1-800-421-3976
Facsimile: 1-480-949-1707
Email: info@poisonedpenpress.com
Website: www.poisonedpenpress.com

Poisoned Pen Press
6962 E. First Ave. Ste 103
Scottsdale, AZ 85251